SANDINISTA

SANDINISTA

A NOVEL OF NICARAGUA

Marie Jakober

NEW STAR BOOKS
Vancouver

This story is fiction based on contemporary history. The Somoza dictatorship and the Sandinista National Liberation Front are real. So are the National Guard, the different political groups and factions, and a few well known persons like Sandino, Carlos Fonseca, and Pedro Joaquin Chamorro. The October offensive of 1977 is a fact of history.

However, the events of this story, though based on that history, are invented. All the characters are fictitious and are not intended to resemble any real persons, living or dead.

Canadian Cataloguing in Publication Data

Jakober, Marie.
Sandinista

ISBN 0-919573-42-8 (bound).-ISBN
0-919573-43-6 (pbk.)

1. Nicaragua - History - 1937-1979 - Fiction.
I. Title.
PS8569.A396S3 1985 C813'.54 C85-091359-4
PR9199.3.J339S3 1985

The publisher is grateful for assistance
provided by the Canada Council.

Printed and bound in Canada by Gagne Printers.
First printing August 1985
1 2 3 4 5 89 88 87 86 85

New Star Books Ltd.
2504 York Avenue
Vancouver, B.C.
Canada V6K 1E3

Acknowledgments

Many people have a share in this novel. They provided me with information, with contacts and practical advice, with unfailing warmth and encouragement. They shared their food and their *flor de cana*, their homes, their jeeps, their experience and their consciousness. I would like now to thank them all: those many Nicaraguans whose paths I crossed but whose names I never learned; and the following: Marco Altamirano, AMNLAE of Managua, Fred and Corinna Beck, Alberto Blandon Lezama, Miguel Bolanos, Manuel Salvador Castaneda Flores, Lizandro Chavez, Luz Marina Davila Escoto, Laura Enriquez, Esperanza Flores Torres, Rafael Gaona, Mary Hartman, Maryknoll Community of Ciudad Sandino in Managua, Joel Mugge, Margaret Navarro, Thelma Ortiz Mercado and Roberto, Lupita Otero, Margaret Randall, Margaret Stothers, Maria Eugenia Urroz, Mariana Yampolsky, Daisy Zamora.

I would like to extend a very warm and a very special

thank you to Sarah Murphy, my translator and very dear friend, without whose unfailing help the research for this novel would have been five times as much work, not half as much fun, and on occasion downright impossible.

I would also like to gratefully acknowledge the excerpts from song lyrics used in this novel:

—Epigraph and page 151: from *Hermano, Dame Tu Mano*, by J. Sosa and D.J. Sanchez.

—Page 23: from *La Pala*, by Victor Jara.

—Page 76 and 152: from *Pancasan*, by David McField.

—Page 191: from *Existen*, by Silvio Rodriguez.

Hermano, dame tu mano,
Vamos juntos a buscar
una cosa pequenita
que se llama libertad.
Esta es la hora primera,
este es el justo lugar...

Brother, give me your hand,
Together we will seek
a tiny little thing
that they call liberty.
This is the hour to begin,
this is the very place...

—J. Sosa & D.J. Sanchez

Prolog
September, 1977

The sun soaked through Daniel's shirt like liquid fire, burned his hands, burned through the thin, taut denim over his knees. From where he sat he could see the cone of the Intercontinental Hotel rising against the backdrop of the mountain of Tiscapa. He had been told once that the hotel was terraced to look like a Mayan pyramid, but to him it looked like an overturned basket, a plastic and cellophane pyramid designed by somebody who had never seen a real one. Not far behind it, close enough to shoot at—someone had already tried it from the eighth floor—was President Anastasio Somoza's bunker.

All around him, except at his back where the Lake of Managua lay befouled and gleaming in the winter light, the city fell away in bewildered, broken pieces: palm trees and *chilamate* and dust, pigs rooting in the ruins a thousand feet from the Bank of America, their bellies as hollow as crescent moons; whole blocks without houses, only the memory of houses; the earthquake had been five years ago but the government hadn't even cleared away the rubble. It lay brazen in the sun, greening with weeds; it grew roots like Somoza's; it would remain as long as he did.

Daniel shook a fly off his hand, let his eyes drift from the ruins to the pyramid hotel and the mountain behind it, to the bunker built solidly into its side. It was long and low; it looked more like a warehouse than a fortress, but that was deceiving. It had artillery emplacements inside and anti-aircraft guns on the roof; it had torture chambers and a well-stocked bar. Higher up were the presidential palace and the infantry training school where the president's son educated the next generation of the National Guard so that, when the time came, the dynasty would pass on smoothly, and he would be elected president in his turn.

You could see Tiscapa from nearly everywhere in Managua—some part of Tiscapa, some inaccessible and enduring symbol of Somoza power. From this particular side you could see the heart of it, the nerve center, just there, naked in the sun, with no grace to it, no majesty, just brute power: arms and arrogance and no end to either, no imaginable end, except to fashion it yourself.

Daniel was not given much to daydreams, but he sometimes thought about the day when they would take Tiscapa, take the palace and the armories and the hated bunker with its warren of secret jails; thought about what it might be like, and how they might feel, and whether anyone, after all these years, would believe that it was possible. Tiscapa had been there for so long. Tiscapa and its fat lord, Tacho, reincarnated in his sons and his grandsons. Tacho one, two, three; Tacho the last Marine who went home only for banquets and guns. (*Nicaragua es mi finca* and I'll sell it to whoever I damn well please!) Tacho *mi general*, Tacho milord, Tacho old buddy you're a son of a bitch but you're our son of a bitch, hail to the *jefe*. Tacho in his glass cage, terrified of the guns of poets, addressing the people of Nicaragua, what people of Nicaragua? There isn't anything out there, just shit. Tacho the god, grown fat from feeding on the people that weren't there, glory be to the father and to the sons, the Holy Ghost left the country forty-three years ago...but not forever, Tacho, not forever. One day, Daniel thought, the people of Managua would walk up the sides of Tiscapa in their bare brown feet and find that it was just another hill, and that it was theirs. God knew when, or how many of them would be alive to see it, but they would take it back.

Tacho, goodbye.

He sat quiet, watchful from habit, from years of habit even though he was still young. The bus stop where he waited was busy enough to provide anonymity; he looked like any of the people around him, dark and lean and poorly dressed, standing in clusters or sitting in the grass, climbing on and off the battered, overloaded buses that would take them into the far-flung barrios of Managua. The heat was fierce but not intolerable, eased as always by wind, by the north-east trades that blew from the far Caribbean, restless with the memory of ancient ships.

He had not been there long when he noticed the man with the cane, picking his way as though he were nearly blind, standing for a while on the corner, afraid; then coming back to the bus stop, to Daniel.

"Forgive me," he said. "The traffic is very bad here, and I can hardly see. Will you help me across?"

Daniel got to his feet indifferently, walked with him to the corner, waited.

"I'm going to see my niece in Altamira," the man said. "My niece Celia; she's getting married."

Daniel looked at him. His hair was gray, but his face, considered closely, did not match it. His sunglasses hid eyes that no doubt could see very well.

"May she have twenty children," Daniel said. I really have to talk to Valerian about these passwords; he's losing his touch...

The light changed and they began to walk, very slowly.

"I can get you everything you need," the man said. "It's ready to ship. Five hundred rounds of ammunition, some small arms, plus the explosives."

"What about detonators, wire, fuses?"

"Yes, yes!" the man assured him. "Everything. I have your list. It will be expensive," he added.

"It always is," Daniel said. "Where are you going to ship from?"

"San Diego." He laughed softly. "Friends where you least expect them, no?" They reached the boulevard as the light was changing. They stood patiently, cars streaming past them in both directions, drowning out their voices.

"I need to tell the boat where to land," the man said.

"We'll tell them where to land," Daniel replied. Casually he slipped the man a paper. "It's a list of fishing ports, with a code for each. The code has no meaning outside of this operation; nevertheless you must memorize it right away and destroy it."

"*Claro, claro*," the man said.

"If you will give me your boat's radio frequency, and the code name it will use, we'll identify the landing place two hours in advance. From Corinto. *Esta bien?*"

He shrugged. "*Esta bien*."

They began to walk. "You people are very careful," the man said.

Daniel was not sure what he meant. If he meant yes, we intend to survive, and no, we are not playing games, then yes, we are very careful. What else did he expect?

The boat, the man told him, would use the radio code La Palma. They should expect it in the region of Corinto around the first or second of October.

They had reached the opposite curb. The man took his hand, thanked him, and made his way clumsily down the street where he stood signalling for a cab.

Daniel crossed back to the stop that he had left and climbed onto the first bus that came. He rode it for a quarter hour and then got off and walked home through the dirt streets, with the sun fierce on his body and the wind tangling his black hair like weeds; with the mountain of Tiscapa lying quietly over his shoulder, forever there, forever but not forever, we'll take it back; it's ours and we'll take it back; it's time, it's hour zero, time to begin.

To begin once again.

1

These were not clouds like any Jadine had known. They were not layered, like clouds at home, but bunched instead into pillars vaster than mountains, utterly motionless, filled by the high sun with a thousand shades of shifting light. The plane moved among them without haste and without effort. Here everything was insubstantial; the wingtips passed through cathedral walls as a sword through a shadow.

If she had been happy she would have thought it magical, would have given herself over to fantasies of queens and beasts of legend, would have given names to the translucent temples and peopled the thundersky with gods.

Once she would have done that, but it was not possible any more. There were no gods left, unless they were gods of nightmare. Down below, in that scrunched-paper landscape laced with rivers, too far for any eye to see and too close for any mind to bear, young men in trim green uniforms were searching for people to kill. They were not particular; almost anyone would do. And back in Kerry Heights, Pennsylvania, her brother had been buried at the crossroads.

"Look." The man beside her, the Panamanian, smiled and gestured toward a small city coming up fast on their left. "Chinandega. We will arrive very soon."

Chinandega. It was only a name to her, a spot on the map she had pored over before she left. She knew nothing about it, or about any of these places with curious names that sounded as if they should be Spanish but were mostly Indian. Jinotega. Esteli. Matagalpa. Matagalpa—the loveliest mountain resort in Central America, the man from Panama said, until the guerrillas ruined it.

"I use to really like Nicaragua." He had told her that at least three times since they left Mexico City. He always spoke English, even though her Spanish was very good. "It was...how do you say?...*muy sencillo*...a simple life here, you know. People were happy. But now..." He sighed and shrugged as it seemed only Latin Americans could, a gesture that could brush away a leaf or comment on the whole of human history. "Now I do not come here except on business. Last summer I go with my daughters to Poneloya, to the beach, and when they play in the water they find three...*cadaveres*...I do not know in English..."

"Cadavers," she said. "It's the same in English."

"No," he said. "You have another word."

"Corpses."

"Yes, yes, corpses. They find three corpses. All cut up. A terrible thing for a child to see. Terrible. I do not bring my family here any more."

Years ago—the Viet Nam years—she would have asked him what about the children who *lived* here? Wasn't it terrible for them and did he ever think about that? But that was years ago. Now she just wanted him to talk about something else.

He picked that up quickly. He was gallant. He talked about all sorts of things and she found herself not listening, found herself remembering the oak-panelled office lined with books and smelling faintly of fine incense, the dignified priest with artist's hands explaining why the Church could not bury her brother in sacred ground.

Her mother understood. Even her father, who didn't like priests much and went to church only when he had to, understood. Everyone understood. It was a question of fundamental moral principles. Holy ground was holy ground. You could lie and steal and commit murder; you could eat or drink or work yourself to death; you could grow fat with so many sins that you wouldn't fit an ordinary coffin. But they'd wrap you in flowers all the same, and march you down Assumption's broad aisle, all in their best black with the organ straining at the windows to let the stench out; and they'd give you a good clean hole at seventy-five dollars a square foot and pray you into paradise. You could do damn near anything and they'd tuck you in like a good Christian when you died.

What you could not do was walk out onto McKinley Bridge at three a.m. and feel the cold that came from the water and the steel mills and the remorseless eyes of cars that came from nowhere and passed into nothing; what you could not do was stand there and look at it all and say fuck you and walk into the river. You couldn't do that and expect a decent burial. It was a question of principle.

She became aware of silence and turned guiltily. The Panamanian was watching her, looking puzzled rather than offended.

"I'm sorry," she said. "I was distracted."

"No matter." He smiled. "You are expected, yes? Someone will meet you?"

She smiled inwardly at all the implications in that. And then kicked herself. He was a nice man. Maybe he was just being nice.

"Yes," she said. "I'm expected. I have relatives here."

"Ah. You are part *nica* then."

She looked up sharply. She had never thought of it that way. Her Nicaraguan grandmother came to the States to study music, married Pennsylvania Irish, and died young. The Hall clan of Kerry Heights had a lot of exotic relatives scattered around the world, to whom it sent occasional Christmas cards and from whom it received an occasional visit. But it never thought of itself as anything but American.

"The *nicas* are good people," he said. He paused, glancing out the window as the plane slowed and circled. "They will soon put an end to this nonsense of revolution. You will see."

Soon? That surprised her a little; she thought they already had. She'd read *Time* and *Newsweek* and all the papers faithfully until she left—mainly to calm her family's hysteria. The press rarely mentioned Nicaragua. A back issue she'd picked up in the library told of a big sweep made last winter against the Sandinista guerrillas. They had killed the guerrilla leader—killed him and taken pictures of him laid out under a mango tree, and chopped off his fingers (some said it was his head) to send back to Managua as proof; she couldn't remember his name. It seemed quite clear that the revolution, such as it was, had been crushed. The government under President Somoza had just ended a three-year state of siege—though, of course, the reprisals still went on. Mopping up, they called it. That got mentioned now and then. *Priest Claims Seven Peasant Families Massacred*—two column-inches on page 37, next to Jackie's flu. Mopping up. Cleaning out the AP/UPI trash bin.

"I thought it *was* over, more or less," she said. "There's been nothing in the papers for weeks."

Her companion smiled, just a little but with a lot of irony. "The papers do not understand Latin America very well." He didn't say whose papers. He didn't have to. "It is better here now. Very much better. But it is not over."

She considered that, less troubled by what he told her than by the fact that he had needed to. It was amazing, she thought. You knew you could not believe the media. You knew it like you knew your own name, yet every time they caught you off guard, you believed them anyway.

"So there's still a lot of fighting, then?" she said.

He shrugged. "To fight much you must be. . . *numeroso* . . . you must have many people. The *guerrilleros* are few, two or three hundred, no more. But there is still very much subversion."

The distinction was less than clear to her, but she did not

pursue it. They were landing. The Lake of Managua dipped into view and swung away again as though a child spun it on a rope. She caught her first sight of the city, Managua, scattered, weed-grown, not a city at all but a huge, permanent encampment, dusty in the sun and muddy in the rain, hot and clamourous and violent. And she was, finally, afraid.

The hot wind hit her instantly as she stepped off the plane, whipping her hair into her eyes and pinning her skirt against her legs as though it were made of canvas. The air was cleaner than she had ever imagined air to be and the light was liquid, drowning everything. The Panamanian carried her tote into the terminal and said goodbye to her in the customs line.

"Good luck, *senorita*. I hope you will be happy here."

She smiled and thanked him. You couldn't tell such a nice gentleman that the very idea was ridiculous, that happiness was the last thing on your mind. Even though he should have known, should have guessed that you didn't come to a place like this in order to be happy.

Precisely why you did, though, wasn't at all clear. You wonder about it while four cousins talk at you at once and the car jolts and veers through streets that amaze and bewilder you with their undirection, with their sheer weight of visual contradiction—streets of shacks and streets of riches and streets of weeds; walls and fences scrawled with paint, with harsh twisted letters screaming at the sky: DEATH TO SOMOZA! FSLN. POWER TO THE PEOPLE! FSLN. *PATRIA LIBRE O MORIR!* Free homeland or death. FSLN.

It stands for Sandinista National Liberation Front; that much you know for sure, and you remember the professor who said that he had never heard of a national liberation front that was either national or liberating, or in front of anything at all. You never liked him and you don't necessarily agree, but the graffiti offends you. It reminds you of Viet Nam: ten long years of dying for *la patria* and killing for *la patria* and all I want for Christmas is my M-16...

No one in the car mentions the existence of a revolution, but you stop at a red light and in a vacant lot beside the road is a smashed car, stripped to the skeleton, laced with bullet holes. You know the Panamanian was right—that it's far from over. You pass ten, maybe fifteen military vehicles, some of them mounted with machine guns and mortars, all of them bristling with men who seem ready to shoot at anything that moves.

You will not be happy here. You didn't come for that. But for what then, to this place of death and light?

2

The lake stunk. In the first heat of the sun coming over its eastern shores one could pick out the thousand variations of its foulness. At least Marcos could, as he wandered just between the water's edge and the long lines of shacks that were the barrios Acahualinca and Los Santos. He could smell mud and petrol and reeds, excrement and rotting vegetation, small dead animals that had somehow escaped the forever foraging dogs. And always the other smell, which grew fiercer as he walked, which came from up ahead, where the pipes from the slaughterhouse spilled into the lake.

He didn't like walking here, but it was the shortest way to Pablo's house, and sometimes there were things to scavenge. He found candy sometimes, or scraps of food. Once, to his great delight, he found a knife, and once a *rojinegro* scarf, snagged in the reeds, a sudden splash of colour and of fear. It was made of the finest cotton, the two pieces beautifully sewn, and he would have loved to keep it, simply because it was pretty, but he knew better. Red and black were the colours of the Sandinistas, and they wore bandannas like this as insignia. The Guard might kill you just for having one.

But today he found nothing. There were other kids on the lakefront, and dogs, and on the path ahead women were making their way to the foul-smelling mouths of the slaughterhouse sewers. They were there every morning, hundreds of them, wading in the lake, or bashing in the concrete pipes with rocks, fishing out the chunks of lung and spleen and gut that tumbled by. They fought over it sometimes, and sometimes threw it at each other and laughed, but mostly they just sat patient as fishers and gathered it into their little plastic pails. Afterward they would take it to the Eastern Market, to the food vendors who mixed it into sausages. They called it Somoza's bread, among other things, but they ate it anyway.

For a while Marcos sat, watching the women, looking for the faded red print dress that was his mother's, wondering if she might have a few tortillas with her. He could not see her, and after a while he went on. Almost always she had nothing. Almost always she yelled at him for asking. Or she cried; that was worse.

But not seeing her made him feel lonely; lonelier still when he got to Pablo's house and found it empty.

"Pablo's sick," the neighbour woman told him. "They took him to the clinic. To Father Pepe." She crossed herself.

He scuffed the dust with his toes, hoping she'd offer him food. Sometimes she did.

"Pablo's always sick," he said. He liked Pablo. He liked Pablo better than anybody. But it was tiresome having to sell papers by himself half the time.

"God will make him well," the woman said.

Well, maybe, Marcos thought. God was certainly taking his time about it.

"Ciao," he said, and drifted away. He did not look back. He could not stand to look at Pablo's house sitting empty like a shoebox, to think that maybe Pablo was going to die.

He sold one batch of papers and picked up another,

working his way towards Ciudad Jardin, hoping he might find the singer he had seen there last week. He had come upon him just by chance, in a maze of streets: a young man with shaggy hair and a guitar that seemed alive. Every day he had gone back, hoping, as one goes back to the place of an apparition or a miracle.

The city spilled and moiled around him, hawkers and buyers, old men sitting and watching with centuries in their eyes, young people restless as panthers, market women screaming their wares, the Guardia, always the Guardia: they were the customs agents and the traffic police and the building guards; they were the dreaded Becats, the special anti-terrorist brigades, riding those infernal orange jeeps. Always and everywhere the Guardia, with their trim uniforms and black boots and guns, with their insolence and their fear. Marcos could smell their fear like he could smell the stenches of the lake; he could measure it in the clamour of their trucks, the loudness of their voices, the tightness of their hands on the grips of their weapons. They were always frightened in the barrios, always alone no matter how many of them there were, always strangers. Somoza sent them to places far from their homes, so they would never feel close to the people they controlled, so they would have no friends, so they would live always in terror of the dispossessed. So they would find it that much easier to kill.

Like everyone else, Marcos watched the Guardia relentlessly—watched them and watched those who dealt with them: the vendors who sold them food, the boys who polished their boots, the *orejas*. The spies. There were hundreds of them, all over Managua, Somoza's ears, some of them brazen enough to openly wear the boots or carry the transistor radios that the Guardia gave them. They were found dead from time to time, in empty lots and ruins, sometimes with their ears and mouths stuffed with dirt; usually it was not the Sandinistas who killed them.

Marcos sold the last of his papers and wandered, looking for occasions to scavenge or to beg, but mostly looking for the young man with the guitar.

It was almost noon when he turned into a cluttered stretch of the Mercado Oriental and heard the music, soft and clean amid the market sounds. He followed it and found the young singer sitting on an upturned crate, clustered round by a small but eager audience. Marcos crept into the shade between a rack of cotton shirts and a stand full of Japanese and American gismos, and sat, his arms wrapped about his knees, totally content.

The singer was good. Really good, not like the sad lot who usually played in the streets, who knew three chords and two verses and whose music was a desperate attempt to beg with dignity. He was twenty-one or so, and street-bred, you could see that; taut and lean as a cat. His hair was black, ill-cut; his face angular, half Indian and half whatever else there was, not handsome but very alive, very intense—the kind of face the *turistas* with cameras loved.

Marcos listened, shutting out everything else: the heat, the clamour of bargaining, the other paperboys pushing their way through the crowds yelling "*Prensa!*" at the top of their thin lungs. The music was soft but rhythmic, subversive as *flor de cana* in the blood. Marcos had never heard songs like these before. On the radio, when he got to hear one in a shop or in someone else's house, they played music from Europe or the United States, or music from Buenos Aires or Caracas that might just as well have been from Europe or the United States, for all the difference there was.

But this youth sang of the fields and the shanties, of women who made clay pots and men who made shoes and kids who sailed palm-leaf boats down the barrio streets when it rained.

He didn't get much for it: a coin here and there, a bit of bread or fruit. Once a young woman bought roasted corn cobs from a brazier down the street and she gave him two, and went away like a dream; he put down his guitar and ate them, one after another, like an animal.

Marcos watched him wistfully. He had, until that moment, quite forgotten that he was hungry. He looked around, looked at the woman in the gismo booth who never stopped glaring at him, never stopped expecting him to try and steal something; looked down the row of stalls where they sold rice and cabbages and *nacatamales* and oranges and soft drinks and watermelon packed in ice. Once he had spent the money from his newspapers on food; his father had beaten him with a board until the neighbours made him stop.

He settled deeper into the shade. The young singer took up his guitar again, but by now the sun was high and burning; the shags of black hair around his face began to curl and mat with sweat.

Me entregaron una pala
que la cuidara pa' mi...

Entranced, Marcos let the words wrap him in melancholy and wonder:

They gave me a hoe
that I should always keep,
that I might water the earth
slowly, slowly.

And they gave me a plow
that I might make the earth cry out,
slowly, slowly.

Yoked by the years now I can do nothing more;
all that I worked for
they took from me,
slowly, slowly...

Who wrote songs like this? Marcos wondered. Who dared to? And where, dear God, where had they been hidden?

Cursed be the dark life
I've had to bear;
but I've seen that the night has begun to lighten
slowly, slowly...

It was the last song. Marcos watched the young man sling his guitar over his shoulder and vanish in the crowd; the heat and the dust closed behind him as though he had never been there at all. Marcos laid his head on his arms, desolate. The emptiness in his belly was turning into pain;

it always did. There was nothing to do, nowhere to go, no more music. Nothing. Only the sun and the noise and the eternal waiting. Waiting for the night and oblivion. Waiting for the morning and food. Waiting for the Guardia.

Waiting for the revolution.

The barrio Los Santos was not the poorest in Managua—not quite. Like the rest of the shantytowns it lived in the dust and the mud of its unpaved streets: a sprawl of shacks crowded amid the bamboo and scrub; small shacks made of nailed-together boards, roofed with pieces of tin weighted down with rocks; roofs that maybe did or maybe did not keep out the rain; dirt floors that maybe did or maybe did not have a mat to sleep on. Shallow ditches served as sewers, the sun served as light and the natural order of things served as an explanation. Only a few of the men of Los Santos had regular work; a few more worked sometimes—a day here and there in the city or a few weeks in the country, harvesting crops on land that some of them had once owned. Most of the rest—the ones who had no work at all—had left. It was a ghetto of abandoned women. Above all it was a ghetto of children. They were everywhere, running and laughing and crying and sitting silently in doorways, tagging after Daniel like the children in the story of the Piper. They wanted him to sing, or at the very least to let them touch the strings of the guitar and see for themselves how the wonderful magic sounds came out. Often he spent time with them, but today he was too tired and too preoccupied, and one by one, as he approached his own house, they fell back and let him go.

He slipped into the shanty and leaned the guitar against the wall. Rosa was asleep. He took a tortilla from the sack on the floor and went back outside.

The yard was small, untidy, fecund. Weeds grew everywhere; hibiscus climbed up the walls and drooped blossoms over the rusty wash-basin. The ground was strewn with flowers from the jacaranda trees and seed pods from the *tabachin*.

Martin was sitting against the wall, carving animals out of driftwood. He grinned at his younger brother. "Well?"

Daniel shook out his pockets. "Two pesos, sixty-five cents."

"Shit," Martin said. "If that's all your voice is worth, you'd better sell your ass."

Daniel ignored that. "Where's Naldo?"

"Who knows? He went out in a rage, the same as he does every day." Martin put down the knife and the silly looking wooden cat. Daniel was good at this sort of thing. He wasn't. "Danito, Naldo's going crazy. He's going right over the fucking wall. One of these days he's going to jump on a Becat and there'll be pieces of Naldo all over Managua."

"I know, Martin."

"Talk to him."

"Talk to Rosa."

"Rosa." Martin sighed. He would have given almost anything for a cold beer. "Rosa's sixteen. She's pregnant. She's scared. She doesn't understand."

Daniel said nothing. He didn't want to talk about Rosa, because he knew that if he did he would say things he would regret. It wasn't her fault. She'd been raised the way thousands of poor girls were raised—yes, and poor boys, too: passive, submissive to every authority, terrified of resistance, terrified of any kind of independent thought; devout to the point of superstition, capable of believing in any miracle except the miracle of her own ability to act. It wasn't her fault. It was Naldo's fault. What man in his right mind brought a timid, resentful, uncomprehending child into a houseful of revolutionaries?

"I've got to get some sleep," Daniel said, turning back toward the house.

"You going out tonight?"

"Yes."

Martin watched him go, afraid and proud and jealous all at once. They were all activists but Daniel just never stopped. God alone knew where he went and what he did those nights upon nights when he disappeared from the barrio. Martin didn't want to know. The Managua underground was crazy, an amoeba with a million nerves, no skeleton, and no readily apparent head. Living in the bowels of the enemy, it was clandestine well past the limits of efficiency and sometimes past the limits of sanity. Its left hand never knew what its right hand was doing, and when sometimes it found out, it found that the right hand wasn't there at all anymore, having been lopped off by the Guardia in the middle of the night.

To work in Managua took a special kind of courage, not least because the heart of the revolution always seemed to be somewhere else. Of all Nicaragua's cities, it was proving the hardest to mobilize. Most of Somoza's friends lived here, or at least owned property; and so did most of the country's criminals: the pushers, the Caribbean and Miami mafiosi, the gamblers and hit men and flesh merchants of Havana-as-it-had-been, who found Managua to be just like home. The city itself was problematic. Scattered and divided, broken by ruins and ravines, bereft of a central core or any kind of ordered structure, it was strategically and logistically a nightmare. Rebel barrios were cut off from each other by craters, by huge expanses of undeveloped land, by middle class districts bristling with fences and fear. And Managua, of course, was the headquarters and the home territory of the National Guard.

The underground never stopped coming apart. Members were arrested with heart-breaking regularity—arrested or simply found dead and mutilated in the reeds of the lake-front. Safehouses fell. Weapons stores were captured. People cracked under torture, and what little they knew—what little they'd been allowed to know—led to twenty or thirty more arrests. The Managua underground never really worked right. . . and never stopped working.

Daniel brooded on all that, lying on the floor a few feet from Rosa, wishing he could sleep. The explosives had arrived, finally. Clariz, the young woman with the gift of corn, had told him that. He thought about her, remembering her eyes, remembering the scent and the taste and the heat of her body when she had lain in his arms. It was so like her to buy him food. There were many other ways she could have passed on the information; all that was necessary was that she approach him, that she indicate a number. That was all he'd been told to watch for, all she'd been told to do. Yet she chose to make it a gift, a perfectly innocent gift that no one would notice any more than they noticed the coins or the oranges or anything else that the market people gave him, yet it was something special, something of herself.

He could not sleep, not with this heat and a hundred kids yelling in the street; not with the thought of her beauty coiling in his brain and in his loins, like a song, like a wound. He looked over at Rosa—sleeping, pregnant Rosa; limp flesh, there for Naldo's asking; alien, but always there. Was that why he chose her? Poor Rosa. Poor dumb Naldo.

He took his guitar and went back outside. He would play a few songs for Martin, for the neighbourhood children, and then he'd go. Tonight it was his and Paco's turn to train recruits; tomorrow he would go to the small garage that was known in the cell as station number two, where they would pick him up to make the bombs.

3

There was so much to talk about. Jadine was on her third *flor de cana* before she got around to telling them about the customs men; by then it seemed quite funny. There had been five of them, no less, all armed to the teeth, going through her lacy nothings and discarded chewing gum and dirty socks, unwrapping the gifts she'd brought and tossing the tinsel into sad little heaps on the floor; squeezing out her toothpaste and lifting her tampons out of their pockets by their tails, like dead mice.

"They're very hard on young people," Beatriz said. "Even North Americans."

Jadine shook her head. She'd had three drinks in an hour and no sleep in twenty-four, and the world was becoming very weird.

"I can see how they might think I had heroin in my vitamin caps," she said. "But my toothpaste? My tampons? *Really!*"

"Not heroin," Yolanda said. "Penicillin."

"*What?*"

"Penicillin." Yolanda's perfectly lined brows arched dramatically. "People smuggle all sorts of things to the Sandinistas that way—in aspirin bottles and toothpaste and such. Medicine, letters, even money. Once they found twenty thousand American dollars inside a baby's dirty diaper. Can you imagine? What a shameless way to use a child!"

"What did they do?" Jadine asked, although she didn't really want to know.

"What could they do? The mother was a foreign agent, a Mexican communist. They wanted to send the baby back to Mexico but no one would claim it—of course, anyone who did would have been implicated in the plot—so the poor thing is in prison with its mother in Granada. If she *is* its mother. If she didn't buy it from a beggar woman. The communists don't care. They'll use anything. They have no conscience."

Beatriz stood up. It had grown dark in the space of minutes, as though the sun had not gone down but had simply blinked out.

"No one in this war has any conscience," she said. Her face changed in the dark. It took on the shadows, the shiftings of the Managua night, the sadness of a city under siege. She came to Jadine's chair and wrapped an arm around her shoulders. "Come. We'll go inside."

Not inside, Jadine thought, surely not? She rose politely, although she did not want to stir. The night was exquisite. There was a moon hanging just over the patio wall and already she could count stars, stars that had long ago disappeared from the rotting skies of Pittsburgh. The air was honeyed with flowers, with *guayaba*, with the muskiness of night. Why in God's name would anyone want to go inside?

Leon put a rock album on the stereo and Pilar brought more drinks. And somehow it seemed like Kerry Heights again. Suburbs were the same all over the world: houses shut away from their neighbours and from the world, houses wrapped around themselves until they suffocated, until no one could remember the way in or the way out.

"Do you like Elton John?" Leon asked, holding up a record.

She didn't particularly, but she said yes, and he smiled. He was handsome. They all were, especially their father, the shopkeepers' son who had married well and grown prosperous, and who now liked to hint that he was descended from an old presidential family. He wasn't, of course, and everyone knew it, but his wife had relatives in the States, and that was just as good. Maybe better.

Leon laid the Elton John record to one side, ready to play next, and sat on a hassock next to Jadine.

"So did they give you all your stuff back?" he asked. "At customs?"

"Oh, eventually. Somewhat mangled, I'm afraid. I never thought I looked that much like a guerrilla." She took a long, pleasurable drink; this *flor de cana* rum was the best she'd ever tasted. "Who are they, anyway?" she asked. "The guerrillas? I couldn't get much out of the papers at home."

"Depends on who you ask," Leon said. "Politics is a volatile subject in this house."

"Oh," she said, ready to drop it like a hot coal, but Yolanda took it up at once.

"They're communists," she said. "Everything they do is planned and run from Cuba."

In the huge chair closest to the patio, Pilar shoved at a planter with her foot, as if in irritation, but she said nothing. She had said very little all evening.

"Are they really?" Jadine asked carefully. "Or is that just one of those blanket labels? Not very long ago all sorts of people were calling me a communist because I disagreed with the war in Viet Nam."

"A lot of them are," Leon said. "And a lot of them aren't. Some are social democrats and some are Christians and some are just fed up with Somoza."

"And the leaders?" Jadine asked.

"The leaders are communists," Yolanda said flatly.

Pilar looked up. "The leaders," she said, "are Sandinistas."

Fact. Perfect circle. A Sandinista is a Sandinista. End of

discussion. Jadine stared at her in soft amazement.

"Sandinistas are followers of Sandino," Leon explained, responding to what must have looked like bewilderment on her face. But she had known that. She had even seen a picture of Augusto Sandino in one of the magazines she'd read: a small, handsome man in an absurd cowboy hat who chased the U.S. Marines around northern Nicaragua for seven years until they gave up and went home, leaving in their place the National Guard and the first Somoza president, who promptly had Sandino shot. And disposed of, Jadine recalled, somewhere under the runways of Las Mercedes Airport. The modern way of burying heretics at the crossroads.

Sandinista, of course, meant follower of Sandino.

"Bandit, patriot, murderer, philosopher, military genius, crazy man," Leon went on. "Again, depending on who you ask."

"I think I won't ask," Jadine smiled.

"Very wise," Leon agreed, and passed her a plate of hors d'oeuvres. She took one and changed the subject, asked about Veronica, their sister who had married a chemist and lived in Costa Rica.

It was Veronica she had met—Veronica and Felipe, the two eldest—back in Kerry Heights, six years ago. The year before the earthquake. The year Alvaro and Beatriz, after a decade of dreaming about it, finally came to the United States with two of their five children. They had marvelled at everything, and she had marvelled at them, wondering how anyone could admire Pittsburgh. But she had liked them. They had a warmth and a charm that transcended Alvaro's pretensions and Veronica's obsession with movie stars, and that took the edge off Felipe's anger at the Viet Nam war. They stayed over a month; afterward she remembered them as generous and untroubled people. But that was six years ago and these were no longer the same Zelayas.

Alvaro, perhaps, was as sanguine and aggressive as always. He had stormed off to Bluefields the day before Jadine arrived, saying he'd get back when he got back, business was business. Perhaps he was unchanged. But

Felipe was dead and Veronica was gone and Beatriz moved like a shadow through a world that was remorselessly coming apart.

Jadine studied the younger children, who all looked older than their years. There had been an innocence about Veronica and Felipe that they did not have. Not even Leon. He was only sixteen, and with his blue jeans and t-shirts and rock music he should have looked like any Pennsylvania teenager. But he didn't. He looked like a grown man playing at youth, pretending to be sixteen because everyone expected it.

Pilar didn't pretend at all. She was nineteen going on thirty and she had eyes that Jadine did not ever want to see angry. She was beautiful. If she had wanted to she could have looked like a Vogue model; she had the colouring for it, the high cheekbones, the eyes and the perfectly curved mouth that Estee Lauder could have turned into a Cleopatran dream. But she plainly didn't care. Her dark hair was cut short; she wore no make-up, no jewellery, no spikes—nothing chic at all, except fashion boots and a musky French perfume. She looked tired, and didn't say much, but to Jadine her quietness seemed not a passive thing but a watchful self-containment, a waiting, a poised unease.

Only Yolanda was almost like she might have been. She was glamourous, like Veronica; fascinated by movies and all things North American. Every detail of her appearance was perfect, down to which shade of nail polish she wore with which Perlini sweater. On her left hand was a diamond—a very large diamond—the gift of Milan Valdez, whose extraordinarily handsome portrait sat on the piano. Earlier, before Leon took out his records, she had played for her guest, and Jadine had watched and marvelled how the light seemed to dance from the diamond to Milan's eyes and back again, almost as though Yolanda were not there at all, as though the diamond and the portrait were sufficient unto themselves.

These were Jadine's cousins, the family Zelaya Perez. Not what she remembered. Not at all what she expected. But then, nothing here was, except perhaps the violence, the void. That was the same because it was the same everywhere. Everywhere and always.

They were about to eat; Jadine excused herself to use the washroom. She took her time getting there, fascinated by the house. It was large and exotic, but to a North American eye it appeared somehow unfinished. The floors were stone tile, the room divisions flimsy. It seemed built neither for stability nor privacy, merely for space and airiness—a palatial tea-house in which to pass your Sunday afternoons.

She could not resist the temptation to go back into the patio; it seemed like just another room. Instantly she could smell the flowers, taste the sweetness of the night. It was so warm. She drifted, feeling an extraordinary inclination to take off her clothes. It was not an erotic impulse, merely a feeling of closeness to the earth, a feeling that here the earth was totally loving. She knew that wasn't true. Five years ago it had heaved up in rage and swallowed a tenth of Managua. She knew that but she could not believe it, could not imagine how this earth that you could sleep on without even a blanket could ever hurt you.

Minutes passed before she became aware of the sirens; after all, they were common enough in Pittsburgh. But the other sound she picked out instantly, sharp and separate from the purr of leaves and the distant vehicles and Leon's tiresome music. The sound of guns.

It was neither close by nor regular. Not a battle. Just somebody shooting, off to the north and west, where the belly of the city was. Once, then again; then somewhere else.

A leaf crunched a few feet away and she spun around, gulping fear. It was Pilar.

"Oh." Jadine laughed uncertainly. "Jesus, you startled me."

"I'm sorry," Pilar said. She didn't sound sorry. She didn't seem to be particularly aware of Jadine at all. She seemed to be listening, listening with her whole body, as though across the miles of darkness she could discover where the guns were.

Jadine waited, wondering what to say. She knew better

than to pretend she couldn't hear. The guns were there, like the earthquake and the Panamanian's three corpses. But what could you say about it? What could anybody say about it that was intelligent?

She remembered a movie she had seen once, some dumb thriller with Clint Eastwood or someone like him, Tarzan in jungle fatigues running through the streets of some South American town, grenades in his teeth and all, single-handedly restoring order to the world.

She didn't know what was going on out there in the streets of Managua, but she knew it was not that. She didn't even want the image in her head.

"Does this go on every night?" she asked.

"Yes." Pilar shifted. Some of the tautness seemed to leave her. "Every night. It was worse before, under martial law. They'd shoot anyone they saw on the streets after dark."

"The guerrillas?"

"No. *La Guardia*. The National Guard."

The National Guard. The government troops, the president's elite private army. The men she had seen in the jeeps and the trucks, with the cropped hair and the uneasy power of the pack. The men who even in sheltered Kerry Heights you heard about sometimes.

"That's why your mother took us inside, wasn't it?"

"Mama hasn't set foot outside of her house after dark for two and a half years. She's even grown to like Leon's music. She used to hate it. Now she lets him play it as much as he likes. As loud as he likes. Mama is determined to grow deaf."

"It's an ambition I can understand," Jadine said.

"Then you are in the wrong country."

Jadine didn't know what to say to that; she was afraid that it might be true.

"Do you think I shouldn't have come?" It was only half a question.

"No. I didn't mean that. I'm glad you're here. Only I'm...curious. This is not a place people come for holidays, unless they are frivolous, and you are not that."

No. Not that. Many unadmirable things, but not that.

"Pilar..." She knew she should not start to talk about

these things. Not before supper. Probably not ever. "Pilar, did mother write you how Eryn died?"

Pilar drew vaguely closer in the darkness. "She wrote only that it was an accident. We thought probably it was a road accident."

"No. It wasn't an accident. He killed himself."

"God in heaven. . ."

"He stuffed his pockets with gravel from a construction site and jumped off McKinley Bridge."

Pilar murmured something; it was soft and muddy and probably purely *nica*; its meaning eluded Jadine completely, but the warmth in it did not. She went on:

"He left two letters—one for our parents, and one for me. I've never shown mine to anyone. It wasn't very long. He just said that he loved me and that he didn't really want to die because it was human nature to want to live. Still, he said, you had to have some kind of reason for going on living, for using up air when there wasn't enough air to go around. . .

"Can you imagine what it must be like to be reduced to that—to believe that you no longer have any right even to the air?" She turned away from Pilar and began to walk, aimlessly, touching plants like amulets.

"Afterward, everyone—all our relatives—kept saying they couldn't understand. Saying that he had everything anyone could want. They acted like he'd insulted them, like he'd dirtied the family name. Not one of them said a word about what he must have gone through. Not one.

"Don't people have a right to die, Pilar? I mean, isn't that the oldest right of all, that you don't have to go on forever and forever in the coil of a nightmare? That you can say no? Even if you can't say anything else, you can say no?"

She could hear leaves shift beside her. Nothing else. Even the guns were still.

"Pilar?"

"I'm here," Pilar said. She did not say anything more for a long time. Then, finally:

"You're right, of course. We have a right to say no. It's the first act of freedom. But is it enough?"

"What do you mean, enough?"

"You begin by saying no to what is there. Then you must say yes to something else."

"There is nothing else," Jadine said.

"Nothing?"

"No."

"Eh, *muchachas!*" They both looked up as Leon's tall silhouette appeared in the doorway, calling them to supper.

"Coming," Pilar answered, but she made no move to go in.

"Come now," Leon insisted. "We're sitting down."

"*Bueno,*" Pilar retorted. "Go sit."

Leon waved black silhouette arms. "Jesus! You're lucky you are a girl, Pilar. In the army they would shoot you."

"No doubt. Go tell mama we're coming. Go on."

He disappeared, grumbling audibly.

"My little brother," Pilar said, "is a great pain in the ass." They began to walk very slowly toward the house. "I know how you must feel," she went on. "When Felipe was killed, I felt...God, how can I say what I felt? We couldn't even bury him; we couldn't find his body."

So, Jadine mused bitterly, the whole world is a potter's field...

"It was Christmas day," Pilar said, "and there were seven, maybe eight thousand dead in the ruins and in the streets. And there were people who asked us why my brother hadn't been at home. Asked us what he had been doing in the barrio where he died, as though simply by being there he had forfeited his right to pity.

"To be dead is to be guilty, Jadine. Always."

That might be true, but it was beside the point. The question was not the meaning of death.

"But Felipe didn't kill himself, Pilar. He didn't turn against life. It seemed to me, when I met him, that he believed in it totally."

"Yes. Yes, he did."

"How could he? How can anyone?"

Pilar paused and turned to her cousin. They were almost at the house; weak light sculpted the taut lines of her cheekbones and her forehead, left her eyes in shadow.

"If Felipe were here to answer you, he would say: How can I not?"

Of course he would. Faith was as self-evident to the innocent as despair was to the disillusioned.

"And you, Pilar? Would you say the same as Felipe?"

"No." She started walking again. "Felipe believed that the meaning of life was absolute, that it was given. I believe we have to make it ourselves. Make it and keep on making it as long as we live, as long as the world turns."

"But do you think that's possible? To *make* meaning?"

"*Claro*. Of course it's possible."

"Of course." Out of bombs and machine guns and *guayaba* and shanties and Molly Hatchett, Felipe devoured by earth and Eryn by water; from the caves to the stars nothing has changed, it's all been rot and poverty and blood, the good die and the mad govern, we dream and grope and blunder and grow old, and one day the universe will implode and begin again, and in the hundred million billion atoms spinning into space there will not be one that will carry a trace of anything we have been or done or thought.

But we will make meaning!

Nice work, she thought, if you can get it.

"You think what I say is foolish, don't you?" Pilar observed.

"No. Not foolish. I think what you say is magnificent. But it's a dream. Purely a dream."

"Well, if it *is* a dream, it's the one that people care about the most, and always have."

"Yes," Jadine said. "But with what result?"

"What would be the result if there were no dreams? If there were no search for meaning?"

"We wouldn't be here. We wouldn't have made it past Sodom and Gomorrah."

"And would that be better?"

"Probably," Jadine sighed.

"Who gets to choose?"

The question threw her. All evening Pilar had been shifting the focus of what she thought they were talking about. This was a totally unexpected shift.

"What?" she said.

"Who gets to choose?" Pilar repeated. "Who gets to say if the world is worth it or not? Children? Old men? Lovers? Beggars? White people? Rich people? North Americans? *Nicas*? Who?"

Oh, ouch! Jadine laughed. "Well, I do, of course. What else are disillusioned wandering intellectuals good for?"

4

Surveillance was the shits. Of all the rotten jobs in the Guardia, it was the absolute worst. Ramon had been here since daybreak, outside this dumb little bakery, waiting for God knew what, playing guessing games as to which of the teenagers and housewives and fat old women who shuffled in and out were really Sandinistas. He'd been here yesterday, too, and the day before that.

The word had come down: Watch the Panaderia Martin. It was always like that. Watch this. Watch that. No explanations, no clues. He'd bitched about it once and Gomez had said quite flatly: "Use your fuckin' head. If we *knew* what they were doing, we'd haul them in."

He was right, of course, but there was no end to it. All the guardsmen in the country, all the police and firemen and customs agents, every God damn public servant there was could be assigned to surveillance and they still wouldn't be able to stay on top of things even in Managua.

Even here, in the capital—forget about the rest of the country. How many streets could you watch, how many houses? How many pharmacies, beer halls, welding shops, shoemakers, taco stands? How many beggars, hawkers, bootblacks, whores, priests, waiters, brats, babes in fucking arms? Nicaragua was crawling with subversion. You couldn't trust your own mother. Hell, you couldn't trust yourself.

But he watched the Martin Bakery like he was told, watched Claudia Martin drive off early every morning with the regular deliveries to the Santa Luisa Hospital and the local restaurants, watched the customers come and go. Everything was ordinary, innocent. But then, it always was—right up until the moment the guns went off. That was what he hated about the guerrillas—and admired, too, just a little. They had poise.

Claudia Martin came and went and came again. She was a pleasant looking woman, plump from too many sweets and a peasant ancestry, but nice. The kind of woman he had once expected to marry. Now. . . he shifted, soaked in sweat and numb with boredom, watching Claudia Martin latch her broken-down garage door and walk into the bakery. Now he figured he could do a lot better.

"*Hola.*" Claudia kissed her husband, took a pastry from the shelf, asked if he had gotten the mail.

"There was nothing," he said.

Her mouth twisted. It was seventeen weeks now.

"We will hear," he said. "Someone will write."

Yes. Someone would write. And she would hand the letter to Rafael with greedy desperate eyes and he would read it to her and it would say: We have seen nothing. We have heard nothing. We don't know where they are.

She poured them each a coffee. His eyes were sleep-starved, like her own. It was not easy to rest with a shipment of high explosives hidden among the flour and the sugar in your storeroom, and with the Guardia camped at your gate.

She did not wait for his question. He asked it every day, in one form or another. Had she spoken to Valerian? To anyone? When were they going to make a move?

"Manolo's in the van," she said, and added quickly, in reply to his instant, unspoken fear: "No one saw him." She sipped coffee.

"Well?" he demanded.

She looked at him. They had worked on a lot of actions and he took what came but he had never liked this one. Partly because he had no control of it. Partly that. And partly whatever.

He was going to like this part of it even less.

"Manolo's making the bombs tonight," she said. "Here. And I'm taking them out in the morning with the deliveries."

Methodically, Rafa ground his cigarette into a black smudge. "Whose great idea was that?"

Actually, the plan was Manolo's, though the order to move had come from Valerian. As he very well knew it had to.

"The *comandante,*" she said simply.

"It's crazy."

"What can we do?" she protested. "What would you do? Wait for a raid?"

He didn't answer. He knew they had to do something, not only to protect themselves, but to protect whatever operation was underway. The explosives were high quality—explosives the Frente could rarely afford. They were clearly earmarked for something big. Something for which many other people were working and waiting and taking risks just like his. Or Claudia's.

Against that collective necessity he had no arguments—none that he could respect. "Well," he said, "I don't suppose Manolo's very comfortable in that van."

Manolo was not comfortable at all. He was lying on the floor, packed around with a variety of crates and trays and several hundred loaves of bread. He had crumbs in his hair and crumbs all down his back and he was sweltering. Rafa cleared away the camouflage and reached quickly to help him to his feet. The Martins knew him well; they had known him for years as Daniel Chillan, but now called him only by his Sandinista code name, or simply, *companero*.

"All right, *compa*?" Rafael asked.

"All right," Daniel said. He rubbed the bruises on his

hip from the three pot-holes Claudia had hit at forty miles an hour. "Your wife drives like a maniac."

"Tell me about it," Rafa said.

"I do not," Claudia said flatly. "It's not my fault the streets of Managua are fit for nothing but oxcarts."

"Even in an oxcart you would drive like a maniac."

"I'll tell you what, Manolito," she said, smiling. "Next time I'll put you in the other compartment. Then you won't bounce."

The other compartment was the storage unit they had built under the floor of the van. It was at best four and a half inches deep.

Rafa looked critically at his comrade. There really wasn't much of Daniel Chillan. Not very much at all.

"God knows, love," he said, "but I think he'd fit."

"Screw you," Daniel said cheerfully, shaking crumbs out of his shirt.

Rafael laughed and embraced him, and they spoke a little of their own lives, and their families. Then Rafa picked up an armful of empty crates and prepared to go back to the bakery.

"The rear door cannot be seen from the street," he said. "But anyone might be watching from the neighbours. You must wait here till it's dark. I'll fetch you."

"*Claro*."

They waited until it was very dark and made their way like a pair of thieves across the ten feet or so of open yard. Even without the presence of the Guardia, Daniel would not have gone openly to the bakery, or to the house of any other comrade. The Chillan name had been in police files for a long time. His brothers had been forced into periods of hiding, and he himself had been arrested twice and had spent most of the thirty-three months of martial law underground.

But things had gotten better over the summer. Somoza had a heart attack in July, and since then his lackeys and his eldest son—the one they called El Chiguin—and the Guard commanders were all jockeying for power. The bourgeois opposition was trying to organize, and the U.S. government was putting the screws on Somoza to let it. Washington called it a human rights policy. Valerian called it toilet water.

"The gorilla has begun to stink," he said, "so they mean to hose him down a bit...or even swap him for a nice clean monkey. They must think we have no brains at all."

It was a lull, nothing more, a strategic retreat. Whatever bargains the ruling class made among itself, whatever bargains Washington made with it, life in the barrios would not change. But the lull was good just the same; politically and personally they thrived on it. Daniel loved Managua, for all its craziness and tears—or maybe because of that—loved the sun, loved the simple animal freedom of the streets. But he was still careful. Very careful. And he knew that it would not last, that one day soon he would have to go underground for good.

At the back of the bakery were the two rooms where Rafael lived with his father, his wife Claudia, and his child; and another, smaller room where the supplies were stored. Into this room they had moved a wooden table, a chair, and a small lamp. Daniel looked around. The building was old and solid, built in better times, with thick adobe walls. From here there was only one way out—back into the bakery. The room smelled of flour and dust; it felt like a closet, like a cage.

"Well," he said. Well. How many times do I do this until it is the last time? "Let's begin, then."

He didn't count the hours; he had no sense of them passing at all. They dissolved into the numbing heat of this room without windows, were lost among the plates and wires, melted into the sweat that ran down his body like rain. As he finished each charge, Rafa and Claudia took it away and packed it with infinite care under the floor of the van.

The light was bad. Not the worst he had ever worked in, but almost. As the night wore on his head began to throb, and at times he was no longer perfectly sure of what he could see. He stopped then and went into the family quarters to beg Claudia for coffee and cigarettes.

She offered him food as well—a rich-looking chunk of bread with a piece of cheese stuffed into it—but he was too raw to eat. He took a cigarette from her and lit it and she saw that his hands were shaking, that his thin cotton shirt was sticking to his body like a rag.

"I don't know about you," she said, "but me, I'd rather be at the beach."

He laughed then, and put his head back and closed his eyes until the coloured lights stopped going on and off.

He had never imagined that he would ever do anything like this. When he was fourteen and the Frente Sandinista was the scattered and bloodied dreamchild of a Matagalpa student with horn-rimmed glasses and the imagination of a poet, Daniel Chillan had wanted only to become a *guerrillero*. To live in the mountains. To do things they would write songs about, as he wrote songs about Sandino.

But he had joined the student movement in high school, and from there was drawn irrevocably into the urban underground. He was good with his hands. More than good; brilliant. And in a struggle like this one everybody did what they did best. Valerian organized. His mother networked block after block of barrio women into cells of resistance. He played music, forged documents, built radios, fixed everything from typewriters to trucks. And made bombs.

"Manolito." Claudia's hand fell lightly on his shoulder. "Coffee?"

He took it and thanked her. She sat on the floor beside his chair, stirring her coffee with her finger. She would have liked to go and bury herself in Rafa's arms, but she was reluctant to let either of them guess the depth of her fear.

"It's time to wake Grandpa," Rafa said. Time to start making bread. Time to affirm that the world was going to go on exactly as before.

Wearily, Daniel got to his feet, drawing the last wisp of life from his cigarette. "I'll be done in a couple of hours," he said.

Rafa came and put an arm gently around his neck. "Easy, *compa*," he said. "Easy. There's lots of time."

The heat of the sun woke Ramon. He sat up quickly, praying that no one had seen him doze. It was quiet on the street, though some people were out and the Panaderia Martin, as usual, was open for business—a service to those who liked to stop for sweets and coffee on their way to work. Office workers mostly, bank clerks and secretaries and the like, people who could afford sweets and coffee but couldn't afford to buy them in a nice place. They came in singles and pairs; then two sports cars drove by loaded with young people and tennis rackets and clamourous with music. The rear car parked suddenly and somebody shouted: "It's open! This one's open!"

The other car braked and crunched into reverse and parked a hairsbreadth ahead, and the whole lot of them poured into the Panaderia Martin. Well, almost the whole lot of them. Two girls, one from each car, preferred to sit on the fenders and gossip. They were wearing short tennis dresses; one of them was blonde and European looking and absolutely stunning. Ramon watched her dreamily. Now that, he thought, was what he would like for himself. Definitely that.

The others came out loaded with pastries and ice cream, and the girls decided that they wanted something after all, and some of their friends went back in. And one young man had forgotten his sunglasses and ran after them, and there was so much coming and going that Ramon never noticed that altogether eight people went into the bakery and nine came out.

The cars went happily on their way, turning onto the Avenida Roosevelt and around Tiscapa to the Masaya highway. There, on a long stretch of open road, one of them parked, and the other drove on, all hands waving.

The driver of the parked car leaned into the back seat, pleased with himself.

"*Bueno*, my friend. Hurry."

Quickly Daniel stripped off the sports clothes he had worn over his jeans and rolled them into a ball with the sunglasses. He handed them back, gripping the driver's hand hard.

"Thank you, *companero*." He shook hands all round, thanked them all. They were all strangers to him except the driver, all students, probably. Kids who weren't exactly revolutionaries but who would load up a car and go if someone said to them: Look, we've got this *companero* who's in a bad spot and we need some help to get him out...

He stepped from the car into the clean morning sun. The driver raised his hand in a quick salute.

"*Patria libre*!"

Daniel replied with an upraised fist. "*O morir!*"

They pulled out fast, vanished quickly along the narrow and winding road. For a few minutes, until more cars came, it was wonderfully still. All along this road were beautiful farms, the *fincas* of the rich and the almost rich. They were green and languourous with shade, bounteous with cocoa palms and corn and cattle. Once, his grandfather had owned a little piece of land. A very little piece, very long ago. He let his eyes drift along the road, over the gates with names and speared fences, to the hills, to the brooding volcano of Santiago, naked and smouldering in its sea of ash. The land was so lovely it hurt to look at it.

A truck passed, loaded with vegetable and *campesinos*. He let it pass and then crossed the road. He was utterly spent. He untucked his shirt and sat on a rock and waited for the bus from Masaya to take him home.

Manolito was gone. Safe. Claudia bowed her head to the painted Madonna, thanked her for that great kindness. Then she looked up. It wasn't much of an icon: a stylized Virgin in blue silks who bore no imaginable resemblance to the peasant girl whose son had taken on the Roman Empire. Claudia closed her eyes, spoke to the woman who had been and who was.

"Please Mary, please Jesus, give us strength. Shield us from the hate of our enemies. Amen."

Below the picture was the wooden cradle where her daughter slept. She kissed the child without waking her, and turned as Rafa came in. He had on a clean shirt and the one pair of good trousers that he wore to Mass on Sundays. He pulled the door firmly shut behind him.

"I'm driving the van," he said.

Jesus. She looked at the baby, at the Virgin, at the wall. Jesus, not this. Not now.

She didn't have the strength to be patient. "Would you like a *rojinegro* banner, too? You can fly it out the broken window."

"Don't be a bitch, Claudia."

"Rafa..." God, it was hard to fight in whispers. "Rafa, for God's sake! You never drive the van. They'll know it's not an ordinary delivery. They'll *know*!"

"Maybe," he said stubbornly. "But I'm not sending a woman out to face the Guardia's guns."

"Women are facing the Guardia's guns from one end of Nicaragua to the other."

"Not my wife. Not while I'm sitting here selling pastries."

Oh, stuff it, Rafael. Just stuff it..."And I suppose after they shoot you they'll come in here and doff their helmets and say we're terribly sorry, *senora*, but we had to kill your husband, have a nice day! In God's name, Rafa, it doesn't make any difference who's out there or who's in here. If they find the bombs they'll kill us all."

He would not look at her, or answer.

"Look..." She wanted to say: Look, I have a right to go. I don't particularly want to, but it's my right. I am a Sandinista. And that means a lot of things but finally it means that I have a right to die like any other revolutionary, and if you take that away you're taking something else, something of my courage, something of my power and my wholeness. You're making me less than you.

She wanted to say that but she knew it would not make sense to him because he would not let it.

"The Frente needs those bombs, Rafael. We have to get them out. God knows we might get caught no matter who drives the damn van, but we have no right to make the risk any worse. We have no bloody right to do that!"

Their eyes met and held. He cursed. "Go then," he said. "If you live to see Valerian, tell him what a fucking asshole he is."

Well, I might tell him what a fucking asshole you *think* he is...

"Ciao, *compa*," she whispered, and walked past him into the bakery. The truck keys were on the counter where Grandpa was counting change for a half loaf of bread. She put them in her pocket, said good morning to the old woman who was about to leave, and when Grandpa wasn't looking, took the nicest pastry from his display plate.

"What shall I bring from the market, *abuelo*?"

He shrugged. He looked spent and sad. He had taught all his children that it was a sin to kill, and now he was helping them to make bombs.

"I'll get a rabbit," she suggested. "A big, fat rabbit. And some tomatoes and squash. We'll celebrate tonight."

"Well, then," he said. "If we're going to celebrate, I want some beer."

She looked at Rafa who stood in the bedroom doorway, watching her but refusing to meet her eyes. "Beer?" she asked him.

"Yes," he said. "Beer is fine."

Claudia opened the garage door and eased the van toward the street and they closed in like hawks; she would not have believed that so many of them could appear from nowhere so fast. Within seconds three trucks had blocked the driveway and the street, and the Guardia was swarming around her and pouring into the bakery.

A man wearing a sergeant's insignia waved her out of the cab. She stepped out slowly, her hands raised, into a waiting circle of guns. The sergeant waved her back, back, back, until she stood in the grass against the fence. He made her turn and lean against it, and he searched her deliberately and crudely, handling her every way he could, while the others watched and laughed, and asked him what she was like, and how she liked it.

She bit her lip and made herself not really listen, not really think about being a woman at all. This was the Guardia and this was war; the hands on her body were weapons like any other. No more, no less. They carried no special, evil magic; they could not touch her soul, no more than a club could, or a bullet. She remembered the woman in her home village near Esteli who had been gang-raped by soldiers, and who worked her fields after and sold her things in the market, with her head up, just like before. And one well-meaning woman had praised her, said how strong she must be to live so bravely with such shame.

And she had looked the woman clear in the eyes and said: "What do you mean, *companera*? What shame do you speak of? Your house was burned by the Guardia—are you ashamed?" She looked around, picking out others who were there: "And your son was beaten, and yours killed. And you were four years in prison, and lost the sight of an eye. Are you ashamed?" None of them answered her.

Oppression was oppression, she said. If you beat a man or raped a woman or starved a child, what was the difference? Shame belonged to the guilty.

You had to remember that, Claudia thought. Always remember that. Always.

The sergeant stepped back and ordered her to turn around. She looked full at his face. He was a very ordinary man. In another reality he would have been a farmer or a bricklayer and he would have had his wife and his friends and his Saturday night beer and he would have never dreamt of living like this.

He questioned her: Where was she going?

"To deliver bread, just like always."

"Where?"

She told him.

What did her husband do?

"He's a baker."

"And what else?"

"What do you mean, what else?" Over his shoulder she could see them searching the van. They were shameless. They threw the baskets of bread one by one into the street, slashed loaves open to see if anything was hidden inside. A tray full of pastries splattered against the grill fence, and some of them hung there like speared birds, and gobs of jam rolled down the rusty iron into the grass.

Her anger grew unbearable, watching that. There was something foul about destroying food, something quite separate from destruction itself. The anger coiled in her belly and dried her throat and crept to the very tips of her fingers, grinding her nails into her flesh. The sergeant saw her anger, and it amused him.

"Look at it this way, *senora*. What you do not eat cannot make you fatter."

She speared him with her eyes and looked away. God help me, Rafa, I'm going to kill the pig. If he says one more thing I'm going to kill him...

But she didn't, not even when he asked her if she was a

communist, if her husband was a communist, if her children were communists.

"My baby is two years old," she said.

That, perhaps, he believed; the child's wailing could be heard in the street. Other sounds, too, from inside the bakery—things being moved, being thrown, breaking.

By now the entire cargo of the van was on the ground, and they were slashing the seats and prying off the hub-caps. The sergeant himself went to peer into the van's belly and then climbed inside. She could hear him say, quite clearly: "Fucking pigs!" She knew what the inside looked like. There was dried-up goo on everything, and crumbs and grass and dirty flour, and in the corners real dirt, and things that looked suspiciously like mouse shit. It didn't look like the floor could be opened; it didn't look like the floor could be *reached* except with scrapers and scrub brushes. Daniel and Grandpa had spent an hour and four jars of syrup to get it into that condition.

The sergeant stepped back out, looked at Claudia with disgust, and went into the bakery. Claudia watched him, her anger slowly melting into fear. God, please don't let him kill anyone. . .please. . .*please*. . .

Inside there was nothing. Flour and sugar and pots and pans, an account book, an old man bleeding from the mouth where he'd been hit and a young man with his hands pressed against the wall. A screaming baby.

"Nothing," Ramon told the sergeant. "Not a fucking thing."

The sergeant began to question Rafael. He got nothing more from him that he had gotten from Claudia, but he was able to vent a good deal of his frustration—which by now was the only remaining purpose of the raid. He left the baker in a heap on the floor and stalked out, waving his men after him.

"Come on! We've wasted enough time on this rubbish."

They left as they had come, quickly and arrogantly. At the last moment the sergeant turned in the seat of his jeep and emptied a clip from his Uzi into the windshield of the van. A closing statement to the Martins and the barrio and all of Managua: We are here. We command. Look how easily we could have killed you all, how easily we will kill you tomorrow if you forget!

Claudia saw the rifle swing around and dove into the gravel, not thinking, knowing that she was dead, trying to formulate some prayer that had no words. It drowned in gunfire and shattering glass, in the sound of bullets hitting metal and earth and grass and wind, spinning off the grill fence into a neighbour's adobe wall, falling silent then, stopping as carelessly as it had begun. She heard the trucks begin to move, heard shouts and running feet. She lifted her head an inch. There was no pain; no blood except a small trickle from her hand where a splinter of glass had struck. Broken glass was all around her. Rafa was kneeling in it, sobbing.

"I'm all right." She said it to calm him, and only afterward realized it was true, and began to cry.

As soon as the Guardia left the people came—women mostly, from nearby shops and houses. They took the still frantic baby from Claudia's arms and made her sit down, gave her coffee, tied a bandage around her hand and another around the old man's head. They collected what food could still be sold and loaded it back into the van; the rest of it Rafa gave to them, and to the neighbourhood waifs who scraped the jam off the grill fence with their fingers and searched for scraps in the grass. Two teenage boys removed the shattered windshield and changed a riddled tire, and left with two sacks of damaged bread.

When they were finished, Rafa walked with Claudia back to the van and kissed her on the mouth, not caring that half the barrio was still in his yard. She smiled at him, then looked ruefully at the mangled truck. It would take everything they earned for months to get it fixed.

"I guess we forget about the rabbit," she said.

"No." He was looking at it too, ransacked and bullet-scarred, still carrying enough precision explosives to blow Somoza's bunker right off the side of its mountain. "No. Buy the rabbit. Buy the biggest rabbit you can find. For some things one must give thanks."

5

They were tearing Somoza limb from limb in the press. Day after day Leon or Pilar would bring home the Chamorro paper, *La Prensa*—the opposition paper—and Jadine would read it in amazement. The attacks were relentless. They accused the National Guard of massacres in the countryside and accused the president of channelling public funds into private Somoza enterprises. They demanded the release of political prisoners, a return to democratic government, an end to monopolies and corruption. And they made it clear that the press was not alone in its protests, that all through the country there were mass demonstrations, sit-ins in churches and schools, spontaneous outbreaks of rock-throwing and bus-burning; that new union alliances were being formed, new action groups, a women's organization. To read *La Prensa* was to see all of Nicaragua in motion; the single target of its rage was Anastasio Somoza Debayle.

Jadine wondered how the paper got away with it. A number of people in the suburb of Las Colinas—including, apparently, Alvaro—seemed to think that Somoza was too tolerant. Leon thought that Chamorro was too famous and too well respected to be silenced. And Pilar said that criticism of the government from within the ruling class had always been permitted in Nicaragua because it never meant very much.

Nicaraguan politics had been a private club for generations, she explained: Granada against Leon, old landed gentry against new moneyed bourgeoisie. Criticism was mostly competition from within; it never implied a change in the structure, merely in the personnel; and it was accepted because neither faction was strong enough to completely dominate the other. And it was useful: it provided a nice facade of democracy.

Chamorro was one of the honourable critics, and he was stepping further and further outside the boundaries of his approved mandate. But he was part of that tradition and therefore he was tolerated. For the moment. Sooner or later, Pilar said, Somoza would re-establish censorship or close down the paper altogether.

This seemed to Jadine to make a certain amount of sense, although her knowledge of Nicaraguan history was slight. She knew that the first Somoza had come to power in 1934, and that the family had ruled the country ever since. There were political parties, of a sort, and even elections, but they didn't seem to mean much. There had been a lot of repression, a lot of cruelty, an enormous accumulation of wealth by the Somoza clan. The first patriarch was eventually assassinated by a poet, only to be replaced by one and then by another of his sons.

But his death had sparked the resistance, and in the early sixties three students, led by Carlos Fonseca, founded the revolutionary Sandinista Front—an organization which, as far as Jadine could tell, was never taken seriously by any of the world's large contingent of guerrilla-watchers; or by Somoza, who regularly assured everyone that it had just been wiped out; or indeed by anyone except presumably the Sandinistas themselves, who kept right on reappearing. Like a bad penny. Or a bad conscience—assuming that the

Somozas had a conscience at all. The question was open to debate.

It was difficult to see the ruling family as anything but a very shabby breed. She had been told, since arriving, that the first Somoza's credentials on assuming power had included experience in counterfeiting and toilet inspection, as well as an excellent command of English; that Franklin Roosevelt had cheerfully referred to him as "a son of a bitch, but he's *our* son of a bitch"; and that the clan consistently enjoyed a good relationship with Washington.

It was a classic case of banana belt politics and American stupidity, she reflected. We always pick the assholes. We must lie awake nights trying to figure out who's the biggest asshole, trying to determine which is the worst of all possible options, and then we defend it to the death. So often and so literally to the death.

She closed the paper and went to the kitchen, craving a drink. Maria was up to her elbows in pastry but she turned at once, smiling, scraping dough from her hands.

"*Si, senorita Hadine?*" She still hadn't gotten used to saying the *J*; the name came out sounding Arabic. Rather nice, actually, Jadine thought.

"It's all right, Maria. I just came for a *refresco*."

"I will make it."

"But you're busy—"

"No, no, I will make it. What would you like? Lime? *Guayaba*? Pineapple? Rum with it, of course?"

Jadine gave up. Servants were a fact of life here. "*Guayaba*, please. And lots of rum; I need it."

"You are feeling sick?" Maria asked, instantly concerned.

"No. Just depressed. I've been reading the paper."

Maria's face curled in scorn. "Papers! I never read the papers."

"Why not?"

She put the jar of *guayaba* down and leaned on the counter. "One paper is Somoza's, and he is president. The other paper is Chamorro's, and he wants to be president. I am a cook, and I don't want to be anything but a cook. *Entiende*?"

"Yes," Jadine said. "I understand perfectly."

She took her rum drink and wandered back to the patio. Already she had begun to feel limited by this house, by this yard with its languid trees and seven-foot stone fence. Beatriz had warned her against wandering around Managua by herself, but she knew that she would do so just the same. For many reasons. For truth—what one could find of it. For experience. For excitement—that too, God forgive her, that sad measure of being alive. For an end. Some kind of end to the void, to the ambivalence that wouldn't just let it be a void, that wanted knowledge even while recoiling from it, that wanted to die but not just yet, maybe there was another way, but of course there wasn't. Yes, an end.

The next morning was Sunday. Jadine hadn't attended Mass for years, but it seemed polite to go along with the family. The priest was a plain man, growing bald and overweight, and he gave a very dull sermon that interested Jadine only occasionally, when he dragged in a little bit of politics. Christians had a duty to live in peace, he said. To trust each other. To put the common good above personal differences or ambition. Christians had a special responsibility to heal and restore this troubled country.

It was all appropriately vague and admirable. Some people seemed impressed, but the Zelaya family, by and large, did not. Alvaro, returned late last night from Bluefields, was half asleep. Leon was palpably bored. Pilar was brooding and Yolanda was regularly and indiscreetly stealing glances at Milan Valdez.

Jadine stole a couple herself, just to confirm her first impressions. He *did* have it all, she reflected: looks, style, rank, money. He had a stunning green Porsche parked out front, a mansion higher up in Las Colinas, a yacht on which he and Yolanda would honeymoon, a completely furnished and staffed holiday home in Switzerland, a condominium in Maui, and a wardrobe to make Prince Rainier weep. Income from his own stocks and properties, according to Yolanda, was around five hundred thousand a year (dollars, not cordobas, she emphasized) and he stood to inherit, with one brother, his father's land holdings in Carazo and Chinandega, a vast array of investments, and most of Santa Rosa Industries, a giant chemical processing plant on the outskirts of Managua.

And on top of all that he was charming.

Jadine sighed, not with envy but with a gentle cynicism. She had known two or three such men herself; none of them ever quite grew up; none of them came to terms with the limitations of reality. She wished Yolanda luck.

After Mass they milled in the yard for a while, Alvaro and Beatriz introducing her to a bewildering number of friends and relatives. Then Yolanda went off with her fiance to play tennis and the rest of them drove back to Las Colinas.

It was a beautiful day. They would have lunch, Beatriz suggested, and let Papa sleep a while; then they would join Yolanda and Milan at the country club.

Maria served them in the patio: fruit juice and rum and salads and lush little tarts stuffed with rice and shrimp. Alvaro asked Jadine about her family, about the World Series just completed (he loved baseball), about her plans. Did she mean to stay for a while?

"I was hoping to," she said. She thought about it, and decided that it was too soon to mention the matter of finding her own place. She knew that families in Latin America—families almost everywhere, in fact, except on her own continent—simply assumed that an unmarried female relative would live with them. They would probably be appalled if she suggested getting an apartment three days after she had arrived. She wasn't even sure if there were any apartments to be had. She would give it some time, she decided, send out a few discreet feelers first. Maybe Pilar would help.

"Actually," she went on, "I thought I'd like to work here for a while."

"Excellent," he said. "You've got a job with Zelaya Imports any time you want one. I can never get enough people who know English—good English, that is. And who can spell it. You must admit it's a beastly language to spell."

"Yes," she said, laughing. "It is."

"I know you need to rest," he went on. "Take as long

as you like. Just let me know. It's there whenever you want it."

"Thank you," she said. God, they were good people, she reflected. Really good people.

The day grew languid, though it was cool up here compared to the searing heat of the city's core. Alvaro settled into his hammock with yesterday's *Novedades*, the Somoza paper. Pilar slipped off to some deep corner of the house to study. Beatriz nodded in her chair.

"We seem to be the survivors," Leon said.

She looked at him. He'd had several drinks and the thing she had seen in his face the first night, the absence of youth, was naked now.

"Tell me something, Leon," she said. "What's going on here? In Nicaragua, I mean. What's really going on?"

He waved an idle hand toward his father, who by now was snoring peacefully, his paper spilled across his breast.

"What's going on? Old men sleep, draped in their illusions like a corpse in a flag."

She waited for him to go on, but he didn't.

"And while they sleep?" she prompted.

He shrugged, and quoted Yeats in a bad translation: "Things fall apart, the centre cannot hold; mere anarchy is loosed upon the world...Have you met my soon-to-be brother-in-law?"

"Milan? We were introduced, that's all."

"And what do you think of him?"

It was her turn to shrug. "He's very handsome. Very poised. Probably very arrogant."

"He's rotten to the core," Leon said.

After all those poetic effusions the blunt statement seemed twice as harsh. "Why do you say that?"

"Just remember that I said it." He stood up. "It's awfully quiet out here. Shall we have some music?"

"Your father's asleep, Leon."

"Yes, I know." He smiled. Winsomely. Bitterly. "If a revolution can't wake him up, how can I?"

Suddenly, harshly, the sound of heavy rock throbbed through every room of the house. Leon again. Pilar frowned and snapped her door shut with her foot. It didn't make much difference—not with the grill above and all the windows open. She laid aside her notebook, wished for night, for human space and human voices, for Daniel's body, Daniel's guitar. She hated this puerile, clamourous music—music that ground away the edges of human sensitivity until the totality of consciousness could be expressed by a drum and a blank stare. She didn't believe the radicals who said that North American music was a capitalist plot to destroy the souls of American youth. It never had to be plotted; it came about quite naturally. She only wished they had kept it at home. If there was one thing Nicaragua didn't need, it was the Grateful Dead.

A light tap sounded on her door.

"*Pase*," she said.

Jadine stuck her head inside hesitantly. "Can I come in?"

"Of course."

"I'm looking for a place to hide before your father wakes up."

Pilar laughed and cleared away the books she had piled on her chair. The room was austere. There were a lot of books and papers, a few small stone carvings, and on the wall were reprints of two magnificent Mexican murals. Pilar was sitting on the floor, texts and dog-eared assignments scattered all around her.

"You know, Pilar," Jadine said lightly, "you remind me of me."

"How do you mean?"

"Ten years ago,"—God, was there that much difference in their ages?—"they called me slave-in-residence at Penn State. They also called me the flying purple paper eater."

Pilar took a package of cigarettes from her purse and shook one out for her cousin. Jadine wagged her head.

"Thanks. I don't smoke."

"Do you mind?" Pilar asked, taking one for herself.

"Not at all."

"What did you study?"

"Languages. Would you believe I wanted to join the diplomatic corps?"

"What happened?"

"Viet Nam."

"Ah," Pilar said.

"What about you?" Jadine asked. "What will you do when you finish? Teach?"

"Probably. But I would like to write. Our country has an extraordinary history, and hardly anything has been done with it."

Extraordinary? Jadine thought. Three hundred years of poverty and bad government, and both getting worse? It was amazing that people still wanted to write history instead of unwrite it.

A crash came from the general direction of the patio, followed by a bellow:

"*Leon!*"

No reply except the drums and hammering guitars, the ya-ya voices building to a howl.

"Leon!" Louder still. "Shut that fucking thing off *now*!"

The song died in midscream. In the sudden silence they could hear birds and a neighbour's dog and Alvaro cursing and storming: Did a man have to live like a God damn animal in his own house?

Pilar drew deeply on her cigarette. "So you gave up on the diplomatic service," she said. "What did you do instead?"

"Went to Europe. Did translations. Lived with a Spanish poet for a while."

"Was he nice?"

"He was all right, but he had a lot of crazy friends. He collected them, you know, like some people collect butterflies. There was an ex-nun and a Rastafarian drug addict and a relic of the Spanish Civil War and a philosophy student who wrote porn for a skin magazine—to stay in touch with reality, he said, if you can believe that. Others, too; I can't remember them all. They'd sit up all night, night after night, and talk about the most amazing things. It was fascinating. But it was—what can I say?—circular, perhaps? After six months or so I realized that they were having the same discussion over and over. All that brilliance, all that creativity, was being spent pretending that they were exploring something new, when all they were doing was going around and around their own private mulberry bush...

"So I got what my best friend used to call a California divorce, and went to Morocco."

"Why did you never come here?" Pilar asked. "The letters you wrote, after Mama and Papa came back—we thought you might both come, you and Eryn."

"We thought about it for a while. But Eryn was still in college and caught up in the anti-war movement, and I was..." She faltered. The truth, if she had spoken it, was simple: I was not the least bit interested in Nicaragua. It was a banana republic—the worst of the banana republics. It had no art, no culture, no history; it seemed the last place in the world that anyone would want to go, except maybe Baffin Island.

"I was fascinated by Europe," she said.

"And now?" Pilar asked, with a touch of irony.

"Now I'm not fascinated by anything."

Silence. Then Pilar said softly: "You were very close to Eryn, I think."

"Yes. Very close...He was...he was *good*, Pilar. One of the few human beings I have ever known who was truly good. And he killed himself." She fell silent, feeling the sun, the light, the falseness of both.

"Was there a reason?" Pilar asked. "I mean a particular reason...something that happened...?"

"No." Jadine looked at her cousin, saw in her eyes the wish to understand, and the absolute hopelessness of it. Some people, perhaps, comitted suicide for a reason; but for most the motive was the complete breakdown of everything that people normally thought of as reasons for anything. And no one who had not been near it understood that.

You simply dissolved, came apart against the absolute emptiness of things. You discovered that living was not enough, could never be enough, because living was essentially meaningless. Nothing you did mattered, or could ever matter. You were a wraith and a slug, you existed only through the gestures with which you tried to affirm your identity. And suicide became, finally, the ultimate gesture, and the repudiation of the world that required it.

It was not a subject they could talk about much. There simply wasn't enough common ground.

"Anyway," Jadine said, "he's at peace..." She picked up one of Pilar's carvings, a swan-like bird of soft gray stone, cut with wonderfully simple, clean lines. "This is lovely," she said. "Where's it from?"

"Masaya."

They talked about Masaya then, for a while, about the work the Indians there did in stone and wood and fabric and leather—magnificent work, Pilar said. They talked about Pilar's murals. Then Beatriz stuck her head in the door and announced that they would leave for the country club in ten minutes.

"I'm not coming," Pilar said.

"Pilar, you must come! You never go anywhere with us anymore."

"I'm sorry, Mama. But I have to take the stuff we collected to Father Pepe."

"You can do that next Sunday."

"Mama! He *needs* those things! You know that."

"Then do it after class tomorrow."

"There's a bulletin meeting after class tomorrow."

"Oh, Pilar...!" Beatriz's hands rose in a gesture of exasperation, fell in a gesture of defeat. She said nothing more.

But Alvaro did, later, in the car. He was not pleased. It was time Pilar understood the responsibilities of living in a family, he said. What the devil did she think she was going to do when she got married?

"You don't have a daughter anymore, Beatriz. You have a visitor who rents one of your beds."

"She works hard," Beatriz said.

"We all work hard."

They drove in silence for a while. Then Alvaro asked bluntly: "Are you sure there isn't a man in all of this somewhere?"

"Oh, Papa, for God's sake," Leon said. "She dresses like a cowboy and fights like a cat. What man would put up with her?"

6

There were weeds where Managua had been—weeds and ruins like those of war. A wall here, a pillar there, an overhang of roof where you hid when it rained. The rest empty; thorns and grass, bits of junk too useless even for the desperate to use, broken stone. Grass and stone, beds of grass for lovers and of stone for the dead.

Pilar had the taxi drop her at the bank building, the wonderful bank building, erected to proper quake-zone specifications, which stood after the tremors with its pictures still hanging on its walls while Managua crumbled and burned all around it. From there she walked, carrying her parcels, donations collected in the parish for Father Pepe's clinic. She was dressed simply but well: a good middle class woman doing her charities; it was safer that way.

She never came here without thinking of Felipe, who was buried somewhere under all that broken stone. It saddened her that he had no real grave, no place to which she could bring flowers. But she did not feel dishonoured by it. Sacred ground was not made sacred with holy water.

The streets were not empty. Squatters clustered around every bit of ruin that had a little structure remaining; for some of them, one wall was enough. Though there was no city left here, hundreds lived in it; and where the ruins ended the shanties began.

The beggars came, of course: she was wearing a hat, good shoes, a linen skirt; and it was Sunday and surely she was a Christian. . . ? They came quietly, remorselessly, holding out their soiled brown hands: for the child, *senora, por favor, senora, algunos centavos por el amor de Dios, senora. . .*

She gave them all something. It was impossible not to, no matter what your priorities were, no matter how badly begging unravelled your soul. Carlos had told them that, in his own fashion, two years ago—the only time she had met him. The revolution is tomorrow, he said, but the pain is now.

Father Pepe greeted her with an enormous smile. He was tall, big-boned, tireless. He was also a Canadian, though that was usually forgotten because he had been there so long, and spoke with only a shade of an accent. He led her past the long line of waiting patients to the room in the back where he ate, stored the medicines, and often slept.

He gave her coffee, thanked her several times for the parcels, and began to unpack them.

"So what did you bring me, *compita*?"

"Children's clothes, mostly. Some shoes. Tools. Pens and pencils. Not much."

"Everything helps," he said. "It's all something. It's all for God."

He looked at everything, thanked her again, and sat down.

She smiled at him. "So, Pepe. How does it go?"

"It goes well," he said. "Do you know, we've started two new Bible study groups. And the barrio committee is forming a coalition with Acahualinca and Ana Chillan's people over in Los Santos. It's really amazing. People start out believing they can do nothing and six months later they believe they can do anything. Faith moves mountains, Pilar, it really does. We're pressing for a second clinic now; after we get that we're going after some decent housing."

She started to compliment him but he wouldn't let her. "I don't do anything," he said, "except maybe give them a little moral support, tell them God says it's okay, you know. And dole out the aspirins. They get all the good ideas. They're inventive as hell. Do you know there's thirty, maybe forty people in Los Santos who've been on arrest lists for a year and the Guardia still can't find them? I swear to God Ana's dug a rabbit warren over there. Have you ever met her? She's amazing."

"No. I've never met her." Which in itself speaks for the nightmare we live in. "I very much want to."

The door opened. It was Oscar Medina, the young doctor who had joined Father Pepe just a year ago, from the university in Leon. He looked tired, but he grinned. He was a handsome man with soft brown hair and melancholy eyes and long, powerful hands. Both of his parents were teachers in Leon: hard-working middle class people with a large family which they had hoped he would help with his earnings as a doctor. But he had come here instead, on a dismal salary from Pepe's missionary box, and they were proud of him for it. Appalled and scared and bewildered, but nonetheless proud.

He was serious to the point of being solemn, but everyone liked him—for what he gave them, partly. And partly for himself.

"This is always how it is," he said. "Pepe gets the coffee and the pretty *companeras* to talk with, and I get all the work."

"*Pobrecito*," Pilar said, laughing, and giving him a comradely embrace. "Come and sit. There's coffee left for you, and I'm sure there's work left for Pepe."

"I'm sure there is," the priest said. She could see that he didn't want to go, that he wanted to talk. They had been friends a long time. But there were twenty people out there, maybe more, all hurting. They didn't come here unless they were hurting.

He got up, thanked her again, made her promise to

come back. When he was gone Oscar went silently to the closet and brought out a box. He laid the contents on the table in front of Pilar, naming them as he did so. Morphine. Penicillin. Streptomycin. Sterile syringes. Water purifiers. Iodine. It was a very small pile. She waited for him to get more. He didn't. He just stood with the empty box in his hand.

"Is that all?" she whispered.

"Yes. That's all." He threw the box aside and sat down wearily. "Cordobas don't buy much in San Jose. Or anywhere else, for that matter."

"Yes, but...but there was another..." She faltered.

"Another shipment. From Honduras. I know. It never got through."

"What happened?"

"Nobody knows. It just...never came."

"*Jesus*." She looked at the pile. Enough to get one commando through one bad night. "Can you...can you give us anything from the clinic?"

"I already did." He looked away. "I'm sorry, Pilar."

"It's not your fault," she said. It was no one's fault. It was just the way things were. There was never enough of anything. Never enough ammunition or typewriter ribbons or shoes. Never enough ink to print the handbills; never enough radios or rifles or cigarettes or bread.

"We'll get by," she said. "We'll just have to pretend that they're loaves and fishes."

She packed the supplies into the church donation bag. He watched her. He was drawn to her, she could tell that; drawn strongly, and wondering things he would not, dared not ask: Was she one of the Sandinistas, or just helping them like so many people did? Like he did? And when the offensive began—the offensive that no one mentioned but that everyone close to the resistance sensed was coming—when it began, would she be fighting? Was this perhaps the last time he would see her?

"Thank you, Oscar," she said. "Thank you."

He held out a cigarette. She hesitated.

"Ten minutes," he said. "Pepe won't die, and neither will the revolution."

7

Three times in ten days Naldo brought home money—always the same amount: fifteen cordobas, of which he gave half to Rosa to keep for the day when they would move, and half to his mother. He made no explanation, and the second time Ana asked him outright:

"Where are you getting this money, Naldo?"

He glared at her. "What's the matter, Mama? Do you think I'm a thief?"

The third time she said nothing, except with her eyes, which he would not look at. She spoke instead to Daniel, when he came to eat cornbread and *gallo pinto* at her stall in the market. He had been out all night and he looked dead on his feet. She fished two small pieces of meat out of the pot of stew she was selling and put them on his plate, too.

He grinned at her, wearily. "*Gracias, Mama.*"

She let him eat in peace, sitting on the ground by her tin stove with his plate on his knees. Then, when he had finished, she sat beside him. Already the sun was high and fierce. She was mountain-born and she had never grown used to Managua's heat. Daniel didn't seem to notice it.

She looked at him with affection. He was a good kid, she thought, a really good kid. All down the years, raising them all, keeping them alive, keeping them fed, keeping them whole, it had been Daniel she had worried about the least—as though everything bad that could ever happen to him had already happened, all at once, that one murderous hour in Diriamba...

"Danito," she said, "Naldo brought money again last night."

He looked at her, and then away, across the market that was filling with people, growing loud and rough. He craved sleep.

"Did he say where he's getting it?"

"No." She drew a deep breath. "He isn't working, Danito. I know there's day jobs, sometimes, if a man's lucky, but that isn't it. He comes home and there's nothing on his hands, nothing on his clothes. Besides, if he was working, why would he hide it?"

Daniel was silent.

"There's only two ways for people like us to make fifteen cordobas in a day. We work like dogs...or we do something illegal."

"Everything illegal is controlled by the Guardia," he said.

She didn't answer. She didn't need to.

"What do you want me to do, Mama? He won't listen to you. He won't listen to Martin. Why should he listen to me?"

"I don't know what you can do," she said. "I just know you have to do something."

He stalked Naldo for most of a day, followed him through the ruins and the plazas and the long streets. It was easy. Naldo did not seem to imagine that he might be followed nor did he seem to have anything to hide. He talked to people. He rested sometimes. Mostly he asked for work. Could he clean, carry, put together, take apart, nail, hammer, sweep, polish, dig, drive, walk, dance, crawl perhaps, *senor*? No, he could not. Go away.

It was late afternoon when his wanderings took on a definite direction, down the Carretera Norte, the long avenue that paralleled the Pacific railway, an avenue lined with Somoza factories and the box-like plants of the multinationals. He turned into the yard of one such building and disappeared behind an iron gate. The gate was chained and guarded; Daniel did not approach it.

The building flew the Nicaraguan flag but had no logo, no name, none of those bright, blatant signs that elsewhere proclaimed the presence of Coca-Cola or Exxon or Schwarz-Schermerhorn. It was a long, low building made of white brick and it looked vaguely like a hospital. Or a prison.

Daniel drifted uneasily along the street until he was beckoned by an old man sitting just off a bus stop, selling pornographic postcards from Argentina.

Great stuff, he assured Daniel. The very best. Want to see?

Daniel looked, wondered how hungry you had to be to pose like that. He made himself smile. Yes, he agreed, great stuff. Considered how he might question the man about the white brick building without being obvious.

"Look!" The man pulled out another card. A girl of perhaps fourteen, with Latin features and blonde hair. A vacant, plastic smile. Legs apart, cunt thrust out like meat on a hook.

This one, the man said, wasn't in Argentina. Did he want her? Five cordobas, that was all. Just five little pesos for all that—

"I got no money," Daniel said, and began to walk away. He was worried about Naldo and tired beyond words; he had no patience left for anything, least of all for this water-eyed, sewer-mouthed, motherfucking pimp.

The man grabbed his arm. "Easy to get money!" he cried. "Easy! Right over there!" And he pointed to the white brick building.

Daniel peeled the man's fingers from his arm. "Look," he said, "don't shit me. The factories aren't hiring.

Nobody's hiring. What the hell are you talking about?"

"That's no factory," the man said. And he laughed. "*Es la casa de Dracula.*"

"What?"

"The house of Dracula. They buy blood. Fifteen cordobas. You get a bonus if you give eight times in a month." He laughed again. "Dracula has good teeth."

Daniel stood voiceless. He'd heard about this place, vaguely; heard that there was a blood bank somewhere where addicts and drunks and totally desperate people sometimes went. He had envisioned some small, dishonourable place. Not this. Not this gigantic million dollar corporation with fences and armed guards.

"Who owns this?" he whispered.

The man shrugged, waving another handful of painted flesh. "Who owns everything in Nicaragua?...Look, *muchacho*, look at this! You like this one better—?"

Daniel didn't even see the postcards in his hand. He was trying to comprehend what he had just learned. There was only a scattering of hospitals in the country; only a handful of people who could afford to go to them. All the plasma they could possibly use in a year could be obtained by a bank like this one in a month.

"What in God's name do they do with the blood?" he asked.

"They ship it to the United States. Or so I've heard. You from *La Prensa*?"

"No."

"I've also heard they pay fifty cordobas a pint for it there. Not bad, eh?"

"Not bad for a *nica*," Daniel said. "They only paid thirty for Jesus Christ."

The man howled, clapped Daniel on the back, and tried to sell him a virgin. He was still making offers, whining lust into the wind as Daniel walked resolutely down the long, dustswept sidewalk, past one after another of the sprawling plants, finally past the gate where Naldo had turned—right past it, keep walking, you can't go in there, you're out of your fucking mind if you try to go in there.

Down the street was a string of food stands selling slices

of mango and watermelon, *refrescos*, corn cobs, peanuts. He wandered into the cluster of people, milled unobtrusively for a while, and found a spot to sit. To wait.

You could tell which ones came from the blood bank. The old ones, unshaven, shuffling; their hands shook as they doled out their coins; the fruit juice ran down their chins and onto their shirts and they grabbed at it with their fingers. After they'd eaten they stumbled away, depressed because they had spent too much, they should have saved it to buy corn and beans in the market but how did you pass a fruit stand when you hadn't eaten for three days and you didn't know if you had the strength to get home?

They came out one by one from a side gate. Mostly they were old, but not all; some were clearly sick. There were drunks and whores and beggars, women carrying babies, a youth with no arms. Some could hardly walk. Daniel wondered how many of them would make it back to the barrios with their fifteen cordobas before the street rats got to them...or the Guardia.

God...

Not the God of the Christians, of the European church—he did not believe in that; he hadn't since he was eight. But the old gods, who lived in the earth, in the volcanoes—he thought about them sometimes, wondered if they were real, if they had ever been real. Wondered if they had hidden themselves away in the bowels of the earth because they could no longer bear to look upon their world.

Then it was Naldo coming out the gate, walking briskly. Daniel got up, moved casually onto the sidewalk as he passed. He saw the clear flash of anger in Naldo's eyes before he fell in step beside him.

"What the hell are you doing here?" Naldo demanded.

"I was about to ask you the same question."

"Look," Naldo said savagely. "I'm not five years old. I don't need a fucking *duena*." He stopped, turning toward his brother. Close up, Daniel could see the sallowness under his dark skin, the muddiness in his eyes. He'd been strong as a young bull once.

"Why did you follow me, anyway?" he went on. "What did you think I was doing—sucking cock? Or maybe spying for the Guardia? You'd believe that, wouldn't you? You're crazy enough."

Daniel's hands closed and opened, closed again. He stuffed them into his pockets. Down the broad avenue, not a thousand feet away, a Becat jeep was spewing dust, coming fast.

"Walk, damn it," he said to Naldo. Neither of them looked up until the jeep had passed.

"If you ever come here again," Daniel said, "I'll break your head."

Naldo laughed. "Sure you will, *hermanito*. And the moon will have kittens. And fish will dance the salsa. And then God knows there may even come the revolution."

He struck aside Daniel's restraining arm, struck it hard. He was still strong.

"Fuck you," Daniel said, smarting.

"Leave me alone, Danito, do you hear? Leave me alone! I've had it with the Frente and I've had it with you. Up to here."

Daniel rubbed his arm. "What the hell's happened to you, Naldo?"

"Nothing's happened to me." They had come to a crossing and turned off the *carretera* into a quiet warren of streets. Naldo's pace slowed. "You think something's happened to me just because I want to live like a human being?"

"You call that living like a human being? Selling your blood to your enemies? Dying by inches to make those pigs rich?"

Naldo looked at him a long moment. Then he sat down in the grass, as though he were suddenly exhausted. "You never quit, do you? To you the whole universe comes in two colours: red and black. *Patria libre o morir*. You're a fanatic, Daniel. You want my blood, too, only you want it in the streets, that's all."

"Naldo. . ."

"I want my life," he said. "I want to sleep nights. I want kids."

"And you think I don't?"

"You want the revolution, Danito. All the rest comes second."

"Yes. All the rest comes second. Look around you, for Christ's sake! Every year the shantytowns get bigger, and the people in them get hungrier. Every year Somoza has another *finca*, and another thousand *campesinos* have no land. Every year it costs more for a sack of corn, and every year there's less work, and they pay you less for what there is. We were always poor, but we lived in a house once; now we live in a fucking box; one day your children will live in a ditch. Our father finished high school; we didn't. Most of our friends never got there. Your kids won't even learn to read...

"It's a closing circle, Naldo. We fight our way out of it or we die."

"We've been fighting for fifteen years—"

"Fifty, Naldo. Exactly fifty."

"All right. Fifty then. And where has it brought us? From Wiwili to Pancasan to Diriamba to fucking nowhere. The Frente gets stronger, the Guardia gets bigger. We use machetes, they use rifles. We get rifles, they get machine guns and napalm. That's a circle, too, and it's getting bigger. It isn't just Somoza out there, *hermanito*."

Indeed it wasn't, Daniel thought. It was empire and multinational capital and the Monroe Doctrine and glory hallelujah kill a communist for Jesus and save the world for Pepsi and Playboy and the twin-party ballot...

"We're fighting against a monolith," Naldo said.

"Yes. We're fighting against a monolith. And the monolith is fighting against history. History will win."

"You *are* crazy."

Daniel shrugged. "Fidel left Tuxpan with eighty men," he said, "and lost over sixty of them in the canefield where he landed. He reached the Sierra Maestra almost without food or ammunition or medicine, with no guides; probably without even a clear idea of where the hell he was. And he gathered his dozen-odd stragglers into that first camp and said: Now we are going to win. And they did. When you hear of something crazier than that, you let me know."

Naldo stood up. "I'm not arguing with you, Daniel. The last time I won an argument you were nine, and you kicked my shins bloody for it."

"Oh, fuck...!"

"Just leave me alone, all right? I never joined the Frente. I don't owe it anything. I won't get anyone in trouble. I just want to live my own life. *Un poquito de paz*, eh, Danito?" He started to walk.

"Naldo!"

He didn't stop, didn't turn, didn't answer. When Daniel got back to the house in Los Santos, he and Rosa were gone.

8

Paco picked up Rafael near the Santa Luisa Hospital, and Claudia just off the Plaza de Compras. He knew them both only by their code names; he never imagined that they were married.

He pulled into a dark side street and, with many apologies, tied heavy black scarves over their eyes.

"You're wasting your time, Paco," Claudia said. "Once the sun goes down and I'm half a mile from home, I'm lost. You could give me a *map* to the safehouse and I wouldn't find it."

He grinned and kept wrapping. "Nevertheless..." he said. He made the blindfolds gentle but secure, and drove aimlessly for a while before guiding the car back toward the Carretera Sur, the southbound highway that would lead, if you followed it far enough, to Rivas and the Costa Rican border. But first it twisted through a long, languid stretch of semi-suburban Managua.

"Eh, *compas*," Paco said, "did you hear the latest from

the Council of Private Enterprise? Front page in *La Prensa* today: Somoza is bad for business!"

"Well, of course he is," Rafa said.

"Oh, bullshit! Arturo Riveras? We're being strangled, he says. At last count he was worth two million U.S. dollars and owned a shopping plaza. Strangled! *Madre de Dios*, what a way to go!"

"But, Paco, don't you see?" Claudia protested. "If it weren't for Somoza, Riveras would be worth ten million and would have five shopping plazas. And no self-respecting businessman ought to be deprived of such possibilities. It's criminal."

"Absolutely," Rafael agreed. "The Council is right. It *is* unfair competition. Somoza has broken all the rules. He was supposed to steal only from the poor."

"*Que barbaridad!*" Paco said.

"Look at it from their point of view," Claudia went on. "Here they are, the great old families of Nicaragua—or half of them, anyway—"

"And the young entrepreneurs," Rafa added.

"And the young entrepreneurs. Here they are. They have it made. An entire country waiting to be plucked. Land to be had merely by pointing out that peasants without a formal deed never owned it in the first place. A work force willing to do anything for two American dollars a day. Impotent unions, and a well-fed, well-armed National Guard to keep them that way. A government dedicated not to health or education or justice but to the gross national product. Friends abroad, very good friends, with Alliance for Progress funds and World Bank funds and just plain fat-cat-from-the-dairy funds. All that... and then Somoza gets more and more out of hand and fucks it up. He won't settle for his share, even though it's the biggest share. He wants it all. Really, Paco, what do you do?"

"Make a revolution," Paco quipped.

"Shit, no," Rafa said. "You steal one. *If you can.*"

Paco laughed, gearing the car down. They were deep in the residential zone now; every few hundred yards a side road wandered off to serve a string of hillside homes wrapped in trees and cool nights and innocence. At one of these he turned. Immediately Rafael and Claudia could feel the car begin to spin and skid. The side roads were narrow and steep, and when it rained, as it was raining now, it was not uncommon to find cars powered out or ditched on a neighbour's yard.

Paco drove fast, very fast, using speed against the slickness of the mud, veering from side to narrow side, missing rocks and gateposts and trees with abandon. The conversation faltered and died. Rafa made the sign of the cross and waited for the inevitable. Claudia, who would have driven exactly the same way herself, was terrified.

"I wish Manolo were here," she said. "He'd never call me a maniac again."

Paco laughed. "Manolo thinks I'm a *brujo*. I drove him once to Jinotega in an hour and a half. By night."

"Jesus," Rafa said. "After that, making bombs would be relaxing."

"He sang all the way," Paco said. "Marvellous songs. Victor Jara. Pancasan..." He threw his head back and belted out a clear baritone:

Hay un clamor que viene de las montanas,
Hay un clamor que se oye al amanecer...

"Of course he sang," Claudia said. "The poor kid wanted to die happy."

"You have no faith," Paco grumbled. He spun the wheel hard, and they skidded into a long driveway and slid to a stop in front of a large, almost darkened house. He shut off the motor and at once they could hear the rain, and around the rain, the sudden, absolute silence. Trees lined the driveway; from their low-hanging branches gobs of water splattered onto the roof and wept across the windshield.

"*Momentito*," Paco said. He got out, leaving the car door open; stood a while, letting his eyes grow accustomed to the dark, letting them drift over the house, the roof, the yard. Then he led his still-blind companions to a side door, pressed the buzzer once, then three times very quickly. A woman's voice came soft from within.

"*Quien?*"

"Paco."

"What did you buy for me?"

He sighed. All was clear. "Paper daisies," he replied.

The bolt turned, the door opened into a hallway that was completely dark. Only when they were inside, and the door was bolted again, did the woman snap on a light.

She was thin, almost gaunt, with strands of gray in her brown hair. Paco introduced her as Lidia.

She was a total enigma to him. Her husband, Edmundo Rey, lived sometimes in Puerto Rico but mostly in Argentina. He still owned this house, a small factory in Managua, and a *finca* in the south, but he had clashed with the National Guard over the distribution of profits from other, less conventional enterprises, and had been forced to flee the country. Lidia lived like a recluse. Her only child was an apolitical student of mathematics at the Jesuit University. Nevertheless, for two years the Managua underground had stored weapons in this house, printed handbills, held meetings, and sheltered their hunted and their wounded. For two years Lidia had quietly sold off the oil paintings and antiques that had once filled the house, and with her son David's help juggled the factory books; the money went to the Sandinistas.

Paco had no idea why. If she had ever talked about herself—to Valerian, perhaps, or to Clariz, who had recruited her—he did not know. She lived behind an impenetrable barricade of silence, behind cool gray eyes that said: Take what I give you, but do not ask who I am.

She greeted them each in turn, offered them sandwiches and coffee. As she served them, a young girl ran into the room; Paco remembered her as Amparo, a militant from the JRS, their Sandinista-based student organization. She was carrying a tray, and she managed to load it, eat a pastry, and hug everyone, all in the same thirty seconds.

"You must come in, Paco," she said. "We've got Radio Havana on, and Fidel's making a speech!"

"*Compita*," he said, "Fidel's been making speeches since before you were born."

"Oh!" She tossed her head scornfully. "That's the

trouble with old people," she said to Claudia. "They don't appreciate anything anymore." And she was gone, all bubbles and commitment.

"*Old?*" Paco said. "Shit. I'm thirty-two."

"In the Frente," Rafa said, "that's old."

It was all in fun; they were laughing, even Lidia. But Paco couldn't laugh. He was holding a cup of coffee and he could see—where the cuff of his shirt didn't quite reach—he could see the scars on his wrist. He'd been in jail. He'd been tortured. He'd been shot three times. He was living on borrowed time.

He was old.

He cursed silently, drained his coffee, turned to Lidia. "Is Valerian here yet?"

"No," she said. "He's going to be late."

He shrugged. Valerian being late was like Fidel making speeches; anything different would surprise you.

"Everyone else is here who's coming," Lidia said. "Do you want to go in?"

They went into Lidia's study, a recessed, den-like room where seven or eight people were clustered around David's short-wave radio. They were all militants, and good ones; Valerian consistently ran one of the best cells in Managua. In this room were all of his key people. Paco had worked with them all. Amparo, of course, who gazed at the radio as at a lover, and who continued to stuff her irrepressible adolescent body with sandwiches. Eduardo, who had come to Managua recently from the north, a man with obvious years of experience and a personality of barbed wire. Julio. Cool, diplomatic Marta, who kept the safehouse in Montenegro. The kid who was thin as a rake and called himself Pancho Villa. Andres. Daniel Chillan, who was known as Manolo. And close beside him, very close, Clariz, whose smouldering eyes had been forged in the depths of Momotombo, and whose body, no matter what spartan things she wore, carried its own clean animal beauty. He always took a second look at Clariz, and sometimes a third. She was lovely, this slender bourgeois girl who took to street life and guns with such disturbing ease. Too wild for him, old man that he was, but lovely: Pilar Antonia Zelaya Perez.

The newcomers were warmly welcomed. Pilar jumped up to hug Claudia; on her cheek was a small but distinct bruise.

Claudia took her hands. "What happened, Clariz?"

"Happened? Oh, that." She shrugged. "Just fighting with Papa again. He doesn't want me going out so much. He thinks it's bad for my reputation."

"God help us, what would he do if he knew the truth?"

"All of it?"

All of it included Danny Chillan—and that, Claudia suspected, would unman the good Las Colinas patriarch even more than plotting revolution. That *was* revolution.

"I don't even want to think about it," Pilar said. "What about you? *Que tal?*"

"I'm all right."

"Have you had any word?"

"No," Claudia said. "No word."

"A thousand things could have happened," Pilar said.

"Yes. And almost all of them are bad. I pray, Clariz, that's all. I pray."

Everyone prayed. It was all there was left to do. Four months ago Claudia's grandparents, two of their sons, and every member of the sons' families, had disappeared from their home outside of Esteli. Simply disappeared, like wisps of smoke. Neighbours had found their huts empty; no one had seen or heard of them since. No one except the parish priest dared to ask about them except in whispers.

"They weren't revolutionaries," Claudia said. "My grandfather always used to say that Sandino was a bandit. They just wanted to be left alone. They were afraid of everyone."

That was the saddest of all, Pilar thought. The hardest to bear. That so many people, thousands of people, believed the lie of silence, believed that if you didn't do anything, then they wouldn't do anything to you. That if you kept your hands at your sides, raised your eyes only to God and your voice to no one; that if you took it all, took the raw labour without food, the nights of fear, the fouled water; took the dying of your children, took it all, all without a protest, without imagining a protest, maybe they wouldn't kill you. And then they did.

The broadcast from Havana ended; Valerian still had not arrived. For a half hour or so the group exchanged news, cautions, and revolutionary gossip. A few who were involved in projects which for security reasons were not shared with the cell as a whole, drifted away to pursue their questions elsewhere. Eventually only Paco, Eduardo, Rafa and Claudia were left in the study, talking about conditions in the north.

"It's a nightmare," Eduardo said. "No one knows how many people they've killed in the last two years. In the countryside there's no one to protest, except maybe the occasional missionary—no one to see, even, sometimes. They wipe out whole families, whole villages. Shoot the old people and the men, rape the women—or the boys, if they prefer. Kill them, too, when they're tired of it. It's absolute tyranny. Absolute."

What he did not add, because he did not have to, was that the victims' property, if they had any, went to the local Guardia commanders—a fact which gave rise to a good part of the nightmare. It was an enormous temptation to see subversives under every bush if afterward you got title to the bush.

They asked him about the Guard commanders. Matagalpa? Bad. Esteli? Worse. Chinandega? Better, now that Valdez was gone—which was not saying much. The north was seething, he told them; it would not take much more. He recounted stories, horror stories, one after another, until the room was thick with smoke and nobody wanted to hear anymore.

Paco was suffocating. He wandered into the kitchen where Lidia and her son David talked with Amparo about the student movement. Was it all right, he asked, to go into the patio?

"Of course," she said.

It had stopped raining but the sky was still wild, tumbling with clouds. Wind tugged at his sleeves. He took a deep breath of the air, and turned abruptly, irritably, to find Eduardo beside him.

"Your *comandante*," Eduardo said, "where the fuck is he?"

"He'll get here."

They moved a ways into the garden. As Paco's eyes grew used to the darkness he could see—five, maybe six yards away—Clariz, wind-haired, pressed against a tree, running her hands all over Manolo's jeans.

He turned, with a gesture halfway between a sigh of envy and a shrug of resignation, to go back inside. Eduardo did not stir.

"Eh, Eddy, come on," he whispered. "Life is short. Let the kids be."

"I'm not bothering them," Eduardo said.

"Asshole," Paco muttered, and left him.

Eduardo stayed for several minutes more, watching; the next day he complained to Valerian that the presence of women in the commando was creating sexual tensions and interfering with the combatants' concentration.

The wind tore leaves from the trees overhead and swept shags of Daniel's hair across her face. She coiled against him, supple as water, greedy as the wind that would not for anything be still.

"Danny..." God, it was good to have this, to have it anywhere, wind, rain, silk sheets, it didn't matter, what mattered was the fire of it, the sweetness, the freedom. The freedom to touch him as she wished, to speak his name against his flesh, over and over, because she wanted to, because it was his name; because they were friends and comrades and they chose to say their names like this.

"Daniel..." Their voices were muffled animal cries of pleasure, their tangled bodies rocking in the wind. It was brief, yes, insubstantial, but so sweet, no matter what lay behind them or ahead. It was good, so good, just to have.

Few people in the cell knew much about Valerian. Paco would not have described him as a shadowy figure—that would have been unnecessarily melodramatic. But he was one of the cadres who kept a very low profile. Though no longer legal, he moved about the country with a surprising degree of freedom, and spent more time in Managua than most leaders of his rank could have risked.

He was very good at disguises; he had a pleasant, nondescript face and a talent for acting; he could appear to be almost anything he wished, and Manolo kept him well supplied with forged identity papers. The National Guard knew his real name—which was more than Paco knew—but it had no picture of him and probably not even a good description.

He was sharp, Paco reflected. Very sharp. Also an unflinching realist. That was often apparent, but never more so than last spring—the last time the entire cell had met. He had come back from a meeting with members of the national leadership in Costa Rica, and had laid out for the Managuans the new strategy that was being developed: a strategy of broad-based alliances and mass insurrection.

The Frente at that time had already been split—badly split—into two factions: the GPP, the Prolonged Popular War faction, to which Valerian and his comrades and much of the student movement belonged, which favoured long-term rural guerrilla warfare; and the Proletarian Tendency, which favoured grass-roots urban political organization. They growled at each other a lot over tactics, but their goals were essentially the same; sooner or later they would have to re-unite. Nevertheless, the last thing the revolution seemed to need at that moment was another faction.

Valerian disagreed. He had laid it out—hammered it out, really—in a meeting that lasted twenty-six hours. The third tendency, he said, the Terceristas, fully recognized the roles of both the rural guerrilla and the urban base; what they saw was a need, a readiness, for one thing more, one thing that could both make the revolution and provide the grounds for Sandinista unity: national insurrection. Their aim was to mobilize—to mobilize everyone, everything, in one great sweep of revolt. The commitment was there; the leadership was there. Above all, the rage was there, the rage that lay on the surface of the land and coiled in the streets, incandescent as a volcano and remorseless as a human heart.

Two huge arguments had erupted in the room that day, as they had and would throughout all of Nicaragua. Were they, in fact, ready? That was the first question, the question of most desperate consequence. Half the art of making a revolution was knowing where the hell you were while you were inside it; knowing what was possible and what was not, what you were ready for and what you were not. Strategy mistakes were always bad; they always wasted lives and unravelled months or even years of careful work. But misjudging readiness, escalating the struggle to a level you could not sustain, was probably the worst strategy mistake of all. There were enough dead revolutions lying around the continent to testify to that.

The second question was an ideological-ethical one: just what sort of broad-based alliances were being made, and how much was the FSLN going to sacrifice of its commitment to authentic social change in order to make them? It was one thing to seek alliances with youth and women's groups, with uncommitted unions, with the left-wing political parties and the student federations; it was quite another matter to bed down with the capitalist-Conservative power block that made up UDEL, the Democratic Union of Liberation, led by *La Prensa's* Pedro Joaquin Chamorro.

UDEL was anti-Somoza; that was indisputably true. Beyond that it possessed no consensus; it included everything from the Nicaraguan Socialist Party, the PSN, to bewildered reactionaries who were fed up with Somoza and had nowhere else to turn. Chamorro himself was a man of integrity and courage, but he was a man of the conservative centre. In so far as UDEL spoke for any unified group, it spoke for those who simply wished that Somoza would go away, like a stomach ache, and take all of Nicaragua's problems with him. Including, if possible, the Sandinistas.

What in God's name was to be gained by working with UDEL?

"They don't want any of the things we want," Paco had said. "They only want to work with us because we have the organization and the skills. We can go into a peasant community or a union and in two months we've got it working like a clock. The Conservatives can't do that; they don't know how. They couldn't organize a birthday party. They want us to do all the fucking work, that's all."

"No, that isn't all," Luisa, the woman from El Carmen, said bitterly. "They want us to take the bullets, just like we did in '67. Have you people forgotten that?"

"It wasn't UDEL that did that," someone said. "UDEL wasn't even formed then."

"No," the woman flung back, undeterred. "But it was the same people. And they want the same damn thing now that they wanted then—they want someone else to die for them. You want to trust them again? After all that? They called for a general strike, remember? And then for insurrection. Everybody into the streets. We were going to take the Guardia post, and then God knows maybe the bunker. And we believed them. We put sixty thousand people into the streets of Managua and there weren't any guns. There weren't any leaders. There wasn't anything. And the Guardia came and cut us down like dogs. There were bodies all over the Plaza Nacional. All over. Afterward they said we'd misunderstood. We didn't misunderstand. They lost their nerve, and we paid for it."

A murmur went through the room, a memory. A lot of them had been there. Daniel Chillan, twelve years old then, with Martin and Naldo, with his parents wary as cats, he wanting to believe and they not believing anything. He remembered his father screaming at them to take cover when he spotted the first green shirt sleeve on the palace roof; remembered his father dragging him under a fence, his father burying two children beneath his body and Ana the other, don't move, don't breathe, don't ask yourself how many machine guns are up there firing and when it's over don't ever forget...

It had not been UDEL, no; it had been the Conservatives, the people who were now the moving force in UDEL, the wealthy anti-Somoza *burguesia*, that had led the people into that massacre. They had fed, and fed upon, the people's passion and the people's need, and when the stakes had grown too high they had retreated back to their fenced and gardened houses and said: We're sorry; you misunderstood.

So much for the bourgeois revolution.

Valerian listened, let the anger crash like water onto stone.

"None of us," he said, "have any illusions about UDEL's revolutionary potential. But if you think about it for a moment, that's one of the reasons we might as well enlist them. They have no program. They have no leadership, except Chamorro, and all he wants is to get rid of Somoza; beyond that he has no idea what to do. They have no basis for unity except their hatred of the dictator. They would love to take the revolution away from us, but they'll never agree on anything long enough to do it."

"Look, *comandante*," Daniel said. "Maybe they can't hurt us. I'm not convinced of that, but I'll accept it for the moment. That's no reason for making an alliance."

"No," Valerian replied. "There are other reasons. And they are reasons well worth thinking about.

"For one thing, although UDEL as an organization is hollow to the core, there are individuals in it who are absolutely sound. We owe it to them and to ourselves to make a place for them. Many of them do not understand the revolution and never will, but they can live with it. They see their children in the streets. They know that Somoza is a monster, that Somoza has to go, and maybe the Frente Sandinista isn't exactly what they had in mind but they'll accept it because it's a thousand times better than what they've got now. Some of them will turn on us, but some of them have a great deal to give.

"The second thing—and yes, you are right, Manolo—the second thing is that the Conservatives are still dangerous—but less dangerous if they are in our camp than if they are nowhere, floating, waiting for someone else to fasten onto their discontent. The closer we get to victory, the more desperately the reactionaries and their friends in Washington will look for an alternative. There is no advantage to us in leaving UDEL out there for them to play with.

"Finally, let's face it: the participation of the private sector will give the revolution an enormous credibility abroad, in that great chunk of the world where, if you are not at least on speaking terms with money, you do not exist. A million ordinary Nicaraguans are ready to die to be rid of Somoza. That is not considered a matter of importance. Nor is it considered to reflect badly on

Somoza. If it's noticed at all, it reflects on us: there go those damned ungovernable Latins again, running around with their machetes. But two hundred respected members of the business community want to get rid of Somoza? My God, there must be something awfully wrong with Somoza! All at once the matter is serious, the revolution is real. One body in the boardroom is worth twenty thousand in the streets. So be it. When the revolution is over, the question will not be who has credibility in Washington or Wall Street. The question will be who has credibility in Nicaragua."

They had fought it out, over smoke and coffee and sometimes tears, for a night and a day. In the end almost half the cell broke with Valerian and stayed with the GPP. The woman from El Carmen left weeping; others left granite-eyed with anger. Those who chose to follow their leader into the ranks of the Terceristas sat around afterward feeling like criminals. It had been awful, totally, unspeakably awful.

That had been more than six months ago and they still felt bad remembering it. Paco hoped to God that tonight's meeting would not be like that. It wasn't. It was strictly tactics.

Valerian greeted everyone, talked quietly and briefly with Marta and Manolo, who were his immediate subordinates and his long-time friends. It was after midnight when the real business of the meeting was finally broached: the Tercerista units of the Frente, he told them, were ready to attack.

"We are about to launch a major nationwide offensive," he said. "We are going to demonstrate to the people of Nicaragua that the dictatorship is not omnipotent; that in fact it is cowardly, demoralized, and stupid; that its armed forces can be hit, can be hurt, and can be stopped. We will target *Somocista*-owned industries, banks, and in particular, the command posts of the National Guard. *Including those in the cities.*"

They had all been waiting for this. They had spent the summer preparing for it: training two, sometimes three times a week; storing arms, medicines and food; building support networks; lining up safehouses. They had been waiting, but perhaps for something not quite so ambitious.

Pilar looked at Daniel, who held up a thumb and forefinger in a small, precise gesture of satisfaction. He had all sorts of doubts about the Tercerista policy of alliances, but none at all about the strategy of attack.

"It will take Somoza two or three days to figure out what's going on," Valerian continued, "that it *is* a large-scale offensive and not just a few isolated guerrilla raids. Once that happens, the repression will be hell."

"We have to start warning people," Claudia said.

"Yes. You all know who your own contacts are. You know who's vulnerable. Get to them and get to them fast. Those who can should stay out of sight; those who can't should stay as public as possible. If they're going to be arrested, let them for God's sake arrange for witnesses!"

"Yes," Daniel added, "if possible a photographer, a reporter, several people with kettle drums, and the papal nuncio."

They laughed, but the laugh had an edge; the matter was too painfully true to be funny. Publicity was the absolute bottom-line strategy against repression. You made public every name of every person killed or arrested or disappeared. You made them public as quickly as you could and you kept on, day after day, until people knew those names like they knew the names of their own children. You used the newspapers, if you could, but you didn't stop there. You painted the names on placards and marched them through the streets; you wrote them on walls; you shouted them from student podiums, from embassy steps, from pulpits. You put people outside the Guardia posts twenty-four hours a day and if prisoners were taken out you followed them—all of which required not only courage but tireless organization.

They spoke for a while about that organization, how sound it was, where the holes were. *La Prensa*, as always, could be depended upon to headline arrests and disappearances. The Tercerista student wing, the Revolutionary Sandinista Youth, could be depended upon, as always, to provide unmeasurable decibels of shouting and unmeasured hours of work.

"We have three clandestine printing presses," Amparo said, "as well as the bulletin. We have access to between forty and fifty cars and vans—any ten of them on a half hour's notice. We have ten health action committees, two literacy committees, and six Christian support groups working in the barrios. We can draw on all of their people as well as our own."

The strengths were many. The weaknesses were basically two, and hardly needed to be discussed: they were short of arms and ammunition, like always; and they had no well-organized base in the unions or the barrios—contacts and support groups, yes, but no real base. That part of the resistance had fallen, partly by historical circumstance and partly by default, to the Proletarian Tendency of the FSLN—the tendency that at the moment was angriest at the insurrectionists.

"They are Sandinistas," Valerian said. "Just like we are. Neither they nor we have ever questioned that. We argue about what it means but we've never denied what we are. I believe that as the need arises they will be there."

"I hope so," Paco said. "We need numbers. We're too damn fucking few for what we're taking on."

"That is exactly what the offensive is intended to remedy," Valerian said. "How many thousands of people do you suppose there are in this country who would like to do something about their misery but who are too afraid? And I don't mean just afraid of being killed, but afraid that it's pointless, that resisting is like jumping into Momotombo—a heroic gesture, if you're into making gestures, but meaningless. Powerless. Changing nothing. But if ever they start believing that it's possible—no, if ever they start *suspecting* that it's possible to change things—then there will be numbers, Paco. There will be so many numbers we'll give up counting."

"You're saying that faith will make the revolution," Rafael said.

"Yes. That's precisely what I'm saying." Then he laughed softly. "With a little help, of course."

Just what form that help was going to take was the next

issue to consider. They were short of medical supplies, for one thing, due to the loss of a shipment from Honduras; they would have to expropriate a pharmacy. In addition, they needed two commando teams.

"One," Valerian said, "to put to good use Manolo's excellent little cache of bombs. The other to join an attack force already being formed to confront the National Guard."

He did not say when or where; he never did. The teams would be assembled on the basis of necessary skills. They would acquire the equipment they needed, if they didn't already have it; they would train and discuss tactics in terms of the general nature of the objective. Only at the latest reasonable point—maybe a few days, maybe a few hours—would the objective be identified.

The sabotage mission would be handled within the cell. Manolo, being the explosives expert as well as the best runner, climber and general street rat among them, was placed in charge of it. Both groups, Valerian stressed, especially the attack commando, should be made up of people who were already underground or who could at least disappear from where they lived for several days. That left out Amparo and Pancho Villa, who didn't mind much; and Clariz, who did.

She hid her frustration from everyone but Daniel; he caught her eyes before they fell to examine a scratch on her hand; caught the disappointed curl of her mouth. He knew the feeling, the feeling that anything less than the front lines was not enough. It was not a demand you made of others—you would not even have considered it, it was absurd—and yet for yourself it was there, always there, the standard against which all your work was measured and found wanting. It had taken him years to learn to deal with it—to learn to more or less deal with it; he never came to terms with it completely. There was a need, some kind of need, and maybe it was not totally admirable, a need to always do more and be more, to matter...to matter perhaps too much.

They tied up the last details by daylight, over still another pot of Lidia's good coffee.

"*Bueno*..." Valerian looked at his watch. "Well, my

friends, by the time you are all at home you should have the news. Our comrades in the north and the south are at this moment in combat with the National Guard at San Carlos and Ocotal." He smiled, raised his coffee cup. *"Patria libre!"*

The October offensive had begun.

9

There was only one word to describe the Valdez estate in Las Colinas, but Jadine couldn't remember what it was. She had read it in a novel—a totally unscrupulous novel about the glamourous rich, of which she could now remember only the title and the fact that it was awful. Perhaps, she thought, perhaps the author could come to Nicaragua and try again. Milan Valdez belonged in a novel.

The family, Yolanda told her, was old. Their first land grants dated back to the 1750's. One Valdez had been a viceroy, another a general in the Spanish army; any number had been governors and mayors.

The house, however, was not old. It had been built by Milan's father when he retired from the National Guard two years ago, and signed over to Milan six months later. The old man preferred his *finca* in Carazo. Managua, he said, was a fucking pigsty; he couldn't imagine why decent people would want to live there.

"I hardly know him," Yolanda said, "but from what Milan tells me, he sounds like a real old bear."

"I do know him," Alvaro said. "And he is."

They both laughed. Beatriz smiled. Leon kept right on looking out the car window.

A steel gate met them, heavy enough to stop a tank, manned by two men in trim paramilitary uniforms and carrying automatic rifles. They were pleasant; the guests were known and expected. But the gate had sharp steel spears top and bottom, and when it clanged shut behind them Jadine felt not fear but a lingering coldness.

Inside everything was sumptuous. There were all the things she had expected: swimming pool and tennis court and outdoor bar; servants; two grand pianos, a European stereo wired to the patio and the master bedroom; servants; paintings, objects of art, mahogany, silver, lace. . . Servants.

"How many servants does he have?" she whispered to Yolanda in a discreet moment.

"Eleven live here," Yolanda said. "I don't know how many come in."

"When Milan farts," Leon said, "somebody is right there to take away the smell."

"Enough, *bastardito*!" Yolanda slapped at him, but he ducked and ran. "By God, I'll strangle him, the little pig!" she cried.

Jadine suppressed a smile. Surely, she thought, surely if you lived this high you could take a joke or two from the nether regions?

Milan was a good host. There was soft music playing, towels laid out by the pool if they wished to swim, luscious tidbits to eat in bowls of Bohemian crystal on the bar, a bewildering array of fine imported liquors. . . and of course, Milan's charm. He greeted them all warmly, especially Jadine, whom he called his cousin. He asked about Pilar—was she not coming?

He asked Alvaro, but it was Beatriz who answered: "She sends her deepest regrets, Milan. She wasn't well enough to come tonight."

He was sorry. He hoped it wasn't serious.

"Not in the least," Leon said. "She's probably recovered already."

This time it was Alvaro who slapped at him and missed.

There was a lovely yard and orchard to wander in, and after they swam and played a few sets of tennis, and her parents were comfortably into their third or fourth drink, Yolanda finally got to go off discreetly with her fiance, leaving Jadine and Leon sitting by the pool.

Jadine leaned her head back, looking at the sky that was already laced with stars.

"Do people from the north ever get used to nightfall here?" she asked.

"Used to it? What do you mean?"

"It's so sudden. It's what—four, maybe five minutes from full daylight to total darkness?"

"Something like that," Leon said. "What about it? What's there to get used to?"

"At home we have twilight. It gets dark very slowly. By tiny degrees. You can drive a car for an hour without lights after the sun goes down."

"God, that must be weird," he said.

She laughed, letting her eyes drift. She had been in a lot of beautiful places, but this one was as fine as any. There was something disturbing about this much opulence in the face of all the misery outside; still, objectively, you recognized it as a magnificent place. The high patio lights played shadow games in the trees, floated on the water like uneasy moons, glistened high on the wall like a spill of diamonds.

"What's that?" she asked Leon, pointing.

"What?"

"Sparkling. On top of the wall."

"Broken glass."

She looked at him. Broken glass lying around in a place as well kept as this? That was absurd.

"It's there for a reason," Leon said. "Every square foot of wall around this property is stuccoed with broken glass. It isn't decorative. Some of the shards are two inches long and all of them are sharp as knives. Would you like to see?"

"No," she said.

"Some kid tried to get in once—no one knows why. It was a cloudy night and he obviously hadn't checked it out first. He tied a rope to a tree and swung himself onto the wall. Of course he couldn't hold on and he fell. They found him a few hundred yards away. He didn't even break his arm. He just bled to death."

Jadine said nothing, only stared into the pool where the lights fluttered and drowned.

"You hate Milan," she whispered finally. "You and Pilar both. Is that why?"

It was a lovely night, he said. Why didn't they walk?

It was a lovely night, but it had an edge now. As they walked Leon spoke quietly.

"There is something you must know about this family," he began. "Yolanda will tell you it's very old and aristocratic, and that's true, as far as it goes. What she will not tell you is that until about ten years ago they were small-time rural gentry in Carazo. Comfortable, certainly, and very much members of what my other sister would call the nasty ruling class. But definitely small.

"All this—" He waved his hand to indicate the whole hillside estate, "came about through the family's connections with President Somoza, and in particular, through Milan's father's seven years as a *comandante* in the National Guard."

"I don't know what military salaries are like here," she said, "but I'm not about to believe they are that good."

"No, they're not. Guardia commanders don't get rich on their paychecks. They get rich on the drug trade, prostitution, extortion, business and import licenses, and the confiscation of property. From subversives, of course. Ennio Valdez now owns some twenty thousand acres in Chinandega—all a tribute to his extraordinary zeal in rooting out terrorists."

From somewhere up ahead came voices, the sound of Yolanda's laughter. Leon turned and they headed back the way they had come.

"It doesn't stop there," he went on. "They take this money—maybe a million cordobas a year—and if they're on good terms with Somoza, they get to share in all of his profiteering. They don't, of course, get to share equally, but they do get to share. They bought earthquake ruins, for example, for a few thousand dollars, and sold them to the government for a hundred thousand or more, for reconstruction. Nearly all the emergency aid money we got from your government went like that. You've seen for yourself how much of Managua has been rebuilt."

He slowed, scuffing gravel with his feet. "You know, my sister says it's inevitable. Pilar. She says if you have capitalism you have this—this kind of greed and corruption. Do you think that's true?"

"No," she said, without thinking about it much. "I think you'll always have greed and corruption. I think bastards are endemic in the human race."

He laughed softly. "That's what I told her, too. She had an answer. She always has an answer. Sure there are bastards, she said; there have always been bastards and there will always be bastards. But we could control them instead of reward them. We could base our society on the best of human qualities instead of on the worst. Capitalism, she said, prepares the ground for men like Somoza. It plants them and it waters them and then it pretends to be appalled when they grow.

"There are times I think she might have a point...especially when I come here...

"These men are not talented. Oh, they may have a certain gall, a certain cunning. But Somoza is a brutal, foul-mouthed, uncultured bully, and Ennio Valdez is something considerably worse. And here they are, cocks of the walk, kings of the mountain, beady-eyed centipigs with all hundred feet in the trough...I really wonder if my crazy sister hasn't got a point.

"I'm no leftist, Jadine. I think you know that. I don't want to see this country run by communists, or Marxists, or whatever the hell they call themselves now. I like my life the way it is. I like to live in a house with floors and beds and a refrigerator. I like to play tennis on weekends. I like to know that when I finish school I can go and study anywhere I want in the world, and that afterward I can have a good career and my kids can have things even better than I did. I'm not about to toss that out the window for some piper's dream of a socialist utopia.

"Only every time I come here I remember what she said: All this comes with it. You choose, she said, but this comes with it."

They walked in silence for a while.

"Does it, Jadine?" he asked. "Does it have to?"

He really wanted to know. He really thought there were answers...the price of being just sixteen. Down the path, still many yards away, they could hear Alvaro raising his voice, banging his fist on a table, cursing the treacherous, godless, murdering Sandino-communists.

Leon wanted all the answers and Alvaro thought he had them all. It was, she thought, going to be a long night.

Under the charm, the easy natural courtesy, Milan was troubled, almost tense. Yolanda sensed it as they walked, but she wasn't sure of its source. He did not discuss it. Instead he made small talk, praised her tennis game, said teasingly:

"Really, *querida*, I am beginning to think your little sister doesn't like me."

"Oh, she does, Milan. Of course she does. It's just all the stuff she's doing—raising money for Father Pepe and working on the university bulletin and God knows what else. She doesn't just miss your parties, Milan; she misses everybody's."

"Does your father permit all that?"

"Papa can't control her. He never could. He's away a lot, but even when he's here he can't do anything. They have big fights and then she just goes ahead and does what she wants to anyway."

He paused to light a cigarette. She wished that he would not smoke; it was the only thing about him that she considered uncouth.

"Did you know that she's very involved with the student movement?"

"Everybody's involved with the student movement, Milan. It doesn't mean anything. Not for most of them. Students just *do* those things."

"You didn't."

"No. I wasn't interested in politics. I was interested in theatre. I wanted to go to New York to learn acting, and I was mad at Papa for two years because he wouldn't let me. Then I forgot all about it. Pilar's the same. For a year and a half her best friend in high school was a shantytown communist who lived on her lunches. She really believed this kid was some kind of genius. She would go on forever about how we had to go into the barrios and teach the people to read because look how talented they were when they had a chance. Well, that didn't last. Halfway through the second year the kid was missing classes and failing everything he touched; one day he just never came back. That was the end of the literacy crusade. Pilar adopted Father Pepe instead.

"She's like that, Milan. It doesn't mean anything. I think it's mostly just a way of being different. She's very insecure."

He considered that. "You're probably right," he said. "But it's unfortunate. These things can drift in very dangerous directions. Your father ought to shout less and govern more."

"Surely you're not suggesting that Pilar would ever actually *do* anything...?"

"Don't be naive, Yolanda."

She fell silent, hurt.

"Anyone can be deceived, *querida*," he went on quietly. "Or corrupted. Or used. Or can simply make a stupid mistake. Your sister is playing with fire; it should be stopped."

"Would you like to suggest how?" she said tartly.

"No." He laughed and mussed her hair. "If I knew, I'd patent it. I could sell it to half the parents in Managua." He took her hands. "Come. Let's go back."

He made light of it for Yolanda's sake, but he was concerned—concerned and increasingly angry. Not one of these slogan-mouthing kids ever gave a thought to their families, to the damage that their reckless idealism could do—if it really *was* idealism. What it was for Pilar he was not yet sure; he would do nothing until he knew, except watch. Likely the National Guard would have a file on her communist friend; if not, it was time they started one.

He smiled as Yolanda fell in step beside him. "I imagine

Pilar doesn't talk much about her genius any more," he said wryly.

"Never. She doesn't talk about putting night schools in the barrios any more, either."

"Perhaps she's come to realize that schools have never yet taught anyone the will to work, if they don't have it in the first place. You don't remember his name, do you?"

"The kid? Daniel, I think. Daniel...Chillan...something like that. He was a total radical. Total. Lunch breaks he'd have his little following in a stairwell or out under a tree and he'd talk about how everybody was being trampled and exploited by the rich—all the while stuffing his dirty little face with his rich girlfriend's sandwiches. It was quite funny, really."

They ate outdoors, under an utterly still and magnificent sky. The food was superb, and as far as Jadine could tell, came from an inexhaustible kitchen. After a time she lost track of how many dishes had come and gone, and finally sat, more than satisfied, looking sadly at a plate of tenderloin which she knew was cut from the best beef in the world, drowning in mushrooms and carrots and onions and cream, with a side bowl of rice and another of plantain, which had just arrived.

"I'm never going to be able to manage this," she whispered to Leon, who was sitting beside her.

"Just dig in," he said. "You'll be surprised."

He was doing all right. Maybe after he was finished one of those wandering guards would fall into the swimming pool and they could switch plates. Or maybe she ought to try and eat just enough of it to be polite; she had no idea how much might be required.

They ate to music. *La Boheme.* Jorge Ibanez. *The New World Symphony*. She wondered what it was like to live like this all the time, what it was like to be really, really rich. She had a feeling she would get bored; at the very least the work ethic would get to her. What do you *do* after you've played all the tennis and eaten all the steaks and listened to all the symphonies you can manage?

"So," Milan said to her, smiling. "What do you think of Nicaragua now?"

"I think it's magnificent," she said.

"Yes," he said. "It is. Our country is much maligned, you know. Many people come here and look only at the bad things. They don't look at the reasons for the bad things, and they don't look at the good things at all. And they go home and say: Nicaragua is a terrible place. Nicaragua is backward. It's not true. I've been all over the world, and quite frankly, I haven't seen a place I'd rather live. I don't think anyone in the world lives better than we do."

"We need more culture," Yolanda said.

"Of course we do. But it will come. Culture is always the last thing to flower in a society. First you build, then you decorate. Last of all you contemplate. The arts are the end point in the progress toward civilization."

"I made a chamber pot," Leon said. "I painted flowers on it. I meditated over it. Now it is art."

"Leon..." Beatriz said wearily.

"What are you suggesting?" Milan asked, unperturbed. "Do you think that culture is possible without a developed economy, without education, without stability, without resources that can be put aside purely for the use of the arts?"

"Of course not," Leon replied. "But it would help if our ruling establishment could tell the difference between a Ming vase and a Coca-Cola bottle. Culture does require a certain—what shall I call it?—a certain sophistication of mind."

"Which some of us have," Milan said blandly, "and some of us don't. That's life."

The maids brought still another wine, condiments, bowls of sour cream. Alvaro took advantage of the interruption to swing the conversation around to the only subject he had talked about for days. What did this new guerrilla offensive mean? How big was it and where the hell had it come from and what was going to happen now and just how bad were things going to get?

Things, Milan said, could possibly get very bad.

"The government is handcuffed," he pointed out. "The president can't do anything. Every move he makes he has to answer to UDEL, to all those well-intentioned assholes in Washington who think they know what's going on here better than we do, to the professors, to the priests, to the international press, and to that irresponsible son of a bitch Chamorro. How can anybody govern like that? It's absurd."

"Oh, come on, Milan!" Leon said bitterly. "Disagree with Chamorro if you want to, but don't call him irresponsible. He's the only leader in the country who has any integrity at all."

"Integrity?" Milan took a sip of wine, put the glass down very slowly. "Pedro Joaquin Chamorro is either the biggest fool in Nicaragua, or the biggest traitor. I don't know which. I don't care which. Either way he is a national disaster. And personally, if it were up to me, I'd have him shot."

"Just like that," Jadine said.

He looked at her. Very briefly. Very calmly. It was a look that said: Listen, little American cousin, do you think you are watching a play?

"Yes," he said. "Just like that."

"It would be no loss," Alvaro said. "He's the best ally the communists have."

"So now even Chamorro is a communist!" Leon burst out. "Jesus Christ! Who's left except you and me and the president's horse?"

"Not a communist," Milan said. "Your father didn't say that. He said ally. And he's right. Chamorro is doing an enormous amount of harm. He is shamelessly undermining the authority of the government, slandering the president, slandering the National Guard. He's deliberately stirring up mob passions and hatred, and encouraging every kind of sedition and terrorism. What does the man think, anyway—that he can tear everything apart and then put it back together again the way he wants it? That he can destroy or emasculate every legitimate authority in the country and then he and his bunch of pantywaist intellectuals are going to hold off the Sandinistas?"

"There wouldn't *be* any Sandinistas to hold off if we had a decent government," Leon said. "The only reason the Sandinistas are getting anywhere is because there's so much corruption and poverty. Chamorro isn't the biggest ally the communists have. Somoza is."

There was a moment of silence. Milan put his knife and fork down quietly.

"Listen, Leon. The communists in Cuba are training and arming guerrilla cadres to send them into every country in Latin America. They are collecting every malcontent and every fanatic they can find on the continent, teaching them propaganda and terrorism, teaching them how to infiltrate unions and youth groups and even the Church, teaching them how to subvert people and organizations and whole countries. Who'd keep them out of Nicaragua if it weren't for the president and the National Guard? They've trained every leader in the Sandinista organization; they provide the arms, they give the orders—"

"Even if that's true," Leon cut in, "—personally, I think you're exaggerating—but even if it's true, how far would these cadres get if the people weren't miserable? Who'd listen to them? Who'd follow them? Go up to some well-fed man who has a bed to sleep in and whose kids are healthy and who doesn't wake up every morning wondering if he'll be shot today—go up to him and hand him a rifle and say: Here, you poor oppressed son of a bitch, we're going to start a revolution—and you know what's going to happen? He's going to laugh at you. He's going to say: You want to start a revolution? You go right ahead. I'll just sit here and pick my teeth, thank you.

"It's your kind of fucking paranoia that's going to do us in, Milan. Your paranoia and Somoza's greed."

"Leon, why don't you shut up when you don't know what you're talking about?" Alvaro said harshly. "You're sixteen years old and you think you know politics? You don't know shit. You're too God damn naive."

"I don't think he's naive," Beatriz said. "I think he's right."

"Beatriz, for God's sake...!"

Milan waved his hand, silencing him. "No matter. Let's hear everyone's opinion. Let's be democratic about this. Jadine..." He looked at her. There was food left on his plate but he had not touched it for some time. He studied his wine glass, turned it round and round in his fingers, looked at her again. She saw that under the surface calm he was strung like a high wire. Angry, but not just angry. Something else. Afraid, perhaps. And something more. Something that made her cold, that made her wish to God that she were somewhere else.

"Well, what do *you* think?" he said.

She chose her words carefully. "I think there's a connection between poverty and violence. I think revolutions grow mostly out of desperation, and that if the desperation were dealt with, the revolution could be defused."

"How would you deal with it?"

She looked at him.

"How would you deal with it?" he repeated. Softly. Savagely. "That's the big question, isn't it? The question the wonderful middle-of-the-road liberal humanists never have an answer for. *If only we could deal with things*, they say. What they mean is, if only they had some magic wand, if only they could hammer out some new formula, if only they could appoint another committee or appropriate a few more taxes or say a few more prayers, then all the shit down in Acahualinca would just—" he waved his hand like a baton—"disappear.

"You're all very generous. You don't want people to be hungry. It's a noble sentiment. It's a sentiment I totally share. I'm just waiting for one of you to tell me how to prevent it.

"In your country, Jadine, they've tried God knows how many things. They've torn down whole city blocks in the slums, and put up modern new apartment buildings with running water and refrigerators—and gone back a year later and found the buildings totally ruined, the refrigerators full of maggots, the toilets stopped with shit, and the people living the way they always lived—like pigs. Is that not true, Jadine?"

"Yes, in some cases. But there were reasons. There were factors that were never—"

"There were reasons. Of course. There are always reasons. The do-gooders will reason us all into the sea. You people have an infinite supply of theories but you don't have any that work. You just have a lot of mush and posturing. You want to have it all. You want power but you won't call it power and you won't take the responsibility for using it. You have no intention of giving up anything you have but you still insist that the rabble ought to have something—you just can't figure out where it's supposed to come from.

"Leon, you say Chamorro has integrity—would you tell me why? Because he's set himself up as some sort of champion of the people? On paper that's easy, and Chamorro has lots of paper. But what's he actually going to do about them? They can't take care of themselves. They live like animals in their own shit. They have no morals at all. The men take up with one woman after another, and leave batches of kids behind them everywhere they go. Half of what they do earn they spend on *chicha*. As for the women, they'll screw anything that moves for a cordoba; in Chinandega the prostitution was so bad that my father tried throwing them in jail. He gave up because he said the jail would end up bigger than the city. What do you suppose Chamorro's going to do about that? Change them all back into virgins? What would you do about it, Leon? Tell me."

"Give them work, for one thing," Leon said.

"Where?"

"I don't know; we could develop some more industries—"

"What industries? With whose money? We can't sustain the ones we've got. We fired thirty men from the Santa Rosa plant last week. Skilled men who know how to work. Do you think we're going to turn around and hire a bunch of whores?"

"Save it, Milan. Save it and sell it to your grandmother. Everybody in the country knows why you fired those men; they were union activists. They'll be replaced before Christmas."

"If production picks up," Milan said flatly, "they'll be replaced. If it doesn't, they won't. That's my decision, and I'm not about to turn it over to you. Or to Chamorro. Or to any fucking communist-infiltrated union."

He ground out his cigarette for emphasis. In the pale

light his eyes were harsh and brilliant. Jadine avoided them, wishing the meal would end. She tried to imagine how Pilar would deal with this man. Or Eryn. And considered how much meaning was packed into the fact that neither of them were there: If you felt about life as they did, you had nothing to say to Milan Valdez. Simply that. You had nothing to say.

There was an end point to debate, unless you became like the Spanish poet and his friends, and made debate an end in itself. There was an end to pretending that words necessarily had meaning. Leon, too, would discover that one day; God help him when he did.

Milan started to speak again. She had the feeling that he had barely begun, and for a moment she imagined them sitting all night, all winter, sitting forever frozen at this table with its linen and silver and light. Forever listening to Milan Valdez. Forever and forever, words and argument, argument and words. Dante should have thought of that.

"No God damn union is going to browbeat me into giving money to people who haven't earned it," he said. He didn't shout, like Alvaro. He spoke with absolute control. "If the man who owns a factory can't judge what a day's work in it is worth, who the hell can? That shantytown scum who couldn't plan it, couldn't build it, couldn't run it for half a day, but always have their mouths open wanting more money, somebody's money, anybody's money? All these people know how to do is make demands. They're totally ignorant. They can't read or write, most of them. Their kids are full of parasites because they don't have the simple common sense to keep them out of the sewers. Those who do work save nothing; those who don't blame everybody and everything in the world for their misery except themselves.

"You spoke of desperation, Jadine. Yes—the desperation of envy. The desperation of stupid and violent people who look around them and see that other people have good things, other people have houses and factories and music and books; other people have the ability to make things work. They see that, and they see that they don't have any of it, that they'll never have any of it because they haven't got the energy or the brains. And they're sick with envy. All they want to do is destroy. That is the motivation of every terrorist in the world: to annihilate everyone who is better than he is; to destroy everything he cannot have.

"You're not going to *deal with* that, my friends. Nor is Chamorro. You can try making pigs into posies, but you needn't think that the communists will copy your mistakes. They're not stupid. They know what pigs are good for."

He paused to light another cigarette. Everyone had stopped eating except Alvaro; there wasn't a sound in the patio except the click of his knife and fork against his plate, and Chopin wandering bewildered into the palm trees.

A servant moved unobtrusively into the circle of light, and bent close to Milan's chair.

"Excuse me, *senor*. There is an urgent call for you."

"I'm eating, Bertran. Take a message."

"I've tried, *senor*. It is very urgent—"

"Don't argue with me."

The servant straightened, and said simply: "They have blown up the factory, *senor*."

"*What did you say?*"

"The chemical plant, *senor*. At Santa Rosa. It's been blown up, *senor*."

A huge curse erupted from Alvaro. Milan was on his feet in a single, powerful motion, striding for the house. The servant righted his overturned chair, picked up his napkin, began to collect plates of cold, unfinished food.

"God in heaven," Beatriz whispered. "God in heaven..."

Jadine sat very still, only half listening to the buzz that came from Yolanda and her father, the quick bursts of unbelieving, unaccepting fury: How dared they, how was it possible, by God they would never get away with it...! She looked at Leon. He seemed...not stricken, exactly, but certainly sobered. God, it was all so stupid, she thought. Terrorist left against paranoid right, everybody else in the middle, trying to make sense and nobody listening—nobody listening maybe because we have nothing more to say, but what the hell have they got? Milan Valdez in here and some bomb-throwing crazies out there; take your pick, world, take your choice!

It was fifteen minutes or more until Milan came back. Yolanda went quickly to meet him.

"Milan, is it true?"

"It's true." He faced them, calmer now. "Both wings of the plant were blown; what's left is burning."

"Sandinistas?" Alvaro asked.

"Who else?" He picked up his cigarettes from the table and put them in his pocket. "I'm sorry. I have to go. You may stay if you wish. Certainly it would be better if the women did. All the main roads are blocked; there may be patrols even out here."

"Pilar is alone—" Beatriz began, looking at her husband.

"Yes," Alvaro said. "I should go back to the house."

"I'll take you then," Milan offered. Pilar was, at least, at home. Milan had not expected anything else, not really, but he had made sure. Her voice had not sounded either sick or sleepy, but it had been her voice, growing more and more edged when he did not reply. She hung up before he could. Just a tense young woman home alone, of course.

Headlights emerged suddenly from behind the house. A dark blue van pulled up to the edge of the patio. Its windows were curtained—like a duke's carriage, Jadine thought. Or like a hearse.

"For God's sake be careful!" Yolanda pleaded.

Milan kissed her lightly and turned to Beatriz. "The house is yours. We'll be back before morning."

She thanked him, but he was already climbing into the van, followed by Alvaro. Over their shoulders Jadine could see men—two of them, or maybe three: dark-clad shadows carrying glinting sub-machine guns. As the tail lights of the van disappeared Yolanda sat down by the table and began to cry. Beatriz went to comfort her; and then, after a bit, Leon did, too.

"It'll be all right, Yolanda," he said. "Probably nobody got hurt. The plant's insured. It isn't as if—"

"Don't you say anything!" she said bitterly. "Don't you dare say anything—not after you sat there all night defending those *animals*! Milan is right. The only way to deal with them is to kill them!"

"I wasn't—" Leon faltered; began again: "I have never defended the Sandinistas."

"No. You just defend every other miserable wretch in the country who does. Maybe now you can see what that leads to!"

Leon didn't answer. Jadine felt sorry for him. In the abstractions of debate the centre was a clean, comfortable place to be. But when the shooting started it turned into a very nasty, very lonely, very unprotected place. On battlefields, the land between the camps was no-man's-land.

It was late; close to dawn, perhaps. Jadine awoke shaking and raw, and sat for a long time, wrapped in her sheet, trying to understand why. There had never been fear—no real fear—until tonight. Oh, there had been moments: on the plane, looking down at the tangled sprawl of Managua. Reading the papers sometimes. There had been that quick jolt, that God-in-heaven-what-am-I-doing-in-this-place? moment of panic. And there had been the accumulated body of conventional wisdom, wisdom that comprised both truth and cliche, as to what the risks were: riding in a bus that's attacked by guerrillas on a mountain road; being in a building when it's bombed; getting caught in a shoot-out. Getting arrested for no imaginable reason, being dragged off by the Guardia to some hole where no one will ever find you, no one even listening as you cry: "But you don't understand—I'm an American! You don't understand! *I'm an American!*"

There had been all of that, but never anything like terror. She was not timid, and she really didn't care that much.

So why was she having nightmares now? Here? Wrapped in perfumed sheets in one of Milan's gracious guest-rooms, sheets that were now drenched in sweat, rooms so still that she could hear her own heart banging on the walls. There was no danger here. This was probably the safest building in Managua next to the bunker.

Next to the bunker...Jesus, she thought. *Jesus...!*

She put her clothes back on, threw the light spread over her shoulders like a poncho, and went outside. She had barely settled herself by the pool when one of the guards appeared. He was young and quite attractive; he was making extraordinary assumptions.

It took some time to get rid of him. No, she did not want a cigarette, did not want a drink, did not want to go for a walk. Yes, she was enjoying her visit. No, she was not married. And no, most certainly no, she was not in desperate need of masculine attention.

She was troubled by last night's events, she told him, and therefore she could not sleep. She was worried about her relatives. She wanted to be alone. She needed to be alone to think.

He went away then, but not far; he found a shadowed spot near the house and smoked cigarette after idle cigarette, watching whatever guards watched in places like this, but mostly watching her.

He was a man, macho and armed; she a woman, a stranger, but a guest of *el senor*; they were balanced, poised, despising each other across a few yards of darkness, both perfectly aware of what would happen if the balance shifted.

She knew then where her nightmares had come from; why they had come. Not from fear of a particular danger but rather from the recognition of a peril that was implicit in everything around her: the recognition that absolutely everything in this house was based on power. Layers and layers of power that doled out the food and the guns and the shelter; power that sliced up the world by the standards of its own perpetuation; power that might or might not protect you, that might or might not turn on you; power that you could cling to and serve and maybe even manipulate but never *have*. You were always, finally, defenseless.

She hugged her knees. If I feel like this here, what must it be like to be in the streets tonight, with the Guardia out, and Milan, and God knows how many like him, answering to nobody? God, what must it be like?

10

Smoke was still drifting over the shell of the Santa Rose plant when the Sandinistas attacked the National Guard post in Masaya, twenty-odd miles from the capital. The raid cost them six fighters, and killed fourteen of the Guard; it left Managua reeling.

Judging from what she read in both newspapers and from what was said in the Zelaya house, it seemed to Jadine that no amount of paranoia had prepared either the government or the Guardia for such defiance. MiGs or warships from Cuba they would have understood. Or guerrilla armies descending from the clouds, perhaps. But not that ragtag commando firing old guns out of the windows of old cars, storming a fortified military installation with a tank made out of a cattle truck; making good their retreat after a three-hour shoot-out down the Masaya highway. Those things did not happen in the real world of million dollar defense budgets; no one had made a provision for them.

There was a kind of heroism to it, she supposed.

Certainly a great many people in Nicaragua seemed to think so. Such thinking depressed her and made Alvaro absolutely furious. At the supper table references to the God damn bomb-throwing, bloodthirsty Sandinistas were almost as common as please and thank you and pass the salt.

Leon argued with him sometimes but Pilar did only once. Two nights after Masaya, Somoza's paper *Novedades* published an interview with their parish priest, a man named Father Rojas.

"Listen to this," Alvaro said to them, reading from it: "'The path of Christ is the path of peace; there is no other. If there are people in this country who say that violence is necessary to obtain justice, those people are not Christians. Violence is the enemy of justice. And those who choose violence are the enemies of God, and the enemies of this country.' You see," he went on, putting the paper down, "even the Church condemns the Sandinistas."

"Father Rojas hardly constitutes the Church," Leon said. "The Archbishop, in case you haven't noticed, has been very critical of the government."

"The Archbishop doesn't understand politics."

Leon raised his eyes to heaven. "But Father Rojas does?"

"Well, it's clear from this article that he does," Alvaro said, loading his plate. "Violence only breeds violence, he says; there is no place for terrorists in a Christian society."

"Has he excommunicated the National Guard?" Pilar asked.

Alvaro glared at her. "No," he said flatly. "Why should he? The Guard uses violence only to defend itself. To defend this country. To defend *you*, while you sit there and bad-mouth it to your heart's content. There wouldn't even *be* any National Guard if it weren't for the fucking Sandinistas. They started all the violence in this country."

"Starvation isn't violence, of course," Pilar said. "Taking the land away from people who lived on it for centuries isn't violence. Using it to grow cash crops that no one can eat and then importing food at prices only a handful can pay—that's not violence. Forcing people to live without schools or medicine or clean water or—"

"Nobody's forcing anybody to live like that," Alvaro said.

"—Or without a shred of dignity—that's not violence either," Pilar went on, unheeding. "Only resistance is violence. Well, you're right about one thing, Papa. There wouldn't be any Guard if there weren't any resistance. That's true. No man ever hired a police force to keep order among his cattle. And that's what Father Rojas wants—not Christians, Papa. He doesn't want Christians, he wants cattle. Dumb, leaden-eyed cattle starving in the fields and stumbling to the block without a murmur, without ever disturbing the sleep of fat little Pharisees like himself with the realities of violence—!"

"That's enough, Pilar!"

"It isn't going to work any more. The people won't take it any more—"

"What the fuck do you know about the people?" Alvaro demanded. "All you do is read books. You think the people want any part of this? They hate the Sandinistas even more than we do. You think those bloody terrorists represent the people? You believe that shit? Jesus! Jesus, Maria, for God's sake get me some coffee. The Sandinistas are nothing but a bunch of fucking Cuban puppets. They ask Castro for permission to piss. Jesus!"

"Castro's nine hundred miles away," Leon said. "Don't you think it could get a little painful?"

Jadine almost choked. But it really wasn't funny; none of it was. In the two weeks she'd been here, no one seemed to talk about anything but politics; the most innocent-seeming conversations ended up there, like spokes of a giant wheel. There were a thousand variations of the same arguments, but nothing ever changed. Nothing was concluded. Nobody gave an inch. There was a grinding futility to it all that left her numb.

But on one matter—one only—she was in agreement with Alvaro and the priest: Violence accomplished nothing. Revolutions accomplished nothing. There had to be another way. There had to be.

"They've been tried," Pilar said. "Believe me, they've been tried."

She was sitting cross-legged on her bedroom floor;

Jadine wondered what she had against chairs. It was late. Alvaro had blustered himself to bed and Leon, too, had finally gone. Only Beatriz still wandered the house, Lady Macbeth with twisting, pristine hands...I must stop drinking, Jadine thought. Really I must...

"Sure, they've been tried," she said to Pilar. "But how much? Everybody tries a little. Nobody tries hard enough."

"How hard is hard enough?" Pilar shot back. "How much blood do we have to give to wash the conscience of the world? Listen, let me tell you a story. One night, ten years ago, a group of men met in a little shop in Diriamba. They were union leaders from all over the country who had realized that even though their unions were allowed to exist, they were almost powerless. They wanted to do something about it. The meeting was private but it was legal. The methods they discussed—if they would ever have had a chance to use them—were also legal. Then the Guardia came. They surrounded the house and dragged the men into the street and shot them, one by one. The leader—the one who'd organized the meeting—they tied to the back of a truck, and made him watch the executions; then they smashed his arms and his legs with clubs, in front of his twelve-year-old son; and finally they shot him. Just for talking, Jadine. Just for asking what might be done. That was ten years ago. How much more is enough? How many generations of us have to die before the great white liberal throws up his hands and says: I'm sorry, I don't have any more bright ideas; you now have my permission to fight?"

Jadine looked at her, and looked away. For a moment she remembered feelings of years before: the passion, the reaching out, the immense driven possibility of meaning. Pilar was young, resilient, beautiful; her strength steadied everything it touched. If Pilar could believe in this, then maybe it was real.

But the moment passed. She'd seen too many of her friends sell their souls to sleight-of-hand philosophers. She had seen some of them go to Viet Nam and come back holding their guns like a second phallus, heard them talk by the hour about standing up like men and fighting whoever and whatever needed to be fought. Give them a bandanna and a Spanish lesson, she thought, and they'd make splendid Sandinistas.

"I don't know, Pilar," she said. "I don't know."

"Nobody ever knows," Pilar said bitterly. "They never have any answers. But they keep right on telling us to listen."

Jadine stood up. "I'm sorry," she said. She had no idea what she was sorry about. Discussing it at all. Being here at all. Not believing—yes, mostly that was what she regretted: not believing anything at all; and yet wishing that she could. That ambivalence followed her long into the night. The ambivalence of an immense, bottomless depression, quietly gnawed upon by envy. It was frightening and sad that someone like Pilar would defend the actions of terrorists, that she would defend the deliberate, conscious choice of violence. But at least she believed in something, cared about something strongly enough to fight about it. A Sandinista is a Sandinista, she had said. The sun is the sun and the moon is the moon and what's true is true and maybe we can find our own answers, thank you very much, world, we've had enough.

Lucky Pilar. Lucky Pilar as long as it was talk and dreams, but what if one day she decided to join the revolutionaries? The new offensive was already capturing the country's imagination—as of course it had been intended to; already a growing trickle of young recruits was slipping away into the mountains. She'd probably go with them, sooner or later, if she kept on thinking the way she did. Beatriz knew that, somewhere deep in her unsleeping soul; that was why she walked. Pilar would go with them, and learn how to sleep in the rain and how to plant mines and how to judge exactly where the jugular was and how to slash it with a nail file...and she wouldn't be Pilar any more. She would be someone else, someone who increasingly resembled those she fought. Because the sun was a small, insignificant star and the moon was a clod of volcanic ash and truth had as many angles as the wind, and as little substance; and what was the use believing when in the end you had to pass from faith to knowledge, and knowledge destroyed you?

God, why did I come here? Why? I can't live here and I won't die—who would bother to finish me? I just go on like a bad play...on and on and on and on...God let it end. Let me find some way to make it end.

11

It took forever to get home, walking with Pablo. Marcos wouldn't have minded, except that he was so hungry, and he knew his mother would give him something extra because he had sold so many papers. Everyone was buying papers this week. Last week the Sandinistas had blown up a factory and three days ago they had attacked the National Guard command post in Masaya. Everywhere, in the streets and the markets and the barrios, it was all that anyone wanted to talk about, or read about. Never in his life had Marcos sold so many papers.

He stopped and looked back at Pablo, who was quietly falling behind again. It would do no good to shout at him. If Pablo hurried, he would merely begin to cough, and little flecks of blood would spatter his hands and then he'd walk slower than ever because it hurt so much to breathe. Once, Marcos had gone with him to Father Pepe's clinic and the young doctor there, Oscar Medina, had told him what Pablo was sick with. It was a long word and Marcos could never remember it.

He sat on a rock and made himself not think about Pablo being that sick. They were in an open field; just ahead, one of Managua's small, jagged ravines lay between them and the next barrio. It was a short-cut home—for him, at least. For Pablo maybe it was just as hard as the long walk around. He took out his sack of coins and began to count them, methodically, one by one.

Pablo sat beside him, grinning. "You've counted them three times already, Marquitos," he said. "Do you think they'll have babies before we get home?"

"Oh, shut up." Pablo could make jokes. Pablo's father didn't beat him if he decided that there weren't as many coins as there should be.

Pablo lay back in the grass. Overhead, very high, a jet passed, leaving a wisp of trail that broke and drifted and dissolved almost as it was made.

"Where do you suppose it's going?" Pablo asked.

Marcos looked up. The plane was so high that he could barely see it, so high he could not imagine it ever coming down. He thought about the farthest away place he had ever heard of.

"China," he said.

He watched it for a while but it made him sad. Planes went everywhere, like birds. Watching a plane was like listening to the singer in Ciudad Jardin—the one he'd seen twice and then never again; it was being reminded that there was something else, something out there, something possible.

Day after day he had dragged Pablo from market to market, ranging farther and farther afield, finding nothing but a few sad old men with broken-down guitars, a few orphans with tin whistles, and one not-too-bad marimba. The black-haired youth was gone—gone like he'd never existed.

"He'll be here tomorrow," Marcos promised his friend, every afternoon. "Tomorrow. You'll see."

When Pablo smiled he had a saint's face: thin, almost translucent, with huge eyes that were always too bright, as if with fever. Every time Marcos made that promise, Pablo smiled; but he never seemed to mind that they never found the singer. And this afternoon, when they had given up once again, Pablo smiled and said they should stop looking, because likely as not the young man had run off and joined the Sandinistas. Pablo was like that—always imagining crazy things.

Marcos shoved his coins back into his pocket and stood up. "We got to go," he said.

The ravine was rough and full of tangled growth but after a while they found a path of sorts and followed it. They were suddenly totally alone; the city that surrounded them might have been a hundred miles away. Pablo began to play at being a *guerrillero*—carrying a stick like a rifle and slinking and dodging behind trees, appearing suddenly on the path ahead of Marcos, gasping for breath but proud of his small triumph.

"Stop it, you monkey," Marcos said. "What if there's Guardia around?"

"There's always Guardia around," Pablo said. "They're everywhere. They grow on trees. Sandinistas, too." He laughed and slipped into the trees again.

Marcos kept walking. Crazy Pablo would wear himself out in five minutes and then Marcos would have to sit with him until he could breathe again. He swore to himself, softly, and kept going until the trail began to turn. Then, in spite of himself, he looked back. Pablo was nowhere to be seen.

"Pablito, come on! It's late!"

There was no answer, no motion at all in the trees. From down here the sun was already hidden, and the silence crept over his body like a cold fog. He could hear insects rustle; and far away, softer than a bee's wing, a truck passing; he could hear his own breath die in his throat.

"Pablo?"

He had meant to shout but it was only a whisper. He took a few hesitant steps back the way he had come.

"Pablo, if you're hiding on me I'll kill you. . . !"

He walked faster and faster until he was running, numb with terror, gulping out Pablo's name, running too fast, the trees going by in a blur of menace. He almost missed seeing Pablo, just a thin shape there among the trees, bent low as though he were doubled over in pain. Marcos crashed into the tanglewood beside him and almost fell over the first of the seven or eight bodies that had been thrown there.

God. Oh, God . . . He did not say it aloud, could not have said any word aloud; horror cut off his breath and drained the strength from his legs. He had seen dead people before—murdered people. Four of them last week in the barrio, lying in the streets after the Guardia had come and gone. But he had never seen anything like this, only heard about it. Heard that they cut ears off and dug out eyes; that they severed hands and genitals and heads; that they raped women and sometimes young men, and afterward tore their bodies open with bayonets or broken stones; heard that they dumped the bodies like garbage and denied that the dead had ever been taken, had ever been seen, had ever existed . . .

God. The thing by his feet, that he had stumbled over, was only a few years older than himself, fourteen perhaps; a naked and bloated ruin from which twisted three smashed limbs; the fourth had been wrenched off altogether. Marcos backed away a few steps, made himself look up, look for Pablo, and saw that the entire grove was fogged with a buzzing obscenity of flies, that there were others and that they were all like this, all horribly destroyed. He threw up then, again and again, until he couldn't any more.

Shivering, he picked his way through the grove to sit beside Pablo, and saw, right at his feet, the body of a man, mangled like the others, black with blood and flies, the upturned face twisted and scarred, but still a face he knew. It was the young doctor from Leon, who three times had kept Pablo alive, the only doctor they had ever had on the lakefront.

No.

He said it over and over. No. Not Oscar. Please, God, not Oscar. He's never done anything, only helped people. Please, God, no . . .

"You got to go get somebody," Pablo said. He sat quietly, tears making a small dark circle where they tumbled onto his knee.

Marcos looked at his friend, looked at the sky. It was maybe half an hour till dark. "You can't stay here," he said.

"Somebody got to stay," Pablo said. He had broken off a tree branch and was gently fanning the flies away from Oscar's body. "You go, Marquitos," he said. "You go. You got to go."

12

There were too many people to fit into the weathered wooden church of Maria del Consuelo—hundreds too many, milling in the barrio streets, clutching flowers bundled in newspaper; clutching banners, placards, crucifixes. Inside, there were only prayers, only a remembrance; the Mass for the dead would be offered tonight in Oscar's own parish in Leon. Four borrowed cars waited outside the church, circled by an honour guard from the University of Leon; they, with Oscar's parents and a handful of friends, would take his body home. All the rest—the hundreds from Acahualinca and the eastern barrios, the Managua students, the people who had known him and the people who knew that it made no difference whether they had known him or not—they would accompany him as far as they could, some of them to the outskirts of Managua or beyond...if the Guardia let them.

Pilar never heard a word of the prayers. She was aware

of Father Pepe's voice, aware of the way it faltered and steadied and faltered again, aware of the swell of voices around her, but the words dissolved without meaning. Felipe was dead. The woman who had recruited her into the Frente was dead. Half of Claudia's family was dead. Carlos Fonseca was dead. When did it end? You were supposed to accept it but you never did; they were all irreplaceable. Every death was an echo of every other; every death made new the pain and under the pain the anger burned and burned and burned...

They carried Oscar's coffin out into the blinding sun, into a sea of faces, hundreds of them wrapped like her own in bandannas, defying the spies and the cameras of the Guardia: you want our names, Tachito? you want our pictures? Very well, come and fetch them one by one!

Solemnly, tenderly, the six youths slid the coffin into a station wagon and the procession began to move into the street. The chant went up then, louder and each time louder: Oscar Medina Farnier, *Presente! Presente! Presente!* Father Pepe walked ahead of the hearse and half of east Managua walked behind it, spilling out of the barrios in a ribbon of bitter and bewildered rage. What had Oscar done to deserve this? they asked each other. What? And what, dear God, what would they do without him? An old woman, parted from her friends or perhaps without any, shuffled beside Pilar just back of the JRS students' banner, carrying a few withered wild flowers. There was no justice in the world, she said. No justice. Pilar could not find words to answer her.

Block by block as they moved the Guardia moved with them. And watched and waited. Hatred hung in the air like dust—hatred cultured in the soldiers, trained into them like obedience and marksmanship. They hated the rabble—they had to—hated their misery and their numbers and their remorselessly accusing eyes. Hated them all the more now, since Masaya, since the Sandinistas had killed fourteen of their men with cunning and contact bombs and cheap pistols, the weapons of rabble.

Pilar could see that many of them were carrying clubs and tear gas, as well as their usual arms. They were ready; they waited only for an order, a provocation, or simply for their own wrath to build. Waited till they were sick of the chants and of the twisted faces of women calling them murderers. Oscar's death had been more than a murder; it had been an attack on the entire community, and it was recognized as one. There was as much rage in this funeral as grief, and the grief was terrible.

Afterward, in Somoza's paper, it was said that the people from Los Santos started the riot, and as an outside possibility Pilar thought that it might be true. That is, maybe somebody struck a guardsman as he went by, or spat on him, or even threw a rock. It was possible. But as to what happened then, there was no dispute. The Guard attacked all along the column, veering their jeeps and trucks across the street to block it, dragging people off here and there but mostly just beating them senseless. The youth banner went down in a tangle of bodies and one of the girls who was carrying it curled into a ball beside Pilar, two guardsmen clubbing her like a snared rabbit.

Rage was a soft cry in Pilar's throat as she bent, grasping the pole of the banner and snapping it with her foot, bringing it up in a savage arc across the guardsman's face. The wood splintered, but he went down. His companion would have shot her then, but he had his rifle by the barrel, using it as a club, and before he could swing it around three students had wrestled him to the ground.

"Run, for God's sake, run!" one of them screamed at Pilar. "They'll kill you! Run!"

There was nowhere to run, but there was still room to move. The students were too many to contain and they fought their way under and over and through the Guardia, finding doorways and alleys and fences to leap over. Pilar dodged a blow and heard it thud horribly against someone else; then a man's hand closed on her hair and spun her to the ground and someone was kicking her, brutally, methodically. She made it to her knees and a club caught the side of her head and she buckled, blind with pain and scared now, really scared, pulling up her knees to shield her belly, an arm to shield her face. She couldn't see who was beating her. From somewhere, not far away, she heard the soft bark of pistols. There was no room to use their rifles in this confusion, but they had handguns, the pigs;

they had everything—a millionworth a year from as far back as the first *vendepatria* among them had learned how to say *gracias* in English. . . God, when did it end?

A man beside her screamed *Jesus!* like a speared animal and fell on top of her, so they hit him instead, not knowing or not caring that he was already dead. His weight stifled her; warm, sticky blood ran from his chest into her hair; but she lay still, huddled and barely conscious, until the violence passed like a wave beyond her, the Guardia still cursing and flailing at anything that moved.

She struggled free of the man's body, fighting for consciousness, looked at his face for a second, only a second, long enough to discover that she didn't know him, to be grateful that she didn't know him. She wiped away the blood that kept running into her eyes, and looked around. The fight, if it could be called that, still raged in pockets, but the crowd was almost dispersed. A Guardia jeep was burning and they were starting to drag people into the trucks.

She was not very far from a fence. She edged toward it. All down the street stragglers were dodging and running. She snaked forward and her hand brushed something hard and cold in the grass. It was a grenade, ripped or fallen from a guardsman's belt without him or anyone else noticing. Just lying there, like a gift from a confused God who couldn't take it anymore either. She tucked it inside her shirt and bolted over the fence; knelt there for a moment, motionless, blacking out and coming back, twice, maybe three times.

Slowly her head cleared; it hurt beyond imagining but it was clear; she could move without feeling that she would fall. The objects in the street glittered like mirrors but they did not dance or blur any more when she looked at them.

Twelve guards, maybe more, clustered around a truck down the block, but it was too far away and she had no way of knowing if there might be prisoners inside. Closer, fifty or sixty feet from the fence, was a jeep, a lone officer sitting in it, talking into a radio. Better, she thought; much better. Take the bastards who give the orders, rather than the poor damn fools who carry them out. Too bad it wasn't El Chiguin. . .

She drew the grenade from her shirt, praying that dizziness would not spoil her aim. Daniel had taught her how to throw grenades—or at least, had started to teach her. The second time out he had just laughed and said: "Fuck it, Clariz; you teach me." She was good at things like that. Not at everything: she hated driving and did it badly; she had a poor stomach for heights. But she was an excellent shot; she could read maps and remember terrain; and she could throw these things more accurately than anyone she'd seen except Eduardo, and he'd been doing it for fifteen years.

She was tugging at the pin when she heard the steps, the soft gulp of horror. She looked up, her body coiling to bolt and run. A few feet away was a man, middle-aged, neither rich nor poor; probably he lived here. The riot was outside his fence and therefore not real, and he was staring at Pilar in absolute, uncomprehending horror. His mouth moved but he did not speak, his eyes were bottomless with fear and hatred. Not for the Guardia. Not for any ugly abstraction like war or violence. For her. For the bloodied, scarved, armed woman in his yard who wasn't supposed to be there, who wasn't supposed to *be* at all.

Pilar patted the grenade. "A friend of mine," she said softly. "Oscar Medina Farnier, *presente*." Yanked the pin, threw with all her strength, and ran.

There were forty people in the hospital emergency waiting room, maybe more. Some of them had been there all day—mostly women with sick or injured children. Two factory accidents. A knife wound. A miscarriage. Some slept, no longer seeming to care if they were tended or if they died. After ten minutes or so, a smiling nurse came to Beatriz and said:

"*Senora* Perez de Zelaya? The doctor will see your daughter now."

Pilar didn't stir. Across from her a pregnant woman clutched her belly, her eyes black with pain.

"She was here first," Pilar said to the nurse. "I can wait."

"She has another doctor," the nurse said blandly. "You may come in now."

And the children? Pilar wondered. The man whose leg,

slashed to the bone, had finally stopped bleeding all by itself? Did they all have other doctors, too? Or just no doctors?

"*Por favor, senorita.*" The nurse forced a smile. "Please come in now." Pilar gave her mother a bitter look and allowed herself to be led away.

The pregnant woman's eyes fell, but not before Beatriz saw them, saw the hope that had been in them quietly die. She fought back shame by remembering fear. Remembering the half hour she had sat in her chair, staring at the catalog from which she was supposed to choose Yolanda's wedding invitations, hearing the shower run and run and run. Remembering what she'd found when she forced the door. Blood on everything. Not a lot of it, but on everything. And Pilar kneeling over the toilet, throwing up like she was going to die.

Still it had been a fight to bring her here—a fight that Beatriz had won only because Alvaro was here in Managua, an hour's drive away. You come with me, Pilar, or you come with him...

Once, in the car—only once—she had asked: "Why did you go, Pilar? Surely you must have known—?"

And Pilar had looked at her with eyes that killed. "What are you saying, Mama? Oscar was my friend. Is it a crime in this country now to bury the dead?"

Beatriz looked at her hands, studied her hands with great care, so as not to have to see the other people, the ones who waited and waited. Steps approached. She looked up thankfully, expecting Pilar, but it was the nurse.

"Will you come in, please, *senora*?"

The fear again. Jesus, she thought wildly, Jesus, what's happened to my child? She blundered after the nurse, terrified that she would find Pilar collapsed on the floor or lying on a stretcher, about to be carried away to the emergency ward. But her daughter was sitting in a chair, clothed and calm. Sullen, perhaps, but calm.

The doctor rose to greet Beatriz, shook her hand politely. His name was Ortiz; she knew him, but not well. He urged her to sit.

"My daughter?" she pleaded, unable to wait. "Is my daughter all right?"

He busied himself with his papers. "There has been no

serious injury. Your daughter will recover from this unfortunate...accident...in a week or two. She will need rest, that is all." He put his elbows on the desk. Looked at her thoughtfully. Pityingly, she suspected. She wondered if he had children Pilar's age, and if he did, how he kept them off the streets in times like these.

"However," he went on, "there is something else. Are you aware that your daughter is almost eight weeks pregnant?"

"Pregnant?" she whispered. She turned to Pilar, who did not turn away. Pilar who never went to parties, never dressed to be pretty, never had time for anything except books and politics? Pilar pregnant? She stared at her, trying to believe it. Trying not to believe it.

"Are you...quite sure...?"

He ignored that as unworthy of a professional response. "I felt it was my duty to tell you, *senora*, even though your daughter insisted that I should not."

He stood up. She saw plainly then that he pitied her. And judged her. She was less than he had believed her to be. The family, Alvaro, all of them were less, markedly and irredeemably reduced.

Pilar sat in the big stuffed chair by the patio window—lay in it, really, her head back, her eyes half closed. The day's last spill of light glinted on the top of her hair, but her face was shadowed. All one side of it was swollen, patched with bandages.

Beatriz poured herself a drink, offered one to Pilar, knowing that she would refuse. She wondered if Pilar ever drank with her friends, whoever they were, wherever they gathered by night to talk about whatever it was they talked about. You don't have a daughter anymore, Alvaro had said to her. You have a visitor who rents one of your beds...

It was her fault, of course. Fallen daughter, failed mother. The natural order of things.

She sat down, ran her hand over her eyes. The rum tasted like water.

"Will you tell me why?" she said finally. "Will you just tell me why?"

"Why what, Mama?"

Why what, indeed? What was it that she wished to know? Why are you not like we need you to be? Did we lose you. . . or did you escape?

"Why you. . ." She faltered. She did not want to sound like Alvaro. "Why you have. . . why you're. . . sleeping with men."

Pilar answered calmly, without anger, without defiance. "Why should I not? I'm a grown woman."

"You're. . . not married."

"You mean there's been no contract? I have not been guaranteed a lifetime of irrelevance and a house in Las Colinas in return for an untouched hymen and exclusive development rights? No, Mama; I'm not married. *Gracias a Dios*."

"You are gross, Pilar."

"No," Pilar said bitterly. "The world is gross. This society is gross. What's a woman in Las Colinas, Mama?—an object, a trinket, a worm on a hook. A mannequin for men to hang their trophies on. A shopping machine. A breeding machine. A smiling machine. The most carefully cultivated piece of capital in the world!"

She reached for her bag, rooted in it—for cigarettes, Beatriz supposed. She wished that she could be angry at what Pilar was saying; it was, after all, offensive. But it only made her sad.

"I'm not supposed to want a lover or a child," Pilar went on. "But the women of Acahaulinca—it's all right for them to take lovers whether they want them or not, in order to eat. It's all right for them to have ten babies by the time they're thirty, and watch half of them die. What else are they good for? They can have all the babies God will give them, and die of the last one; after all, we need a labour force, and we need a fresh supply of young girls to stock the brothels, since they're ugly by the time they're twenty-five, and their teeth are gone, and they've got syphilis. Barrio women are good enough for that, Mama. And we, God knows, we are too good for anything except to pray and paint our nails, and keep our bodies chaste for some man who is not chaste and who would laugh at the idea of it. Do you think Milan is chaste, Mama? Ask his maidservants.

"That's no life—no life for anybody. The poor are

slaves and we're pets; our men shut us away from the misery they create and tell us we're fortunate to be protected; if we don't like it, we can always go and live in the shantytowns. And if we get out of line too far, we can count on ending up there.

"You'd be surprised how interchangeable we are, Mama —how tradeable, like all good property should be. There's only one world and that world runs on our flesh—packages it, markets it, prints it on billboards and grinds it up in factories; takes our children and sorts them like peas: a few to have everything and the rest, nothing; takes our bodies for bait and rewards and status symbols and scapegoats and then says we're free because we can choose whose status symbol we want to be, what kind of bait, scapegoat for which sin! What's it worth, Mama, to be a woman in a world like that?"

Beatriz stared at her glass, looked up sharply as the flare of a match played briefly on her daughter's face.

"And in your world, Pilar? What is a woman in your world?"

"I don't have a world," Pilar said. "Yet."

Silence, then. No sun anymore. No light at all except what Pilar carried in her hand.

She's one of them, Beatriz thought. The revolutionaries . . . one of them already . . . The thought was paralyzing but oddly familiar. It had been with her for a long time, just inside the surface of her mind, waiting for her to be still long enough to hear it.

Her daughter a Sandinista. And the young man, too, of course; Pilar would never choose anyone else.

She stood up, cold all over. How would it end? In one of those bullet-laced streets that every night crept up against the borders of her peace? Or in some worse place, some place that even nightmare did not admit to? Wherever it ended, she knew that it would be in a world she did not know and could not reach. She was a mother of Hamelin now. They all were, staring at the mountains and wishing to God they had paid the piper when they could have.

She poured herself another rum, wishing that she could get drunk, wishing it were not such a tiresome, disgusting thing to be a drunk.

"It wasn't a happenchance thing, then?" she said. "An . . . accident? You have a lover."

"Yes."

"What does. . . what is he like?"

She could see that Pilar was surprised. And touched.

"He is. . . gentle. Very gifted. Very. . ." She hunted for a word and Beatrtiz supplied it calmly:

"Very dedicated."

"Yes."

Yes. He would be that. They always were. Like Felipe, Felipe whose bones were pressed like flowers under the tomb that was Managua. The things we love best in our children, she thought bitterly, are the things that kill them.

She wished that there were something she could say to her daughter, something that wouldn't be either a platitude or a lie, something that would reach across the space between them, a space that was huge now and yet not empty.

But there was nothing; it was best to return to realities at hand.

"How do you mean to deal with your father?"

Pilar dropped her head back against the chair. The simple mention of that seemed to exhaust her.

"Are you going to tell him?" she asked.

"Mother of God, child, you can't have a baby in the broom closet."

"Are you going to tell him?"

"One of us will have to." And God, what a scene that would be. What a nightmare. What a howling, ugly, barbarous nightmare. She wasn't at all sure that she could face it.

She went to stand by Pilar's chair, touched her face lightly, her shoulder. "*Pobrecita*," she said. "You should be in bed. Go, before your father comes. I'll bring you something to eat. I won't tell him anything tonight. You need to rest. Do you want some soup?"

Pilar shook her head, wrapped her arms around her mother and hugged her long and hungrily. They had not embraced like that for years, Beatriz reflected sadly, watching her go; not since Pilar started sneaking political pamphlets into her bedroom at the age of twelve.

She sat for a while, a very little while, before she walked over and picked up the phone, dialed it methodically, remorselessly, as though she were someone else watching herself do it. It took five minutes to book the flight, an hour to get through to San Jose, listening over her shoulder all the time for steps coming up the walk. Veronica's voice was faint and broken by static; she kept asking what was wrong.

Nothing was wrong, Beatriz said. Nothing. "Pilar and I want to buy some things for the wedding. Will you meet the plane? At three on Friday?"

"*Claro,* Mama. *Claro*."

So easy. Sweat was running down her body and her hands were shaking, but it had been easy. They would go to San Jose. They would put their heads together—she and her daughters. They would think of something. Alvaro would never know.

She mixed another rum to calm down. She had never deceived her husband in her life before, never disobeyed him, never done anything behind his back. She was amazed that it had been so easy. The world said women were weak, she reflected; it was more careful what it said about mothers.

The house was still dark; she had never bothered to turn on any lights except the small one by the phone. She went to Pilar's room, wondering whether to tell her now or wait till morning.

The room was empty.

She knew, even before she saw the note pinned to the pillow, knew that Pilar was not in the patio or in the bathroom or in the kitchen looking for something to eat. She was gone. Gone into that soft, terrible night, the night that belonged now to the children of the *rojinegro*. . . only to them.

The note said: Mama. I *do* love you. Please don't try to find me. I'll be all right. Goodbye.

She went into the patio; there seemed no reason not to any more. The night was silent as an ambush, all shadows where everything breathed but nothing could be identified. Over the patio wall she could see the black lace of her neighbour's trees.

She knew Pilar had not slipped past her through the house; she had gone this way, over these seven feet of stone. Bandages, baby, and all. Beatriz wondered if she could ever have done that. Maybe once. There was a time when she could play tennis all afternoon and then dance all night, when she could ride any of her grandfather's horses as fast as they could run. She stopped that after Alvaro slapped her for it; he did not want her killed, he said. She rode only ponies after that. One grew up. . . or at least, one called it that. Maybe one just grew. . . empty.

A voice boomed into her melancholy, a door banged. Where was everyone? Where was Maria? Where was supper?

Alvaro was home.

Pilar would have liked to go to Lidia's house, not least because Daniel was likely to be staying there, but it was too far to walk and there was no other way to get there except by taxi—a risk she would not take. She took a cab instead to the Plaza de Compras, and from there a bus. People stared at her bandaged face and she realized that she was much too identifiable to go anywhere near any of her comrades except in careful stages, and on foot. She walked for what seemed like hours, picking her way like a thief, hiding from everything. There was no curfew now but the years of living with one had honed her senses, honed her nerves to a sharp, unremitting edge of watchfulness. Everything that moved was menace, and shadows that did not move were a different, potentially more dreadful menace. The *orejas* were patient as owls, watching the streets; and some of them had radios to the Guardia patrols.

She had been out alone at night before, on missions, but never running; never without somebody else knowing she was out there, ready to look for her or cover for her if something went wrong. It was different to be totally on her own, to be unsure even of what she did, unsure if she were right to be doing what she did.

She never saw the car—or rather, she saw it but she did not really notice it, notice that it was different, that it was not parked and empty like the others she had passed. She was only a few feet from it when it turned its lights full onto her, blinding her, framing her like a target in a spotlight.

"Oh, Christ! . . ." She spun out of the light, bolting into a gloom of papaya trees, the shadows of a house; over a ditch, under a clothesline with a few ragged shirts, expecting with every step to hear the slam of car doors, the shouts, the guns. She ran until her breath came in gasps, until her head felt as if it would shatter from the force of her blood. But there was no outcry; no one followed her. They had not been spies or Guardia after all, only people, ordinary people, lovers perhaps, heading for home. She would never know.

She slowed her pace to a walk. She was weary now, all but exhausted, and no closer to the safehouse than she had been an hour ago. She walked numbly until the barrio she was crossing curved into a hill, uninhabited and ragged with shrubs. She crept gratefully into the depths of them to rest. The branches scratched her hands and snapped cruelly against her injured head. She huddled, hugging her knees, letting small hot tears tumble unheeded onto her sleeves.

She could have been at home, in her bed, Beatriz bringing her hot soup. She could have called Amparo, darling Amparo who seemed so young and bubbly but who was sharp as an arrow, who would have gotten word to Marta, to Valerian, to Daniel, to somebody. By dusk tomorrow there would have been a car five blocks from the house in Las Colinas. She could have waited. Surely she could have waited a day.

But she had lain on her bed, not sleeping, not even thinking of sleeping, and felt a fear more absolute than any she had ever felt in the streets. Her father would know what had happened at the funeral—all of Managua knew by now. He would take for granted that she had been there. Suppose he stormed into her room over Beatriz's protests, and saw her face? Suppose he called Dr. Ortiz? Suppose Yolanda chose to remember her old, dangerous friendship with Daniel Chillan? Suppose Alvaro called Milan?

She had lain still, watching the last traces of the sun

vanish, and acknowledged how deep after all was her fear of her father—not merely of him as a man, although that was real enough, but of him as a part of his world—a world that would support him in anything he chose to do to her.

There was no question, as men normally judged such things, that Alvaro Zelaya loved his daughter. That he considered it his duty to support and protect her. That he would, under certain circumstances, have done so at enormous cost to himself. He loved her; that was one of the reasons why he consistently blinded himself to the realities of her personality and her life, why he persisted in misinterpreting her radicalism as a youthful and misguided idealism—not such a bad quality, after all, in a woman; a little charity looked good on them. Felipe had never gotten off as easily as she did.

Alvaro was not a wicked man; he was simply a violent man. Not intentionally perhaps, not out of deliberate malice, but out of rage: the rage of power, the rage of men who could not accept that they no longer commanded, men who would destroy what they had sought to control rather than let it go.

She'd gotten up then, taken her toothbrush and her manicure set, her book of Neruda poetry, the perfume Daniel had given her, one change of clothing, the knife and the money she had hidden away, at various times and in various places, for an hour just like this. She had stuffed them all into a small bag, written a note for her mother—her mother who even now was phoning Costa Rica, fashioning a rescue for her that touched the deepest places of her soul, but that she did not want and could never want—pinned the note to her pillow and walked into the night, not knowing if it was sound instinct that she yielded to, or raw cowardice; knowing only that it said go, go now, don't wait, run, for God's sake run! they'll kill you, run. . . !

She wiped her eyes and her nose and looked at her watch, but she could not read it in the darkness; she crawled out of the shrubbery, began to walk. Just walk, one foot in front of the other, that was what you did in the mountains, just walk, ten times around the earth and back again; one block, twenty blocks, forty, she stopped counting, the stars moved west and she no longer knew if the earth turned or if she'd walked that far.

She came into Montenegro from the north, a barrio of simple homes and small tradesmen's shops. It was a late and very still, only the rarest light could be seen in a window, none at all in Marta's rented house, not a light or a sound or any sign of life. She was terrified that it had been abandoned, but after gentle, persistent knocking she saw a curtain shift slightly; then Marta's voice came soft through the door:

"*Quien es?*"

"Clariz."

The door opened. She slipped inside and almost fell. Marta held her for a long moment, like a sister. With her last strength she steadied herself and spoke:

"I'm going underground, Marta. Can I stay here? For a few days? Please?"

They were supposed to find their own hiding places; it was safer that way, and easier on the Frente's limited resources. But nobody was going to send away a comrade who had nowhere to go. Marta took her into the kitchen, stuffed her with chicken soup and aspirins, and then led her to one of the two rooms where the people who stayed there slept. There were no beds, only bedrolls. Beside one of them was a pack she recognized. She looked sharply, questioningly at Marta.

"Manolo's here," Marta said. "Didn't you know?"

"No," she whispered. Through the wall she could hear the sound of muffled, patient voices—teaching voices, saying things over and over; the sound of bodies struggling; suddenly, unexpectedly, the sound of laughter.

"Julio's in there," Marta said. "And I'm supposed to be. Manolo's gone to the country. He should be back before morning. How's your head?"

"Better. Thank you."

Marta laid out some blankets for her and turned to go. At the door she looked back.

"They blew up a Guardia *comandante* this afternoon with a grenade. Somoza's radio says it was a woman that did it."

"Even Somoza's radio sometimes tells the truth."

"That's what I thought. Good night, *compita*."

She went out like a snuffed candle, hearing nothing more of the training or the easy talk that followed it; not a sound of the *companeros* who slipped in quietly to sleep. But sometime deep in the night she awoke. She was not sure what it was that she recognized—a voice, a scent, a way of moving, something.

"Manolo?" she whispered.

"*Si*." He knelt beside her, reaching with desperate care because he did not know how hurt she was, reaching for her hands, her face. "Are you all right? Marta said you were beaten in the riot—"

"Yes. I'm all right." His fingers were like feathers against her cheek; she prisoned them in her own, unbearably grateful for the simple fact of his existence, of his presence beside her. "I'm all right. Where were you?"

"Getting us a truck to move some guns."

"New ones?" she asked hopefully.

"Yes." He eased himself down beside her. "Thirty brand new Belgian FAL's. . . if they ever finally get here." He found his pack, dug a smoke out of it, lit it. They shared it quietly.

"I was scared for you today," he said. "Do you get that scared when I go out?"

"How scared?"

"Like you wish you'd gone along, no matter how dumb it would have been, no matter if you got killed for it?"

"Yes."

The cigarette was almost gone. He gave her the last of it and found something to put his head on; she turned to him, wanting to be held, wrapped herself against him, nestled her face—the side of it that wasn't battered—into his body. His flesh smelled of dust and sweat, felt hot through the thin cotton, hot and hard, not a soft hollow anywhere to curl into, just bones and fire.

"Sleeping with you is like sleeping on a rail fence," she grumbled.

He laughed. "Well, you know what they say about these Sandinista women: they'll go to bed with anything."

"Oh, shut up."

After a long while he said again, very softly: "Are you sure you're all right?"

"Yes." She was very all right. She hurt all over; and she was, when she thought about it, still afraid, still devastated by Oscar's death. Yet she knew that she was finally where she belonged; and that she was, in a certain sense, totally safe. She was happier than she had been for a very long time.

13

All his life Father Pepe had been strong. It was a gift. Some people could make beautiful things and some people could add columns of figures in their heads and some people could sing. Father Pepe could work sixteen, eighteen hours a day, day after day, and never really notice it. Nobody had ever kept up with him—certainly not the lay missionaries who came sometimes to help him for six months or a year. Not even Oscar, who had wanted to but never had a hope of it, who used to sometimes fall asleep over the table with a half-eaten sandwich in his hand.

But now Pepe was tired. And he knew it wasn't the work. It was the pain. The pain of Oscar dying like a dog. The pain of looking every day into faces pleading for help he couldn't give them. The pain of smiling at government functionaries who could not comprehend why it mattered if the barrios had doctors or not. Pepe was so tired that he could not keep track of where he was in his breviary except by reading it aloud.

"Hello."

He muttered quite a few words more before he realized that someone had spoken to him. In English. He looked up. There was a woman standing a few feet in front of his rock, wind-haired, smiling at him. Behind her, the lake of Managua glimmered in the sun.

"You're an American," she said.

He smiled, closed the breviary. "No," he said. "But you are."

She studied him. "You're not British; I'd know the accent. Not Australian, either."

"No."

"New Zealand?" she asked dubiously.

He shook his head. "A little up and to the right. About ten thousand miles."

"Good God. Canada."

"Yes. People eventually remember that it's there."

She laughed, found a piece of ruin for herself, and sat. "So what are you doing in Nicaragua?"

"I'm a priest."

"Good," she said.

"Why is that good?"

"Because now I can talk to you without wondering if you're wondering if I'm trying to pick you up."

He smiled faintly. Somewhat sadly. All his life he'd had women friends. Good women friends. He was nearly forty before he realized that being a priest had had a great deal to do with that. It had been a depressing discovery, not so much for himself, but for what it taught him about the world.

"And you?" he asked.

She shrugged. "Officially, I'm visiting relatives. Unofficially, I haven't really decided yet. Do you teach?"

"No. I run a clinic."

"A clinic?" She looked at him in amazement. "You're Father Pepe!"

"And you're the American cousin, right? Pilar Zelaya's cousin?"

"Yes!"

They shook hands, rushed through the inevitable how-are-yous, I've-heard-so-much-about-yous. How was the family? he asked her. How was Pilar?

Fine. Everyone was fine, she assured him, but she could not quite meet his eyes when she said it. He did not press her, merely talked about other things. Twenty minutes passed and he began to feel guilty. He had to go back.

"Can I come with you?" she asked. "I'd like to see the clinic. All the time Felipe was in the States he was going around collecting money for it. We organized a coffee-house for him at Penn State; I think we made nearly two thousand dollars."

"Felipe did so much for us," Pepe said. "And the North American people, too. One parish in Toronto bought half of our equipment. It was all destroyed in the earthquake; we had to start over with nothing. The new place isn't much more than a shed. But you're welcome, of course. Can you make good coffee?"

"I haven't poisoned anyone yet."

"Then I'll let you make us some coffee. I always ruin it. I used to have two lay missionaries, you know. And after they left Oscar made the coffee..."

His voice trailed away. He began to walk; he was a big man, rangy but not without grace, something like the moose in the Manitoba hills where he came from. Jadine fell in step beside him.

"I'm sorry," she said. You always said that. Somebody died and you said: I'm sorry. And it wasn't that you didn't mean it. You did. But meaning it didn't mean anything; it was a word in a void.

"Do you understand any of it, Father? Why they killed him? Did they think he was a Sandinista or something?"

"Would that make it right?"

"No. Of course not. But that would make it...comprehensible."

"Comprehensible? Yes, I suppose so. We've learned to comprehend inhumanity very well. I think sometimes we've almost come to consider it normal."

Well, isn't it? she wanted to ask him. But the strain in him was visible, almost naked. She had no right to lay her own dark thoughts on his head. Not now. She asked him instead about his work; and he talked about that freely, even cheerfully. She listened, thinking how good it was just to use her own language again, and to hear it spoken; no matter how comfortable you were in another language you eventually got lonely for your own.

And it was good, too, to be out of the troubled Zelaya house for a while. Indeed, it was the need to escape, as well as her own growing curiosity, that was sending her wandering around Managua nearly every day. She shopped a little, wandered the markets. Tried out the food at Los Antojitos and the beer at a pleasantly scruffy *cerveceria* where two off-duty guardsmen tried to pick her up.

Just this afternoon she had dropped into the bar of the Panamerican Hotel, and felt at once as though she had passed through a space warp; as though by simply walking into that room she had left Nicaragua, left it for a place that had no identity, that could have been anywhere but mostly seemed to be nowhere at all. The bar was chilly and dark and she felt an unexpected revulsion for its dim lights and naugahyde chairs, for the coldness that made her wish for a jacket in the height of the Managua afternoon. She drank her beer and shivered, remembering wistfully the wonderful sidewalk cafes of Europe with their parasols and street singers and vibrant mingling of humanity. *That* was cafe life. Not this. This was merely the North American obsession with conquering nature. Of course it was hot outside. But only people who needed to prove something would build this absurdly overchilled and overpriced cellar, and inflict it on a city of eternal summer, just because they could; only they would think it chic to entertain guests in a place where the rest of the world would store potatoes.

The waiter seemed to expect her to stay for the afternoon, drink more than was good for her, and eventually take up with the blond Australian journalist sitting three tables away, who looked almost as bored and isolated as she was. When she asked for her check the waiter pretended not to hear; when she insisted, he sulked.

She went into the lobby where they sold shabby post-cards of the hotel and the Corn Islands. She could not shake the sense of alienness, the sense that this building and everything in it was an aberration, and had gotten here somehow by accident.

She bought a *Time* magazine and went outside to read it. There was not a word in it about Nicaragua. Nothing. Not even in the news briefs. None of the things happening around her, presumably, were real. Or if real, they were of no conceivable importance. She considered writing a letter to the editors. Gentlemen: If you're not using your reporters do you suppose we could borrow one of them for a while?

She began to walk, wondering what to do about the beggars; they just kept coming. The first one, a girl of ten or so, got her magazine and grinned from ear to ear. It was new today and clean; with luck she'd get a dollar for it. More than she'd get for selling her body, if she was into that yet.

The broken core of the city drew her like a magnet. Beatriz, accepting finally that her cousin would go out alone whether she approved or not, had warned her—warned her every single day—to stay where it was safe. The lakefront, the shantytowns, the ruins were not safe. Especially the ruins. She must never, never go into the ruins. Beatriz did not say why, but Jadine did not find it difficult to guess. Thieves, Guardia, and dead bodies were the likeliest risks, probably in that order. But she had not run into any of them. Only into a tall, tanned man sitting on a rock reading aloud from a strange-sounding black book. Reading in English. Filling her with a bewildering and unexpected loneliness.

The clinic was, as Father Pepe had said, little more than a shed. There was a long line of people waiting and a harassed-looking medical student from the university was tending those she could. Jadine made the coffee and asked what she could do to help.

Pepe paused in his work long enough to look hard at her.

"How much help?" he asked.

"I don't know. Lots. I don't have anything special to do."

"Will you write letters for me?"

"Letters?" She had expected almost anything but that.

"Yes. Begging letters. I have no shame at all anymore. I

ask for anything I can get anywhere I think I can get it. I just don't have time to write the letters. And the people here can't help me with that. You know, half the time I don't even get to write the thank you's. Can you write some letters? Make stencils?"

"I...I guess so...But what will I say?"

"Work with us for a few days," he said. "You'll know what to say. After three days it'll be easy."

"You're doing what?" Alvaro demanded, forkful of beef poised halfway to his mouth.

"I'm helping out at Father Pepe's clinic."

"He can't hire anybody. He doesn't have any money. He owes bills all over Managua."

"Oh, Papa, really!" Leon groaned.

"Look," Alvaro said. "Don't misunderstand me. I'm all for charity. We make a donation to the sisters every month. A nice donation. But nobody ought to be expected to work all day every day for nothing."

"It's just for a couple of weeks," Jadine said, wondering why she was apologizing. "He's in a bad spot right now because of...without...a doctor..."

"Well, it's up to you. You're our guest, of course; you can do as you like. But if you wanted to do charity work I wish you'd have spoken to me. There are a couple of very fine missions here. The Sisters of Saint Martha run an excellent girls' school in Altamira. I'm sure they would have been delighted to have you."

"Father Pepe was delighted," Jadine said.

Alvaro put down his knife and fork. "Jadine, I hate to criticize a priest. And I'm certainly not going to say that Father Pepe isn't a good man. I think he is. But he just doesn't understand Nicaragua. And that could—well, that could cause difficulties for you. The man's been here twenty years and he doesn't know anything; he still thinks he's in Canada, where you can just snap your fingers and money comes up out of the ground. This is a poor country, an undeveloped country. It's crazy to expect to have everything rich countries have. But Father Pepe expects that, and whether he means to or not he encourages people around him to expect it, too."

He paused, picked his front teeth very discreetly and quickly with his thumb. "What I'm trying to say, Jadine, is that I don't think the clinic is a good place for you to be—for anyone to be who doesn't have a lot of solid experience in this country. Not because of Father Pepe—don't misunderstand me. But those lakefront barrios are rough, and they're full of troublemakers. The people are dirt poor and ignorant, and the communists exploit that every way they can. Father Pepe's in the middle of it and doesn't even know it. What do you think that doctor was into that he got himself hauled out in the middle of the night and shot? Those people don't play games."

"Probably he gave an aspirin to a Sandinista," Leon said.

Every plate on the table shook as Alvaro's fist struck it. "*Basta!*" he cried. "By Christ, that's enough! I've heard all the shit I'm going to listen to in this house! First your sister. She had a smart mouth about everything, too. She had all the fucking answers. She could figure out everything except how to keep her own legs closed. Don't you start now, Leon; don't you ever start. I don't want to hear any radical crap from you, do you understand? You kids think you can play with life and make up the fucking rules as you go along. You think you can change the world with some birdseed and a big mouth. Well, let me tell you, the world was the way it is before you were born, and it'll be that way long after you're gone."

He began to eat again, savagely. Next to Jadine, Yolanda picked at her food, close to tears. Any mention of Pilar's lost virtue distressed her, and she hated people shouting.

"I hope to God," Alvaro went on, more calmly now, "if you insist on going down there, I hope to God you'll be careful. The damnedest people turn out to be subversives and if you give them half a chance they'll drag you in with them."

"I'm not interested in politics," Jadine said. "Really, *tio*. Not in the least."

He grunted, and she realized that that had not been a good answer. You were supposed to be interested in politics; supposed to understand whatever it was that

Father Pepe didn't understand; supposed to have all your antennae out measuring the current levels of subversion. If you didn't you weren't a realist, and if you weren't a realist you got hurt. Or pregnant.

She looked over at Beatriz, smiled, made small talk about the wedding. That would cheer her up. Yolanda, too. With luck they'd get through dinner without another outburst.

That's how things had been in the Zelaya house since Pilar left. At first they told Jadine that her cousin had gone unexpectedly to Costa Rica to visit her sister, who was sick. She had half believed it because it was reasonable, and half disbelieved it because the tension in the house was palpable and raw. Then Milan Valdez came unexpectedly one evening and closeted himself for two hours with his parents-to-be. After he left, Yolanda, with many tears, told Jadine the truth. Pilar wasn't in Costa Rica. No one knew where she was. She had run away. She had gotten herself pregnant by some *cochino* and run away. Milan was outraged, Mama was heartbroken, and the wedding was only three months away and God, it was awful, it was so *awful!*

Even Leon took it badly, charming Leon who had sometimes seemed to her the only sensible person in the house. Leon didn't think it was immoral; he thought it was tacky. His bright, controversial sister who might have made ambassador one day had just reduced herself to the level of an afternoon soap opera. It was such a dumb, melodramatic, *female* thing to do.

"I really thought she had more class," he said.

Jadine didn't want to listen to any of it. There was still one political issue that touched raw nerves in her, that made her want to strike out with words and sometimes with more than words. A woman had a right to her own flesh. To have a lover if she wanted, and to have whoever she wanted. To be chaste, also, if she preferred. To have babies or not to have them. . . to choose, damn it, that was all. To choose. There were rules for it, yes—rules for people, not for slaves or stable stock. Rules of good faith, not laws of male power. Pilar's choice was Pilar's choice; it was not subject to their outrage, their wounded sensibilities, their worship of hymens or reputations or styles. The body was not negotiable; she'd be damned if she would discuss it as though it were.

Of them all, only Beatriz seemed genuinely concerned about Pilar's welfare, about real things like whether she had a decent place to stay and enough food, and whether she'd have a doctor when she needed one. And it was Beatriz who absolutely refused to permit them to report Pilar as missing, or to call in the Guardia.

"She threatened to leave Papa," Yolanda told Jadine. "Can you imagine? She said if he or Milan sent the police after one of her children she would divorce him. She said the police think anyone who runs away from home is a Sandinista."

"Well, don't they?" Jadine asked.

"Of course not. Mama's just in shock. She'll get over it.

Jadine did not reply. She wanted a drink. She felt the way she sometimes felt reading the papers. Oppressed. Weighed down by air and earth and sky and time, unable to generate a fragment of energy against the enormity of human ugliness. Call in the Guardia, Jesus, whose denatured mind would even think of that? Appeal to men who routinely killed fifty or a hundred people every month, to find your daughter? Perhaps after they raped her twenty times she would learn how to keep her legs closed?

She escaped from Yolanda into the patio. She would be left alone there; it was pouring rain. She stood in the rain, feeling cleansed by it, and sheltered. It shut out all the city's light, and all its sounds. She could imagine peace, even though she knew the guerrillas were likely to be out in force. They liked rain, Leon said. It gave them cover, wiped out their tracks, kept the idle and the curious indoors, and made the soldiers love Somoza less. They were out there, but she didn't have to think about them—either of them. Only of the rain pounding in the trees. And of morning. In the morning she would go to work. It would be hard and probably ugly and she wondered why she was looking forward to it so much that for hours and hours she could not sleep.

14

The coast was jagged and rough. Half a mile away was a fishing village, small and lonely, no more than a few huts; here there were only rocks and trees. They waited for the last, blurred light to dissolve on the horizon, then Daniel and the old man carried the boat to the water's edge and looped it to a tree. It swayed there, gently—a vague black shape at seven feet, invisible at twenty. The sky was overcast and threatening rain; there was no moon.

Pilar wrapped her arms about her knees. Waiting was sometimes the hardest thing of all, but here it was not hard. It was languid as the sea, easy with insect sounds and water sounds and the warmth that wrapped the land at night. They could not talk much or smoke at all, but the time did not seem long. The old man leaned against a tree; he seemed asleep, but she knew he wasn't. Nearby, Eduardo brooded like a rock. He had not wanted her along. He had made it very clear, in a dozen subtle ways, that he did not think she could be depended upon; that Daniel had brought her only because love was rotting his brain.

He had no reasons for that belief; her record in the organization was solid, and so was Daniel's. They liked to work together; that was only human. But they had never chosen to do so when it was impractical, or unwise, or when their comrades or their superiors elected something different. None of that mattered to Eduardo. His mind was made up, based on centuries of accumulated myth and decades of self-perpetuating experience. Pilar would have despised him except that he seemed like such a dinosaur, such a relic of the old absurd belief in the revolutionary as rogue male, as *caudillo* in rags, as the enemy not merely of a repressive society but of all society. Coming up here, just through this bit of woods, she had watched him sometimes, watched the way he moved, the way he instantly became part of the forest; he had been a *guerrillero* so long that she expected him to grow leaves. And he had carried his harsh, narrow sense of life with him all those years, like his boots and his rifle. He had learned from his comrades an amazing range of skills but there were other things he had never learned from them, and never would; he was, finally, a product of the world he fought, a scarred man. One of many who would carry their scars to their graves.

She sighed faintly, and ignored him. Disliking him was as useless as it was inevitable.

Beside her, Daniel was restless, rarely watching anything except the sea, the lights of boats that wandered past.

"Coast Guard's out there," he muttered once.

"*Si*," the old man said, and laid his head against the tree again.

Eduardo looked at her once, briefly and challengingly, as though he expected her to say something timid, to say maybe they should give the mission up for lost.

Fuck you, she thought, and rested her chin on her hands, and stared at the sea.

They waited.

That morning, at the farm house where they had picked up the truck, they had talked about gunrunners—about who they were and why they did it. Some did it for adventure; it was like big game hunting or climbing Everest. But most did it for money. They made good money trading in death. They sold to anyone, anywhere, for any reason; it made no difference. This year they sold to the revolution; next year, if the Sandinistas won, they would sell to the counter-revolution.

But there were a handful who were different—revolutionaries in their own right, to whom supplying arms to the Sandinistas was a logical extension of the most elementary kind of human responsibility. People were hungry, you gave them food. They were sick, you gave them medicine. They were being starved and tortured and murdered, you gave them weapons to fight back. It horrified a lot of people, especially those who had never been starved or tortured, those to whom guns were sold in sporting shops along with tennis rackets and skis. But in the south of Nicaragua a *campesino* priest turned guerrilla blessed every battered rifle and every box of shells and every apron full of contact bombs that came to him, just as he blessed the crops and the calves and the medals of the Virgin. He considered it a completely natural thing to do.

The Coast Guard boat passed twice and then vanished, heading north toward Corinto. With luck, it would not come back till morning. Further to sea, a holiday yacht gleamed with lights, not moving at all. A yacht like Milan's, Pilar thought, or maybe bigger. She had been on Milan's boat once, the night he and Yolanda announced their engagement. A boat of tinsel and dreams, anchored just off Poneloya, wafting Maria Callas out to the fishermen as they drifted home. It had been lovely, like so many things around her that were lovely but that were priced beyond human paying. She would have loved that boat out there dancing with light—loved the pure freedom of it, the wind and the running sky. Boats were gorgeous; the sea was the belly of God. Run the coastline all day and fuck Danny on the open deck all night, all the way to Tierra del Fuego, to Buenos Aires, Caracas, Havana; home up the San Juan River to Granada, over the sunken bones of the *conquistadores* and the gold-rushers and William Walker's broken-down army. . . Someday, she thought, when it's over, when we're free, I want a boat. Never mind the champagne glasses or Maria Callas; I don't care if it's a scow, just give me a boat and let me go...

The old man saw it first, leaning forward from his tree. "*Miren!*" he whispered. "Over there!"

A small light was flashing, low over the water, on and off, three times very quickly. Daniel stood up, answering the signal with a flashlight, waiting for the launch to confirm. Four small stabs of light replied, and the sea fell dark.

"Let's go," Eduardo said harshly.

It was a Venezuelan boat, ugly as a mortal sin; Pilar doubted that anyone could have read its name even in daylight. The captain was known to them only as Chema. He was a wild-looking man, bearded and filthy as his boat; his right hand was gone and he greeted them eagerly with his left. Years back—no one knew just where or in what circumstances—he had met Valerian and became his friend, and adopted the Sandinista revolution as his own.

He embraced Daniel, whom he had met once before, and asked about *el comandante*. How was he? And when was he going to come to the coast himself? Had he grown too important now to speak to a poor smuggler?

He was joking, but not entirely. There was a desperation about the man that Pilar found poignant more than frightening.

"Valerian is well," Eduardo said, before Daniel could speak. "Where are the arms?"

"*Aqui*," the captain said, waving at a pile of crates nearby. They loaded quickly, methodically. It was not a large shipment, but it was valuable, and like nearly everything they got from outside the country, its origins were complex: Belgian rifles and ammunition purchased in Africa with money raised in West Germany and Holland, flown out in a Cuban plane, delivered in a Venezuelan boat piloted by an exiled Colombian guerrilla.

He helped them load, using his hooked stump almost as well as a hand, making jokes: *Companeros*, he said, what is the definition of foreign aid?

"You tell us," Daniel suggested.

"Very simple," he said. "The king loans money to the duke so the duke can buy pheasants from the king, and both of them beat the shit out of the chimney-sweep until he pays the loan back."

He laughed, and the laugh hung across the still waters like the mocking of a sorcerer. Pilar paused in her work to look at him. He was ugly, ugly and mutilated and probably a little mad—later that night she would learn from Daniel that he had spent eleven years in a Colombian prison, that he had lost faith in his own country, or, perhaps, he had embraced a faith that transcended country. He no longer cared whose revolution he served, as long as it was a revolution of the people.

They stacked the last crate into the guerrillas' all but overloaded boat. Daniel turned to thank him.

"*Algo mas*," he said; and he pulled from his jacket a bottle of liqueur. "Some French brandy to shut out the rain. You and your comrades can drink tonight. To the death of Somoza, yes?"

Daniel hesitated. It was a very generous gift.

"Take it," the captain said. "I have three cases of it. Tell Valerian that if he comes to see me he can have one. When we are all very old and very safe, I will tell you how I came by it." He laughed. *"Hasta la victoria!"*

They climbed into the fishing boat and pushed off, oars dipping into the water with barely a sound. Until the darkness swallowed him, launch and all, they could see Chema standing on his deck, staring after them as though they were his children.

It was very good brandy, one of the kinds that Milan Valdez brought back from Paris every year and served when he entertained ambassadors. They shared it in Lidia's study, after wolfing down her offerings of bread and cold chicken and coffee. Valerian was there, fresh from a meeting with regional organizers, pleased with the meeting and pleased with them. He sat relaxed against the wall, his big, booted feet stuck out in front of him, wanting to know everything they could tell him about the Colombian.

"He saved my life once," Valerian said. He did not

elaborate. He wanted only to know that Chema was well, that he was with them, that he remembered; and the answers seemed to please him as nothing ever had—nothing, at least, that Pilar could remember. Only after they had exhausted every detail of the encounter, every possible detail, did Valerian stop asking questions.

It was close to morning; the city was still and washed with rain. Very still. Here, high on the Carretera Sur, there were only faint murmurs of traffic from the highway that curled beneath the hill, very faint, if one troubled to stand outside and listen. Inside, there was no sound of the world at all. Valerian laid his head back against the wall.

"Sing us something, Manolo," he said.

Daniel did not need to be asked twice. He reached eagerly for his guitar, ran his fingers over the strings like a lover. It was hard to choose at first; there were so many songs, more than anyone had voice for, or time. They grew out of the fields and the rivers and the volcanoes; more than anything they grew out of the fighting; the whole continent was alive with songs, songs as lush as its fruits and as fierce as its mountains, songs of love, of rage, of hope; songs of revolution.

Hermano, dame tu mano
Vamos juntos a buscar
una cosa pequenita
que se llama libertad. . .

Pilar settled back in her chair, warm through and through with brandy. The first time she had ever heard Daniel sing it had been this song. It was at a student rally in high school, in a small room packed with people; it had seemed that no one even breathed until he finished. It was a magnificent song, at once powerful and tender, a call to arms by a piper of love: Come, for I carry a people in my voice. . .

She sipped her brandy, half lost in the music, half watching him. She had not chosen him for his voice, for the magic he could work with that incomprehensible instrument, for the passion that coiled in everything he sang, sometimes riveting and sometimes just barely there.

Talent, like beauty, was a gift; she had chosen him for other things. But she revelled in this, drank it like spiced wine, yielded up her mind and her senses in a single, prisoning pleasure. It was not like sharing soul thoughts, or building the revolution, or making love; it was a little like all of them.

She watched him, watched his body shift subtly with the rhythm of the music, watched the way his hair kept falling across his face, black and wild and tangled. She wanted to touch him, wanted terribly to reach out one hand and play it in his hair, for all that Eduardo was sitting there like judgment.

He went from song to song, almost without stopping; she joined in sometimes, and so did Valerian. Eduardo, wonderfully mellowed by a safe mission and brandy, drummed his brawny hand on the table at his side, keeping smooth and cunning time with Daniel's guitar.

Hay un clamor que viene de las montanas,
Hay un clamor que se oye al amanecer...

She sat up sharply, clapping her hands. This was *Pancasan*, the song they loved perhaps most of all, the song about the battleground of '67, where the Frente Sandinista was almost destroyed—and from which it never looked back. Pancasan was the baptism of fire, the Moncada of the mountains; and the song that remembered it was defiant and irresistible:

There is a clamour coming from the mountains,
There is a clamour that is heard at daybreak;
It says this:
Revolution, revolution, revolution...!

It was splendid. They sang and stamped and clapped; even Lidia, who always left them alone, was lured to come and stand in the doorway and to cheer with them when the last chord was played.

Daniel grinned and reached for his neglected brandy. "You know what I'd like to do once?" he said. "Sing that in the dining room of the Intercontinental Hotel. With a whole band—drums, marimbas, everything. At a meeting of the international bankers' association."

"You realize," Pilar told him, "you wouldn't make it through the second verse before you'd be propped up against the seafood bar and shot. Splat. Right into the shrimp cocktail."

"Yes," he sighed. "But it would almost be worth it."

"*Bueno.*" With obvious regret, Valerian stood up. It would soon be light; he had to go.

"A word, Clariz," he said.

She followed him into Lidia's kitchen. He sat down, tired, looking at her critically.

"You were very valuable in the JRS," he said. "Why did you run?"

She told him, simply and briefly, altering nothing except the nightmare edge of her fear, telling her reasons as though they had all been thought out with great care.

He knew better. "It's always best to take a decision like that with support," he said. "You could have been arrested ten times over."

She said nothing, and he added: "We would, of course, have advised you to get out. Quickly. Very quickly. I know something of your father's reputation for exploding." As for the reputation of the family Valdez, no one in the Frente needed to speak of it at all.

"When will you have the child?" he asked.

"In May."

He made a vague sound in his throat but said nothing, merely studied her, not lewdly but frankly. She did not like it. He knew, of course, that she was sleeping with Manolo; everyone did; they had never been secretive. Knew that sooner or later of course there would be a child, and of course we accept it, it's part of life, but damn it, it's inconvenient.

She felt intimidated by his scrutiny, by his silence. Damn men, she thought; damn them anyway. Every last one of them wanted love, or at least pleasure; and most of them wanted children, but Christ, it was inconvenient!

"Have you thought about what you will do then?" he asked finally.

She looked at him. The question surprised her; angered

her, even. Did he not know that she was a Sandinista, always a Sandinista, that she would go on fighting? And then she caught herself. She was being unfair. It was his duty to ask. He was her *responsable* and it was his duty to ask, to make no assumptions.

"I will stay with my comrades," she said.

He nodded. He had known; yes, certainly, he had known.

"Do you have anyone who can care for the child?"

"No." There was Veronica perhaps, Veronica who would never mean her any harm, but who would not know what to watch for to prevent it; Veronica who had left her country, and who no longer understood—if she ever had—anything that was happening there. She sighed and shook her head. "No one that I can really trust. I thought perhaps Claudia...or Manolito's family..."

"Claudia may have to go underground herself soon," he said. "But we'll work something out. There's time. Depending how things are in April we may send you to Costa Rica for a while. There's a safehouse there that some of my friends have started calling the Sandinista Hatchery...they are very rude, these friends...but they do have a point."

He smiled then, and she forgave him. Whatever he thought—and he had not said what he thought—he was assuring her that she would be protected; that the organization itself would protect her; that was part of its commitment.

"Thank you," she said simply.

He went on to the issues at hand. "We're setting up a new cell in Open Tres. I'd like you to work there for a while. Propaganda and political education, mostly, though we'll be moving into insurrectional strategies as fast as we can. The people there are very ready. What do you think?"

Open Tres. The wart on Managua's heel. The barrio that even God forgot, dumped into the hills, created out of earthquake refugees and greed; the saddest, poorest, most exploited of all Managua's shantytowns. Also the angriest. It would be a challenging place to work. And it was miles from Las Colinas, from the university; miles and centuries from the world of the family Zelaya Perez. Certainly she could not be safer anywhere in Managua.

"I can do it," she said. "Where do I go?"

"Station three. At eight tonight. Claudia will meet you there."

He stood up. As they walked toward the door he laid his arm lightly around her shoulders. Was she happy? he asked.

"Yes."

"And Manolito? Have you told him yet?"

"Yes, of course."

He called Daniel into the hall then, hugged him and mussed his hair and slapped his back, hugged her, too; wished them *muchisima felicidad*. And she decided that she didn't understand Valerian at all, but he was all right. He was really quite all right.

The world felt of sun and wind, smelled of rain and *guayaba*. Pilar let herself waken slowly, let sleep turn to languor and languor finally to sadness. Daniel still slept, lying face down, very still. She touched his hair with her fingers, his shoulder with her lips, lightly, so lightly that he would scarcely have felt it even if he had been awake. Across the room, the patio curtains filled and fell, filled and fell like a ship that could not sail.

They had so little time, always so little. They took their love like thieves, in back yards and back rooms, and somehow it was enough, it sustained them. But they craved more time, craved real time, like today, and found that to have it at all was merely to crave it more.

The morning must one day cease to be a temptation. Carlos had written that, or said it; she did not remember where; she remembered only the words, words that spoke to her, spoke to all of them of the hopes they dared not have and could not live without: The unbearable temptation to imagine that if you planted seeds you would eat; if you bore a child it would live; if you could reach out now and touch your lover's body, feel the sun warm in his hair, then you could touch him so tomorrow, and the next day; he would be there. The illusion was irresistible.

She nuzzled Daniel gently but he did not stir and she did

not have the heart to wake him. She slipped from the bed, pulled on her jeans and shirt, and went to the patio. It was late afternoon, brilliant with light after the rain, extraordinarily still. Somewhere there were cars, a murmur in the distance; close by, the scattered barking of some neighbour's dogs. Nothing else, not even a stir of wind in the brooding mango trees. Here, even more than in her own house, you could live the myth of apartness. You could watch the city turn to blood and ash all around you, hold out your hands in bewildered innocence: Why are they shooting at me? I never did anything. I only lived here and tended my garden...

The trap of innocence. The terrible trap. There was no innocence, except that of children and of the mad. Everyone else made choices. Always, some kind of choices...

She remembered her one long talk with Lidia, the Lidia nobody knew, who was linked by cell gossip with Valerian but who in fact did not have a man and did not want one; Lidia who poured every fragment of her waking energy into a revolution she did not understand. They had sat here in this patio, a year ago perhaps, very late, and Lidia had unravelled her soul like an old scarf and wrapped it up in a ball and put it away again.

"There is only one thing I will regret when the revolution comes," she had said. "Only one thing." She was staring into her glass, bitter with wine and memories. "Edmundo will not be here to see it."

Pilar had seen hatred before. Too many people had suffered too much for it not to be there; but the hatred in Lidia's eyes amazed her.

"I would like my husband to see it," Lidia went on. "All the street rats with their guns. All the cheap little factory girls. All the kids. All of them free, out of reach like birds: It's our country now, *senor padrino, senor* pimp. What are you going to do about it?"

Hour by hour she talked. About her life, her marriage, her husband. Her husband, who was in Argentina now, dealing—so she had heard—in pornographic movies. The husband who had almost killed her for having an abortion.

"He called me a monster. How could I, he said, how

could I take a child, his child, and throw it in a trash can? His child, that most sacred thing of all, that divine gift? I was foul, I was despicable, I deserved to die, for having shown such contempt for the sacredness of life.

"Ah, the sacredness of life! Beware, Clariz, of any man who speaks to you of the sacredness of life! Ask him in what field he tends it...

"The children I should have borne Edmundo were sacred. But the children he bred of factory girls—the children he forced on them, whether they wished it or not—they were not sacred. When the girls began to show, he fired them; he threw them out to starve with their sacred offspring.

"My husband's children are rotting in the streets of Managua, Clariz, scavenging the dumps and the sewers; they are prostituting themselves, dying of dysentery and malaria and hunger. Maybe some of those that lived are Sandinistas. I hope they are. I hope they all are."

Innocence? Pilar thought. No, none of that. Neither in the gardens nor in the streets. She stuffed her hands into her pockets and walked idly. She loved perfume, and this garden was wrapped in it. Flowers were everywhere: flowering vines even crawled up the walls, as lush as weeds. Lidia almost never left her home. She raised her son and her plants and her revenge with the same meticulous care, in the same desperate isolation. No innocence here; not ever again.

"Clariz?"

She turned sharply. Lidia stood in the open parlour doorway, paler in the downing sun than she had ever seemed in lamplight, translucent almost, as though her flesh was no longer quite real.

"Paco is here," she said.

Pilar sighed. She had hoped he would not come so soon. "All right," she said. "I'll wake Manolo."

He lay as she had left him, naked and content. She sat on the bed, played her hand in his hair, ran it over the length of him, right to his toes, back again. She liked that thin, taut body very well. He was not beautiful—not as magazines judged beauty. Proud Yolanda would have dismissed him with an airy wave of one perfectly manicured hand: street rat. Even in high school, when Yolanda had not yet met Milan Valdez, and was therefore much less proud, she had shaken her head at her younger sister's taste—or rather, at her lack of it.

"If you have to hang around with radicals, Pilar, can't you at least find some that are *clean*?"

That had stung. It still did. "Danny's not dirty," Pilar had flung back, "he's just poor. And anyway, he's bright. He's got brains in his head—not popcorn and tennis balls, like all your friends!"

They'd had quite a scrap that day. They had a lot of scraps, and always at the end of one Yolanda swore that she would tell Papa that Pilar was lying to him. That she was always lying, saying that she was studying when she was really organizing demonstrations or sitting under a fence somewhere talking communism and other insanities with the likes of Daniel Chillan. Yolanda promised to tell on her a thousand times, but she never did.

Pilar smiled to herself and bent to Daniel, nibbling his back, teasing him shamelessly with her hands until he stirred, grumbled, and turned to her finally, sleepy and irritated, but fired as well, wanting her; it took so little.

"Paco's here," she said simply.

"Shit."

He reached, tumbling her down beside him, undoing her clothes, not rough but greedy, as though he had never had enough of her, and was sure that he never would.

"Manolito," Claudia had said to her once, "Manolito believes so fiercely in the revolution because it's the only thing he can be sure won't be snatched from him, won't be destroyed, won't die in the dirt at his feet the way his father did."

She had thought then and many times since that that was true. Daniel spoke about his father quite a lot, about his ideas and his work, but of his father's death, of the butchery in Diriamba, he never spoke at all, not even once. And she came to understand that he could not. It lay shut away in some back room of his mind, less a memory than a perception of the world which would cripple him if he let it, undo all his joy in life and all his capacity for love. He'd survived—survived quite splendidly, Pilar thought; Ana had seen to that—but the memory was there, the old terror of loss. He cried sometimes after he lay with her. She never asked him why; she never had to.

They made love quickly, without any of the languor and laughter of a few hours before, but it was still good. Simple and animal and good. She did not stir while he dressed, just watched him, watched the last failing light glint and shift in his hair and spill over his skin like running gold, skin the colour of fine copper and damp now with sweat.

No, she thought, he was not beautiful, just alive, just taut and splendid with life. Graceful, yes; they would have to grant him that: he was graceful and quick. He could run like a fox and climb like a monkey, and he had amazing endurance. Nothing else that anyone would notice. Blood with all the fire of the Managua sun in it; a mind that knew the world and eyes that could laugh; hands that were endlessly subtle, that could make music and weapons and love. Just that. To her so much; to the world so little.

15

Paco dropped Pilar a few blocks from the taco stand where she was to meet Claudia, and took Daniel to the safehouse in Montenegro. On the way they talked about all sorts of things; Paco did a lot of travelling for the Frente and he always had a fresh batch of gossip—who had a new lover or a new baby, who was mad at who and why, and what crazy things were happening this week between the factions.

Everyone, it seemed, was mad at the Terceristas. The GPP had lost several people because of the Masaya raid. They had not known the attack was planned, and the Terceristas had not known they had a safehouse in the area; they were holding a meeting there when the Guardia swept through the countryside and simply walked in and took them captive. It was a hell of a thing, Paco said, but it was no one's fault. And now the Proletarians had their noses out of joint, too: they had condemned the new offensive in an open document, full of angry accusations of Tercerista opportunism, and Chamorro had blazoned it across a half page of *La Prensa*.

"I know," Daniel said. "I've seen it." He did not want to talk about it. He accepted the factionalism within the Frente as more or less inevitable; he had, after all, switched tendencies himself. But for the tendencies to fight in public, to lay out their disputes in full view of Somoza and the bourgeois opposition—that was something he did not accept. It violated every notion of organizational discipline he had even been taught. At the best of times he found it hard to deal with; just now he did not even want to try. His mind was elsewhere.

If Paco noticed his mood, he ignored it. "You've got to admit some of it's pretty funny, though," he went on. "Like yesterday: we raid the Matagalpa National Bank at ten thirty and the Proletarians raid it again at twelve. The safe's bare as a *campesino's* cupboard; one teller faints and the other two get the giggles. I'm sure the Tendencia Proletaria de Matagalpa won't speak to us now for a hundred years."

"Christ," Daniel said. "This is insane."

"*Claro, claro*. It's very bad. It's terrible. But. . .it's also very funny, no?"

"Funny for Somoza. Jokes like this make his day."

Paco looked at him, and looked away; after a long silence he said: "I get very tired, Manolo. Very tired and very sad. I like to laugh—even at us. Don't you ever laugh?"

"Yes. . .At some things."

"When you're an old man like me," Paco said, "you'll laugh at everything."

He drew into a dark side street. "Close enough, I think." He turned in the seat, gripping Daniel's shoulder hard. "*Bueno, compa*. I'll see you next week."

"Next week? Where the hell are you going? Guatemala?"

"Almost. *Hasta luego*, Manolito."

Daniel hopped out, ruffed his hair through the open window. "*Vaya bien*, Paco. Ciao."

He walked twice around the block before knocking at the safehouse, partly for security, but mostly just to think. He missed Pilar already.

Eduardo said that it was crazy for a revolutionary to care much about anyone. He was right, of course, Daniel reflected. It was totally crazy. But then it was just as crazy to be a revolutionary in the first place, to ever imagine that you could do anything, or be anything, or have anything except the dirt it took to bury you. It was crazy to write songs, or to sing them; crazy to live at all, like a weed on a rock, surviving from raindrop to raindrop, wanting to live and ready to die, always ready, accepting it as the price for having any life at all.

Stability did not exist in his world, had never existed. Still, he did not want to be like Eduardo. Eduardo had given up living until after the revolution; Daniel was quite sure that by then he would no longer remember how.

The night was breathless. From somewhere not far away drifted deep currents of jasmine; and all around a great jacaranda tree hundreds of fireflies hovered and veered, tiny guerrillas of light that appeared and vanished and appeared again, innocent guerrillas, exquisite in their mastery of the night. Managua by day could be harsh, but Managua by darkness always had this extravagant, sensual stillness. Daniel was rarely unaware of it; tonight he was aware of very little else.

He had spent most of the day in Lidia's house with Pilar, drunk with desire and brandy and time, so much time, hours and hours to tease out every strand of pleasure to its last muted sigh. Hours to make love with her, like animals, like children, like sleepwalkers; afterward to lie wet with the city's heat and their own, and share a cigarette; talk of the world or themselves or nothing at all, maybe sleep then, but more likely start to tease and search and taste and want it all again.

He never really understood any of it. As a revolutionary, as a trained and trusted member of the vanguard, he felt a considerable sense of worth. But that sense of worth was communal and political; it did not quite translate into personal confidence. She was beautiful and free; she had many men to choose from. It seemed always an extraordinary and bewildering thing that she was with him.

He had met her not long after the earthquake, when Managua was tossed between the nightmares of its memories and the dreams of an absurd and false prosperity. Money poured into the country; everyone talked about the future; everything was going to be rebuilt. The money and the promises soon dissolved, vanished into the cavernous mouths of the oligarchy, into the ever-fattening belly of the president and his relatives and his flatterers and his whores. But for a while there was plenty of work. The construction industry boomed, and so did all the trades that served it. Martin and Naldo both had good jobs—underpaid, of course; everyone who worked was underpaid, but the building trades paid best. Ana's little food stall thrived. For the first time in many years the Chillans ate three times a day and wore decent shoes; they decided, to Daniel's overwhelming happiness, to send him back to school.

He did well there. He was bright, insatiable, what his teachers called "surprisingly disciplined," whatever that meant. He was older than most of his classmates, whose schooling had never been interrupted—three years older than the slender, bourgeois girl with brooding eyes and an undefined, untested coil of violence in her smooth, fox-like body. Her name was Pilar Zelaya. Her family was purebred Las Colinas—the two girls came to school in a chauffeur-driven car; they were one of a handful of wealthy Managua families who did not send their children to elite private schools. Their father had summarily pulled them out of their posh Catholic academy two years before, when the oldest sister started talking about becoming a nun. Nobody, he said, *nobody* was going to be allowed to brainwash Alvaro Zelaya's kids.

The eldest, Veronica, outgrew her fascination for monasteries, graduated, and got engaged, but by then the pattern was set; and in fact, the young people liked the freedom of the public school far more than the rarefied air of the convent. They were very different. Yolanda wore Paris fashions and talked of holidays in Naples and New York. Pilar talked politics, talked black and bitter anger, talked revolt. Her brother was dead, and that death walked in her eyes.

Daniel had lost no one from his family in the earthquake. But he had seen it all: seen the houses tumble and fold upon themselves like houses of cards, seen whole blocks devoured in a single sheet of fire as the gas lines broke. When the city was ash and ruin the National Guard and the U.S. Marines came and burned the bodies with gasoline and flame-throwers. They had to, of course; there were thousands of dead; nothing else was possible. He had stood near one of those pyres, watched the bodies blacken and dissolve until the limbs separated and fell away, tumbling with a little shower of sparks, and the soldiers picked them up with forks and threw them back again. And he knew that he was watching the most final and absolute statement that could be made about his people or himself.

Nothing surprised him after that—not the planeloads of relief supplies stockpiling at the airport while the Guardia sold Coca-Cola for twenty-five cordobas a bottle. Not the sixteen-hour line-ups for half a piece of bread. Nothing. The dying just went on. The Guard shot starving looters while their own trucks emptied department stores and jewellers as fast as they could load. The American doctors set up elaborate field hospitals under the shade trees on Somoza's estates, but no one seemed to notice that most of the people who needed them had no way to get there.

All around him Daniel heard the cries of unbelieving and bewildered pain: Why was there no help, no food, no medicine? Where was their government and where was the western world and where in God's name was God? He listened and wondered how it was that anyone still needed to ask.

It was the Cuban doctors and nurses who came into the barrios, who set up their little tents among the ruins and tended the wounded almost where they fell. And it was the church people who built temporary shelters and found ways to subvert Somoza's machinery enough to get some of the relief supplies through. There were a million acts of intended generosity, but finally nearly everything the Managuans received that was of use to them came from the Cubans or from the Church. That was something Daniel never forgot.

It was against the backdrop of that time, and what it had taught him, that he returned to school. He was already an active collaborator with the FSLN, and he threw himself headlong into the student movement. His strongest and most dedicated comrade was Pilar Zelaya Perez.

Sometimes, remembering those early months at the Institute, he did not know whether to laugh or to cry. They had been drawn to each other from the first, but their friendship began uneasily, snarled in obsessions of class that no amount of socialist passion was going to erase in a week or a month or maybe ever. Sometimes they walked around each other as though they walked on glass; sometimes they quarrelled. She called him a shantytown bourgeois more than once; and he told her that if her idea of revolution was taking home stray dogs she could forget it. Exhaustion, rather than wisdom, put an end to the silliness: they needed finally to trust each other, and they found that they could.

His own feelings at the time were hopelessly confused, the political and the personal all tangled, impossible to separate. He never allowed himself to believe that they would ever be more than friends, more than comrades; she was so serious, so committed, so unconsciously beautiful. At times he would work with her and think of nothing but the work; at other times he did not know what in God's name to do with his eyes or his hands or the flushed yearning in his loins.

Then one day, a day just like any other, Martin Chillan fell from a rotten scaffolding and broke both of his legs. The union met to protest, demanding better safety standards. The company would not even talk to them. Naldo organized a strike committee and was fired three hours later.

In days, the Chillan world simply splintered and came apart. They ran up brutal debts just to pay for Martin's doctors; Naldo's union could not protect him, and when he looked for work elsewhere he discovered that the label of communist followed him everywhere, like a congenital disease. Fourteen months earlier, hungry for skilled workers, employers might have ignored a man's personal or family history; now the boom was fading and the first people to go were the troublemakers.

Ana tried valiantly to keep Daniel in school but it was a

sacrifice beyond her strength to give or his willingness to accept. He worked nights for a while in the Managua slaughterhouse; what he earned there fed only himself, but that, at least, Ana did not have to do. He dragged himself to class where he barely managed to stay awake; to political meetings where he took his share of the work because nothing else was thinkable—he could have asked to be marginated but he would not—finally, failing and exhausted, he left the school.

He went there for the last time very late, when no one was about except a few weary teachers, the cleaning woman. . . and Pilar. God knew where she had come from, or how she had known he would be there. She watched him with black, stricken eyes; silent until the last scrap of paper, the last stubby pencil was stuffed defiantly into his worn paper bag and he was turning to the door.

"Danito."

He did not want to talk to her. All the barriers between them, the barriers that he had imagined were overcome, stood restored and huge as mountains now. The mere fact that she could stay in this room, and he could not, made her an enemy.

"Danito, let me help. Let me do something. *Something*. Please."

He stood silent; numb and shamed—shamed not so much by her words as by what they touched in him, a thing that he had never admitted to but that was always there. That she could help him. She was Pilar Zelaya. She was proof against the terror he lived with, the terror they all lived with, of the day when there would be no work, no food, no morning. She could help him; she had power. It did not matter that she had not chosen it, did not want it, had never used it against him or against anyone; it did not even matter that he had grown to love her, that everything they believed in denied the validity of that power. It was simply there. *I can help you*. I have the magic words; I have the world on a golden chain. All he needed to do was ask her. She could probably feed his whole family on her weekly pocket money.

"Danny. . . ?"

For the first time in his life he wished that he could die. He looked at her—a long look, as though he would burn forever into his memory the image of those huge and haunting eyes, of that taut, splendid body that he had never tasted.

"Danito, please...!" She started to move toward him.

He tucked his bag under his arm. "No doubt we'll see each other from time to time," he said.

She did not come any further. Two small tears were creeping out of the corners of her eyes, waiting to spill down her cheeks like broken beads. He did not want to hurt her but he was too destroyed himself to prevent it.

"You'll keep working, then?" she whispered.

"Of course. And you?"

"Of course."

He did see her from time to time, mostly at rallies where he had been asked to sing. Invariably they would gravitate to each other, eager to talk, to be reassured that the other was still out there, not too terribly far away, still fighting. Then the Frente gave him full status as a militant and sent him to the coffee highlands to help organize *campesinos*. He did not see Pilar for over a year.

When he came back the country was reeling under martial law and half the Managua activists had fled. Valerian rebuilt his cell out of the remains of three scattered ones. Daniel and Pilar were working together again and nothing had changed except that they were older, more sure of themselves and of what they wanted. They mated almost the first chance they had.

She was gone now, again; not far but out of reach. As he walked, the darkness wrapped and held him; its peace, like their own lives, seemed a thing of desperate impermanence. You took what there was and you went on; every time you went on. And if finally there was nothing more you also went on, because going on was all you could do; of that worlds were made, and revolutions, and songs, and children. It wasn't much, but it was all you had, and it would have to do.

Once, foolishly, he had spoken about such thoughts to

Father Pepe, and the priest had smiled at him with the most benign irony and said that he had an extraordinary lot of faith for a godless Marxist.

He'd been piqued. "Marxists have always had a lot of faith," he said. "Faith in life, in people, in the earth, in everything real."

"And what do you suppose God is, Daniel? That silly old man in the pictures?"

He said he didn't know, and that was the truth. He didn't know. Nearly everyone around him was a Christian, even in the Frente. He had no quarrel with that; he simply did not share it. And he did not particularly want to share it. There was a clean, animal simplicity to his life and he felt nothing lacking except the right to live it. Maybe God affirmed that right, like Father Pepe said, but only the revolution would make it real.

16

The room was hot, smelling of sweet bread and coffee, smells which Pilar would associate with Claudia until the end of her days—Claudia with a red scarf around her hair, smiling happily as she shoved food at her beautiful, owl-eyed baby.

"It's amazing," she said. "I'm fat and Rafa's ugly and this kid is gorgeous. How did that happen, do you suppose?"

Pilar laughed. Claudia was exaggerating on all three counts, but not by much. She leaned back in her chair, wishing for a cigarette. There were none in the house; no one had the money to buy any. It was new to her, not even having pocket money. For years she had lived austerely on principle; she had routinely used her clothing allowance to buy stencils and gasoline and medicine; she had given her comrades her lunches and her Christmas presents. But she had always had money for bus fare or cigarettes. Until now.

She looked around, studying the place for the first time in daylight. It was a shabby excuse for a bakery; a wayside oven, that was all; it didn't even have a name.

Claudia, noticing her scrutiny, said sadly: "It isn't much, is it?"

"It's something."

"Grandfather cries every morning when he gets up. He'll never accept the fact that we sold the other place."

Sold it for almost nothing, Claudia had told her last night as they drove here from the contact point at station three. The Guardia had come back; the second time they had wrecked everything and beaten Rafa senseless. There was nothing to do but leave, change their names, keep moving. His cousin Bartolo said they were crazy, that they should leave the country like he was doing. He'd sold everything, even most of his clothing; he'd found a dealer who was going to smuggle him into the United States.

"Rafael just laughed," Claudia recalled. "He said if he was going to pay taxes for the benefit of Somoza he might as well stay here. Bartolo wasn't very pleased."

Pilar smiled wryly but said nothing. Several members of her mother's family were talking about leaving while they could still sell their property for a good price. They considered themselves refugees.

"Anyway," Claudia went on, "Open Tres may be a hell of a place to make a living but it's a great place to make a revolution."

"You don't suppose the two things might be connected?" Pilar said, deadpan.

Claudia laughed, and retrieved a spoon with which her daughter was trying to destroy the table.

"Sometimes yes," she said. "And sometimes no. People have to know why they're miserable; otherwise no amount of misery will move them." She poured Pilar more coffee. "Did Valerian tell you what we're doing here?"

"No, not really."

"All right. Mostly it's two things: we organize block committees and we teach skills. Reading, public speaking, civil defense, first aid, printing, making barricades, making tunnels—are you tired yet?"

"Claudia, I was tired in the JRS—tired of not doing enough. Tired of being half a Sandinista."

"Want a muffin?"

"Why not?"

"You know what amazes me?" Claudia mused. "Assholes like Eduardo who think this is easy. Who think that when they rattle their sabres in front of a Guardia *cuartel*, they're the only real revolutionaries, and everybody else is just a support worker."

"Don't tell me about Eduardo," Pilar said. "I've had Eduardo up to my eye-teeth." She picked apart her muffin, nibbled a piece. It was good and she began to eat the rest of it. "He spent a whole evening in Marta's safehouse telling us about the Yugoslavian underground in World War Two. How fierce they were, how disciplined. How they permitted absolutely no personal relationships to interfere with their work. Combatants who got emotionally involved with each other were separated; if they persisted in their bad habits, they were shot."

"You're not serious."

"I'm quite serious. And so was Eduardo. And so, apparently, were the Yugoslavs."

"They shot them?"

"It seems so."

"Holy Jesus. I always knew that Europeans were barbarians." She reached, wiping crumbs from her daughter's mouth and giving her a sip of water. Laughed suddenly. "There wouldn't be too many Sandinistas left, would there?"

They worked through until late afternoon, sharing a coffee and some personal talk now and then but mostly making plans. They were meeting tonight with barrio leaders, most of them women, to discuss needs and set priorities, to figure out how four or five people would do the work of twenty, and how next month twenty would do the work of a hundred.

Customers started coming then, buying a few rolls or a loaf of bread for their suppers, and Claudia went into the front room to tend the makeshift counter. Pilar laid aside her notes and rested for a moment, hearing the easy talk,

Claudia laughing and making jokes with everyone who came. She was glad that she had Claudia to work with—earthy, practical Claudia who could barely read and who thought that maps were something you started fires with if you ran out of *Novedades*, but who knew the barrios and knew people.

The next customer was a man, his voice tired but strong, asking for a *panecito*.

"This one?"

"No, no," he said. *"Mas pequeno. Pequenito.* Have you heard about the raid?"

A breath of silence. "What raid?"

"The Becats are shooting the hell out of a house in Montenegro. It's on the radio. That one—yes, that's fine. How much?"

"One cordoba."

Coins fell with painful slowness onto the counter. Pilar stood frozen, her knuckles pressed against her teeth, forcing herself not to make a sound, not to move, not to run up to the counter and grab the radio from the shelf and shake the words out of it.

"*Gracias*," the man was saying. She heard his steps, heard them stop, as though he were turning, looking back. "What good does it do?" he asked. "All those kids getting themselves killed? What good does it do anyone?"

The door closed and even as it did so the radio was spitting out static and the sound of gunfire, staccato and thin, cutting off fragments of words, leaving the rest sharp and brutal, edged with a peculiar, detached excitement.

"...a few minutes ago. This harmless-looking private residence in the barrio...negro has apparently been used...center by the Sandinista National Liberation Front ...believed to contain a large supply of weapons. Colonel Armando Davila of the National Guard estimates that at least seven or...terrorists are trapped inside the building. Additional Special Brigade units have been called up and all streets heading into or out of Montenegro are—"

There was a burst of machine gun fire, drowning everything.

"Oh, God, Clariz," Claudia whispered. "Oh, Jesus, they're all in there...Manolo...everybody..."

"No," Pilar said. "No. They're not all in there. They can't be." Paco was on the road and Valerian was in Leon and Rafa was in a house three blocks away. But the others...Daniel...She turned the radio up as loud as it would go.

The remorseless, disembodied voice went on:

"...seen as a major breakthrough against the Sandinista terrorists. Colonel Davila...confident that this will mark the end of the so-called October offensive—"

Pilar turned away. She was cold all through. Her stomach hurt, hurt worse than when they'd beaten her. She wanted to vomit.

"What time is it, Claudia?"

If there were many of them, she thought, and if they could hold out until dark...?

"Five. A little after." Claudia looked at Pilar for a moment, only a moment, and looked away. Tried to imagine what she would feel if Rafael were in that house; tried and could not. The reporter was still shouting over the sound of the guns. Claudia pulled a blind down over the window and hung the *Cerrado* sign on the door.

"We'd better go," she said.

Go and hide. Find a house with a telephone. Get out their legals, send messages, warn everyone they could, cover their tracks, listen to the radio, and wait. Wait until their friends or their enemies told them the number and the names of their dead.

The third time the Guardia megaphone blared out its demand for surrender, Eduardo took one of the red and black scarves they had hidden with the printing press and the guns, and hung it from a wire out the front window. The Guard shot it to tatters but it stayed there until a mortar took out the wall.

"We won't last till dark," Marta said.

"We'll last as long as we last," Eduardo said. He looked at her kneeling by her window, blood quietly soaking her shirt from the wound in her shoulder. She didn't seem to notice it much. In the next room he could hear Manolo dodging from post to post; he was not the world's best shot but he was very fast and the Guard obviously thought there were three of him. And two of everybody else. They were stupid, he reflected. They really were.

He ducked a volley, fired, ducked again. They had done all right. He would not have chosen these two people to be trapped with in a shoot-out; he would have chosen almost anybody else. But they had done all right. He felt warm toward them, and wished that there was a way that they might escape. But there wasn't—not after the Guardia brought in the tanks. For himself he was resigned, almost happy; after so many years it was important to die well.

Another shell rocked the house. Plaster tumbled onto Eduardo's head; when he looked up he saw Manolo crouched against the wall beside him. He was breathing in soft gasps and gesturing vaguely toward the room he had fled.

"Wall's gone," he said harshly. "If we're going, we go now."

Eduardo looked at the woman. "Marta?"

She threw a quick shot out the window and crawled toward them.

"You still want to try it?" he asked.

Her face was drawn and hard, empty of everything except pain and will. "What else is left?"

Acceptance, he thought. And saw in their faces that for them there would be no acceptance, not now and not ever. He had believed it weak of them, wanting to run. Now he was not sure.

"*Bueno*," he said. "Let's go."

The back door opened on a cluttered yard and a line of small adobe houses. Guardia fire had come from inside three of them; how many men they had in the yards and alleys and roofs beyond no one could guess, or wanted to.

Eduardo lined up the battery of molotov cocktails they had prepared for this moment. One through the window of each house, one on the roof at the left—there was a sniper up there, not in a hurry to do anything, but up there. That, and what cover he could give them with an automatic rifle. . .He shook his head. They would never make it; but then neither would he, so there wasn't much merit in thinking they were crazy.

It was still full day, but the sun was low and at street

level there were deep shadows. It would help. Daniel stuffed a spare handgun into the waist of his jeans, wishing bitterly for one of those new FALs in Lidia's basement. They had only one automatic rifle between them and Eduardo, quite reasonably, would keep it; he was by far the best shot.

"Ready?" he asked Marta.

She nodded.

He looked at Eduardo, met his eyes openly—not long but very openly. They had never liked each other; Frente discipline was all that kept them civil, and lately Eduardo barely had been that. Neither considered the other to be an authentic revolutionary.

All of which was quite beside the point now. Daniel offered his hand. "Thanks, Eduardo. *Suerte.*"

The northerner laughed. "If I had any luck left, Manolo, you could have it. But I think it's all gone."

Daniel could run like a wild animal, like one of those wild animals that lived by their feet, by their capacity not merely for speed but for a bewildering unpredictability of movement. The soldiers, caught by surprise, got only a few wild shots at him before he had thrown himself between a parked car and a wall, and turned to help cover Marta's flight.

He knew as soon as she broke from the door that she was in difficulty; she was hurt and running badly, running slow. He fired frantically, raking everything in sight with bullets. She was twenty feet from him when she stopped. Simply stopped, crying something, neither a scream nor a word, just a cry, animal and awful. She fell brutally, twisted as though someone had thrown her. They kept shooting. Bullets spattered the ground and shredded the grass around her, impacted like blows into her body that was somehow still alive, still coiling like a worm on a stove.

Daniel closed his eyes. Oh, you bastards, you dirty, murdering bloody bastards!

He shoved shells quickly into the gun and looked toward the safehouse.

"Eddy?"

"Move your ass, damn it!" Eduardo shouted back. He

wasn't coming. He'd meant every word he'd said: he would stay until they shot the house down around his ears, and take as many of the sons of bitches with him as he could.

Marta was lying very still now, and all the fire was coming at Daniel, zinging off the car and chipping the adobe wall behind him. It took a moment—how long he did not know, but some small fragment of time—to ready himself to run again. He was raw with fear, hurting with it as with blows, and it was all that much worse now that he was alone.

It was a short run to the back door of the next house. If it were not locked, if there were no guards inside, if there wasn't a truckful of soldiers stationed in front of it...if, dear God, if...He wiped his face on his sleeve and ran, bent and dodging like a hare. A bullet grazed his arm, others splattered the walls around him, spewing broken adobe, leaving sudden clean scars among the marks of last week's shootings, or last month's, or last year's. He veered as if he would pass the house and then he leapt for the door, flinging himself through and rolling clear of it as it slammed on a spattering of shots.

He rolled to his knees and found himself a hand's reach away from the face of a girl, a beautiful face, huddled under the family's sagging bed. Behind her he could see bits of sleeves, shoes, children's eyes, God knew how many of them, motionless with terror. He wanted to say something to them, some small thing, at least that he was sorry, that it wasn't his fault; but he could only keep running, pausing at the front door just long enough to place the Guardia patrols. He came out firing. One Guard went down and the others dove for cover. The surprise of it and his own fleetness were enough to get him across the street and into another yard and over a wall, into a fresh warren of houses—houses inhumanly still, dirt streets bare of everything except jeeps and trucks and men with guns.

"Jesus." He leaned against a wall, gulping air, scavenging the street with his eyes for something, anything, that might offer a place to hide. Finding nothing.

He could, of course, try a house; could simply run

through a door and throw himself on someone's mercy. This was a working class district and the people were mostly sympathetic to the Sandinistas. But the Guardia controlled the barrio; they would determine quickly enough the general area where he had disappeared. And they would take it apart. Quite literally, they would take it apart; the safety of these walls was pure illusion.

He went on, running softly, staying to what there was of cover and shadows. He had lost them for a moment but he knew it was only for a moment; he could hear them everywhere. A jeep screamed to a stop in the street to his left, disgorging still another patrol, so close now that he could hear their orders, hear one of them laugh, laugh easily, as if in a game, and maybe it was a game to some of them, an afternoon's hunting and at the end of it a bag of trophies for Tacho's wall: what do you think of these, not much but they did put up a good fight, would you care for a brandy?

He never knew who shot him, or from where. Most likely it had been a hasty shot, thrown from a bad angle: the Becats shot to kill. But the bullet smashed his ankle and he fell hard, gulping the dust that spun into his face. He tried to get up and the leg just buckled; he did not try again.

The shouts came then, the running feet, the unbearable memory of Marta's twisting rag-doll body, laced with so many wounds that pieces of flesh and bloodied clothing were torn off and scattered in the grass. He dropped the gun and drew his hand away. He had done what he could to live; they would now do as they wished with his life.

They approached warily, circling like wolves, weapons trained and ready until one of them kicked the handgun aside and they dragged him to his feet. Facing him was a Guardia captain and perhaps a dozen men, all wearing the insignia of Somoza's Special Anti-terrorist Brigades. They searched him roughly; when they had finished the captain stepped toward him and without either haste or hesitation, smashed his pistol across the side of Daniel's face. He tottered, thrown off balance by the blow and unable to put any weight on his wounded ankle. They laughed, shoved him from one to the other. He was no threat now; none of these terrorists were anything once you took their guns away.

"Christ," the captain said, "they get rattier and rattier all the time."

He kicked Daniel's good leg out and caught him in the groin with his boot as he fell. The others joined in quickly, pack-like, with their feet or with their weapons, with jokes and eager snarls of hatred, some of them not quite sure why they were doing it, but everyone else was, and in any case it didn't matter.

There was no way for Daniel to shield himself. They were too many, and they kept at it as though they could beat him into non-existence. He could feel things break: teeth, ribs, God knew what else. He was choking and convulsed with pain, swallowing his own blood, swallowing sounds that were no longer human. He began to retch. Vomit spilled over his face and his body and some of it spattered onto the captain's impeccable Spanish leather boots.

"You *swine*!" the captain cried, and cursed him, cursed his mother and his father, cursed every filthy, miserable communist pig in the whole filthy, miserable, fucked-up country. With every curse he kicked the prisoner brutally. When he quit, blood was running quietly from Daniel's nose and his mouth and he was no longer moving at all.

17

Milan Valdez was miles from anywhere when the call came. He was riding his father's favourite horse in the far reaches of the ranch in Carazo. The land here was splendid, wild and speckled with gray cattle, the highlands laden with coffee and scattered with flowers—different ones month by month as the year turned in its unfailing and abundant fertility. Here, on a hill like this one, breathing the wind, he could understand his father's hatred of Managua—Managua's dust and stinking old buses belching out black diesel, its tiresome noise, its corrupted and corrupting violence. Managua was unclean.

Here there was only sky and freedom, absolute freedom. His body was taut and perfect in the sun, his life utterly his own, circumscribed by nothing, the land falling away like wind. He enjoyed the house in Las Colinas; he could not have lived, like his father, outside the nerve centres of national power. But it was only here that he felt truly himself; only here that the nature of that power defined itself. Here he knew what he was, and what he had a right to be.

He was alone, as he wished. He'd brought some *gauchos* with him for safety, but he'd left them down in the valley, where they would smoke and scratch themselves and talk about sex for as long as he left them there. He took a cigarette himself and that was when he saw the rider, far away still but coming fast, coming from the direction of the ranch-house, bringing Christ knew what fresh trouble. He waited, eyes narrowed with watching, and the magnificence of the day drained quietly away. It took very little now to remind him that everything was at risk: a late phone call, an unexpected visit, a car on his road that he did not recognize. Since Santa Rosa he knew, and the knowledge never left him: if they could, the revolutionaries would destroy everything. Splinter and steal and shit upon everything. Take the land and the culture and the souls of the children, break everything that was honourable and proud, everything that worked; ruin the best so the worst might admire itself. They would leave nothing of Nicaragua but wreckage.

He cursed quietly and tossed the cigarette away and galloped headlong to meet the rider. It was one of Ennio's young security guards; he had no news, only an urgent call from Yolanda.

"*Yolanda?*"

Milan left him, left them all, spurring the horse until it all but threw him, racing the long, falling sun. He savoured the fierceness of it, and grew calmer as his anger grew more sure, more directed. Whatever happened he would deal with it. He would deal with anything they threw at him.

But what he had to deal with, when he called Yolanda, was not quite what he had expected. Her voice was strained but steady. It was obvious that she had cried a lot but she was past it.

"Milan? Oh, please, Milan, can you come? They've arrested Mama!"

"*What?*"

"The National Guard. They came here looking for Pilar

and when Mama couldn't tell them anything they took her away. Milan, you've got to do something—"

"What did she say?"

"Mama? Nothing. She just told them that she didn't know where Pilar was. They didn't believe her. They seem to think Pilar is a terrorist—I don't know what she's done, but when I see her I'm going to strangle her. Can you imagine? Poor Mama being taken away by the police because of her!"

"Does your father know?"

"No. He isn't home yet. I'm scared he'll have a heart attack."

"Tell him to do nothing. *Nothing*, do you understand? I'll take care of it."

"Milan. . .?"

"Don't worry, Yolanda. It's some kind of crazy mistake. I'll take care of it."

He hung up, and made two more quick calls: one to his lawyer, just in case. The other to his father's long-time friend, Colonel Armando Davila, who had thirty-two prisoners on his hands and more coming in and who was talking only to the bunker and to God, in that order, but who nevertheless was persuaded that yes, he would spare Milan Valdez five minutes of his time when he arrived, purely out of the great regard and esteem in which he held his most illustrious father, the noble and respected *comandante* of Chinandega, retired.

18

Daniel had no idea when he regained consciousness whether one hour had passed, or many; whether it was night or day. He was lying on the floor in a small room lit by a single sallow bulb. He was not alone. One prisoner lay almost against him, unconscious; two more sat against the wall, awake but unmoving; another whimpered in the corner behind him.

For a long time he did not try to move. Everything hurt; he could hardly swallow or bear to breathe; every pulse shattered the inside of his head and left it spinning with pain. The wound in his ankle had not been tended at all and it burned as though a heated spear were turning in it.

He moaned without knowing that he did so, trying to move, to ease himself. Trying to think. The attack on the safehouse had come so quickly, and had thrown them into such immediate and desperate peril that no one had had time to wonder why it happened. He tried to go over the day in his mind, tried to remember what they had done, what they might have done, what anyone might have done that had betrayed them. But he was in too much pain and nothing would hold together in his brain long enough to make sense.

A guard came in, kicked him lightly to see if he was awake.

"All right, you, on your feet," he said, but he didn't wait for Daniel to make the attempt, merely reached down and hauled him to his knees. Another guard came to help; a third stood at the door with a sub-machine gun cradled in his arms.

They cuffed Daniel's hands behind his back and tied a hood over his face; it was thick and heavy; it smelled of sweat and vomit and it sent a shock of terror through his body like a knife. Just before they put it on he could see the two prisoners watching him with an identical, sullen expression of pity and relief; the one in the corner did not look up. It was a girl, much younger than Pilar, still huddled, making small animal noises inside herself. Her clothing was torn and bloodied and he did not need to look at her closely to know that she'd been raped.

They dragged him out, through a long corridor and down some steps and through another long corridor. Somewhere, muffled by walls, nameless, genderless even, someone was screaming. Screaming and screaming and screaming, stopping maybe for breath, for the smallest bit of breath, that was all. He tried to fight his own fear but the sound of that terrible screaming honed it to a nightmare edge.

They took him into what he knew was an interrogation room, turned him over to other men—men whose faces he had not seen. They unlocked his wrists and shoved him into a wooden chair, waited beside him. He heard the sound of papers, of a man shifting by a table.

The man spoke as though reading. He spoke clearly and well—an educated man, probably an officer.

"Daniel Chillan Santa Cruz. Twenty-two years old. Member of the Sandinista faction which calls itself the Terceristas or Insurrectionist Tendency...you people really dream up extravagant names for yourselves, don't you?"

If Daniel's jaw hadn't been broken in two places, he might have answered that, but it wasn't worth the pain.

"It goes with all the revolutionary rhetoric, I suppose," the officer said. He tipped back his chair and read on:

"Mother: Ana Santa Cruz, food vendor, barrio Los Santos. Father: Martin Chillan Torres, labour agitator and communist agent, killed in a shoot-out with the National Guard, Diriamba, 1967."

Shoot-out? Daniel thought. You damnable pigs, how do you have a shoot-out when only one side has guns?

"Joined the FSLN in 1969 with the code name Manolo, and took part in the following criminal activities against the security of the government and the people of Nicaragua: anti-government demonstrations and incitement to treason. Arms smuggling. Organization of terrorist cells in Diriamba and Rosario through 1974 and '75. Occupation of the Jackson-Perez cannery in 1975. Robbery of the National Bank in Altamira, the Bancamerica on the Avenida Roosevelt, and the National Bank in Diriamba. And the bombing of the Santa Rosa Chemical Plant in October of this year."

He paused, put the paper down. "You keep busy, don't you, *cochinito*?"

Daniel barely heard the insult. Small beads of sweat ran down his face and tumbled silently into the hood. How did they know all that? It was too much for them to have pieced together by luck, by their own hit and miss investigations. They exaggerated, of course; they made it sound as though he had single-handedly carried out actions that were in fact the work of many people. But the account was basically accurate—incomplete, but accurate. Jesus, he thought. Oh, Jesus...For a moment he was almost glad of the hood. He would be silent, if he had enough strength, but he was not stoical. He was sure that the impact of their words showed naked on his face. He did not want to think about what else they might know. What they might know about other people. He steadied himself then, a little, with great effort.

"I'm sure you realize," the officer went on, "that these charges are enough to imprison you for the rest of your life. Without even mentioning the National Guard personnel who were killed by you and your associates this afternoon in Montenegro.

"This confession outlines the charges I've mentioned. Sign it, and answer a few questions, and we'll deal very leniently with you." He placed a clipboard on Daniel's lap, pressed a pen into his hand, guided it to a spot near the bottom of the page.

Daniel sat unmoving.

"If you don't sign it," the officer went on, in the same quiet voice, "if you don't co-operate with us, we'll kill you. By inches. By half inches. Do you understand me, Chillan? We'll leave you in so many pieces God won't find them in time for Judgment Day. Sign it."

Daniel drew a deep breath, bent over the clipboard, and wrote quickly: *Somoza is shit. So are you.* Handed it to his tormentor, wishing for the tiny satisfaction of seeing his face.

It was stupid, of course. He was swallowing blood when they picked him off the floor, dragged him to a metal frame by the table, strapped him down on it, naked and dazed. It was stupid, yes, but that didn't matter. It didn't matter in the least if you were stupid, if you cried or fainted or pissed yourself. All that mattered was silence, staying together, staying whole.

He wished just then that he believed in God, that there might be someone he could pray to for strength—a person that really existed, not just a dream whose existence depended on the ability of people to create it. Such a small dream, in a place like this.

A man leaned over him—not the officer, someone else; he was big, sweaty; he exuded energy—the hard, practical energy of a man who did difficult work and did it well.

"Do you know what this is, little swine?" he said. "It's electricity. It makes even wire sing."

They began. The shock went through his flesh like a thousand invisible knives. He was sure that they were killing him. His body arched of its own will, twisted like a cat on a wire, fell back shuddering. They attached the electrodes to his genitals, to his shattered ankle; they lifted the hood and forced them into his mouth. The voice, always the same voice, pounded at him in an incessant rain of questions, curses, demands. Even if he had wished to, he could not have understood them all. Where was Valerian, where were the safehouses, where were the guns? Who wrote this leaflet, who printed it, who threw it out of bus windows all along the Carretera Norte? Where did they get the money, the radios, the trucks? Where did the boats from Cuba land? Where was the sun and the moon and where were Sandino's bones?

Daniel said nothing. They began again. And again. And again. The pain was so terrible that he could not comprehend it, could not respond to it, could not deal with it in his mind at all, except to salvage each time the tiny victory of silence. Each time anew, as though he had not suffered it and salvaged it before.

Nothing in his experience had prepared him for this, or could have. He knew that they used torture, but he had not known, and did not even now quite believe, that he could be reduced to this. That his own body could be so degraded and so savaged, that the bestial screams that sometimes filled the room could be his own. That everything he had ever done or learned or loved or tried to be could finally come to nothing more than this.

He did not know how long the encounter lasted, or when it became the next one. They mauled his mind as well as his body; they mocked his loyalties: You think you're protecting your friends, little fool? Do you think they care? Do you think they protected you? We know everything about you—who do you suppose told us?

They knew about Pilar, too; they had her picture. The fat sergeant shoved it into his face, grinning: A classy looking bitch, that one. A little high for the likes of you, but then, you didn't think you had her all to yourself, did you? She's fucked half the Managua underground. Fucked Valerian, too, your fine *comandante*—didn't know that, did you?

He knew that they lied, that they always lied; they'd been lying for a thousand years. But in the isolation of his cell the words would come back, would gnaw at him in the silence where nothing human spoke, where nothing human was there to contradict them. Maybe one of his comrades had betrayed him. Maybe all of his comrades had betrayed him. Maybe Pilar...maybe...The words would come back, and sometimes he could not make them go away. Yet cruel as they were, they were phantoms; they had no power to persuade. In the violence of the interrogation room Somoza's men were real. They were the grinning bullies who came to Los Santos to collect their bribes from the shopkeepers and their cut from the brothels; they were the men who burned villages, who raped and trampled where they pleased; the men who smashed his father's arms and legs until the pieces of his bones stuck out like broken pencils. Facing the Guardia, even the bitterest of the doubts that had slivered into his mind in the silence of his cell simply dissolved. The terror remained, always the terror; but no more questions. He knew these men too well, and he knew why he fought them.

"You're very young," the sergeant said. "Why should you die for people who don't give a damn about you?"

They understood nothing about the revolution, Daniel thought. They really imagined that his commitment to the Frente and to his people would unravel like an old sock if they told him that a friend had betrayed him or his girl friend screwed around. They were liars from birth and he did not believe a word they said, but if he had believed it all, it would have made no difference. They measured the Sandinistas by their own small souls...so much the worse for them.

"Eh, *cochino*," he whispered. Pig. It wasn't much more than a soft growl inside the hood, but he knew they could hear him. "Go fuck your grandmother, pig."

The sergeant hit him, cursed, hit him again, very hard.

"So you can talk, can you?" the sergeant said. "That's good. Now you just need to learn what to say, yes? You will learn, I promise you. You will learn."

It was not possible to sustain his defiance, to sustain even dignity, to sustain anything but silence. It simply went on: began, ended, began again. They tried other things: beatings, live cigarettes, sexual abuse, more beatings. They made him walk. They held him down on the floor and stamped on his hands and his feet. They shoved a piece of metal from a bicycle frame into his ass and fed current into it until he passed out.

There was no light in his cell, no water except the wetness on the floor, no human presence except the stench of urine and the muffled sound of other people screaming. He was cold, shivering, his body huddling into itself like an animal's.

His comrades had talked to him sometimes about torture. Paco once, too. At first, Paco told him, you're scared that you'll be really hurt, that you'll lose your eyes or your balls or your mind. Then you're just scared you'll die. And finally, you're scared that you won't. . .

How long did it take? he wondered. How long, Jesus, till you died or they let you be? Or until—no, there was no other until, no third possibility. Till you died or they let you be, that was all. *Los hijos de Sandino ni se venden ni se rinden.* The children of Sandino do not sell out, and do not yield. He turned his face away from the door, from the sound of their boots coming down the stairs, from the sight of them framed in the sudden harsh light of the opened cell:

"All right, you cocksucking bastard. Mama wants you. Care and feeding time for little terrorists, right? Let's go."

Valerian was back in Managua before the sun—almost in Managua—in a quiet house in the hills just off Open Tres. He met there with a small group of people, most of them legal. It was they who would have to mobilize the city in defense of its prisoners. But he talked first, briefly and alone, with his core people who were there: Pilar, Claudia, and Rafael.

In the years that she had known him, Pilar had seen him defeated and weary and sick, had seen him cry, but she had never seen him as he was now. He was shattered. And the reasons were more desperate than they had even imagined.

The safehouse off the Carretera Sur, he told them, had been raided almost at the same time as the house in Montenegro. Everything in it, including the shipment of new weapons, was lost. Lidia was arrested; her son David panicked and tried to run; they machine-gunned him to death on his front steps, in front of his mother. They had Amparo, they had Paco; they were looking for Clariz. Marta and Eduardo were dead and Manolo was missing and probably captured. That was the fate of the cell itself; as for their contacts and support people, they were being hauled away all over the city. The number of arrests was likely to reach a hundred.

After he had spoken the silence lay like marsh air, too heavy and too foul to breathe. Somebody had to ask. Somebody.

"What happened, *compa*?" Pilar whispered. "What the hell *happened*?"

He did not look at anyone. "They got to Paco. They picked him up on a routine road block ten miles from Managua. By the time anyone missed him, he'd told them everything he knew."

"Paco?" Rafa said harshly. "No way. I don't believe it. Paco was solid gold."

"Nobody's solid gold," Valerian said. "Not you. Not me. Nobody. Don't you God damn ever forget that!"

"But so soon?" Claudia said. "Couldn't he have bought us a little bit of time? My God, just a day...?"

Forty-eight hours, Pilar thought. That was the unwritten law; you owed that much, no matter what; that much, to give your people time to run. Just forty-eight fucking hours...

"He broke, that's all," Valerian said. "He'd been through it before and the first time he stayed together, and the second time he didn't. We can curse him to the last circle of hell but what's the use? What's the use?"

Rafael simply sat there and shook his head. He'd liked Paco. They all had. But Pilar was not thinking of Paco at all.

"Don't you have any word on Manolo?" she pleaded. "Not anything?"

"He was in the house when Julio left at noon. That's all we know. The Guardia has officially reported various weapons and equipment seized and two guerrillas killed. Nothing else." He paused, and went on unhappily. "Julio told me Manolito had a lot of work to do. It's likely that he was still there."

"But he could have escaped? He could be hiding?" Claudia insisted.

"It's possible," Valerian said.

But it was a gesture and Pilar knew it was a gesture. How did anyone escape from a house surrounded with machine guns and tanks, from a barrio with every street patrolled and every house subject to instant, murderous search? She covered her face with her hands. She would not think of Daniel dead. She would not. But if he was not dead, then he was a prisoner, and prisoners the Guardia denied having were almost always prisoners they tortured and killed. Their mangled bodies turned up in lime-pits and ravines, or just never turned up at all...

Valerian came and sat beside her. He did not say that he was sorry; to say that he was sorry was like admitting that Manolito was dead.

"You can't stay in Managua any longer, Clariz," he said quietly. "Every Becat unit in the city has your picture. Julio's too. I'm sending you both to Granada."

He handed her a packet of documents. "Your new identity. Someone will be by later this morning with some appropriate clothing and a wig. She'll help you work out a history to match. The car for Granada will pick you up after dark tonight. *Esta bien?*"

She opened the packet. It contained a complete set of papers for a twenty-year-old legal secretary named Consuelo Chavarria Ross. They were meticulously done. The data had probably been typed in this morning, but the signatures were sure to be Daniel's work, done weeks ago in some stuffy room with bad light, without knowing who would use them, or for what need, just making sure they would be there.

"Did Manolo do these?" she asked.

"Yes," Valerian said. He laughed then, softly. Sadly. "The kid could forge the ten commandments, I think."

The house was nestled in the curve of a hill; by mid-afternoon it was drenched in heat. Claudia and Pilar were alone, waiting for darkness in the room that had the largest window; it was not wise to go outside. For a while, at Claudia's insistence, Pilar had tried to sleep, but all that came to her were images of death.

She sat now with Claudia, sat in her pale blue linen dress and spike shoes, soft brown hair falling to her shoulders, hair that was not her own, like her name and her clothing and the streets she walked on.

There was a song that Daniel sang, she remembered, one that he sang often:

It's not so bad that they exist
those who have nothing to lose
not even death...
It's not so bad that they exist
to create us...

Songs, she thought, dear Jesus, they were all that you had; you lived on a handful of songs. Everything else belonged to your enemies.

Everything.

You forgot that sometimes in the strength of your defiance: forgot the immensity of their power, forgot how much you could be hurt. You had to forget, had to and could not and must not. You said that they could not defeat you, and that was true; you only grew stronger for their trying. They broke lives and bodies and you gathered the blood like a sacrament; you made it a song and you made the song a weapon; you cried *Presente*! until the last cold stars could hear it; and in the end they had to fight a myth a thousand times stronger than any human person. You threw the lie of death back into their teeth and said: Yes, and what can you do to us *now*?

But they could do anything. Anything at all. They could wipe you off the face of the earth, and all that would be left was a handful of songs.

And Daniel, wherever they had taken him, to whatever foul and brutal place that also did not exist, what of Daniel? What of the songmaker in a world of cries and silence?

"He's so alone," she whispered to Claudia. "No matter where he is, he is so alone."

"There is always God," Claudia said softly.

"Manolo's not a Christian, Claudia. He doesn't believe. God is no comfort to him."

"I'm not at all sure God cares about that," Claudia said. "He loves the people; he loves those who defend the people—whether they notice it or not. God will look after Manolo. I know he will."

Pilar spared her comrade a small, melancholy smile. "*Puede ser*," she said. Perhaps. She stared at her nails—beautiful painted nails that belonged to a woman she always was and never had been, a woman of chauffeurs and Chanel, a woman of the world, some other world, not this one—certainly not the driven and unsheltered world of Danny Chillan.

"You know, Claudia," she said sadly, "I don't think he's ever been completely sure that I wanted him for himself, that it wasn't some kind of political gesture, some way of proving something to myself or to the world. There's so much we never talked about. We had no time ...and I suppose we were scared to..."

Yes, Claudia thought, and who could blame you? What you had was good; maybe it was steel and maybe it was spidersilk, but it was good and you just held on to it and didn't ask questions about a future you might never have. Who could blame you? And who could blame you if maybe it *was* all tangled up with politics and proving things, with the need to know what you were and what you could be? That didn't make it any less real.

"What's ever sure, *compita*?" she responded. "I know Manolo well enough to know that he's happy. He believes in nothing, totally, except the struggle. Yet he loves you, and he's happy. What more is possible?"

"I don't know...Probably nothing. Only I keep thinking that there should be more...that I should have given him something...solider."

"There isn't anything solider," Claudia said. "People who think there is get married, and find that everything's still the same. You live one day at a time. You're happy or unhappy one day at a time."

"I didn't mean marriage."

"No. You meant a miracle. You're only people, Clariz. Two people in the middle of a war, with a little space in which to live. And that's all there is, Clariz. There are no talismans. There's no magical thing you could have given him that would shield him now. Or that anyone could have given him. In that sense, yes, he is alone. We all are."

"God," Pilar whispered. "Oh, God..."

She did not cry—not then. Not until two days later in the hideout in Granada, when someone brought her a day-old copy of *La Prensa*. A burning bus lay right across the top of it; stories of protest and demonstration filled the first three pages. In one corner of the front page was a small story with a very large headline: *Authorities Deny Holding Missing Activist*. She looked at Daniel's picture and came apart.

19

No one slept in the Zelaya house that night. Long afterward Jadine remembered how they brooded and paced, how they ran to greet Milan's heavy blue van when he finally arrived some hours after midnight, how they hugged Beatriz and asked her: was she all right, was she all right, was she *really* all right? And she wondered how they rationalized all that anxiety in a society where decent people had nothing to fear.

Beatriz, however, really was all right. The Guardia had spoken to her and ordered her about as though she were an animal, and would not even give her a drink of water, but she was unharmed.

"It was all a mistake," Milan said. "As I was sure it would turn out to be."

"Some mistake," Leon said.

"They're edgy, damn it," Milan said. "The Guard has lost over fifty men since the beginning of October. Did you know that? It gets to them. It would get to anybody." He disengaged his arm from Alvaro's and wrapped it around Yolanda as they walked back into the house.

"Who did you see?" Alvaro asked. He had no contacts in the Guardia through his own family, only through Beatriz. Some of them had considerable influence, but he was surprised that any of them could have gotten her released in a matter of hours.

"I spoke with Colonel Davila."

"Armando Davila? You saw Davila himself? In the middle of the night?"

"He's an old friend of my father's. They trained together in Panama."

"By Jesus," Alvaro said cheerfully to his wife, "he'll be talking to the president next!"

"Nicaragua is a very small country," Milan replied. "Especially at the top."

They went inside, settled Beatriz into a chair, plied her with rum and sandwiches. In the first bit of silence she touched Milan's arm lightly and said:

"Milan. . . when you spoke to the Colonel, did you ask him. . . did you have a chance to ask him. . . about my daughter? About Pilar? Why they're looking for her. . . ?"

"They're concerned about her political activities."

"What. . .*political activities*?"

He met her eyes, then shrugged when she would not look away. "If they believe they have reason to question her, then I'm sure they do."

"What reason did they have to question me?"

"Beatriz, for heaven's sake, be reasonable," Alvaro said. "Considering the mess this country is in, the authorities are behaving very well. They make mistakes, of course. And they correct them. If anything, this whole affair proves how fair and reliable they are."

"Mama," Yolanda said, "you said yourself no one harmed you in any way."

Beatriz did not look at them. "They were beating people," she said. "In the room next to where I was. They were beating people all the time I was there."

"And how the hell do you know that?" Alvaro demanded.

"I could hear it. We could all hear it. We sat there like

little well-bred mannequins and pretended that we didn't notice a thing. We told ourselves that they were moving furniture. Or maybe playing tag. Grown men playing tag and crying out in pain when they were caught, yes? We could believe that. We can believe anything except the truth."

Alvaro turned, flailing one arm in sheer exasperation, the other reaching for the *flor de cana*.

"Damn it to hell, woman, what do you expect? The fucking Sandinistas are tearing the country apart—bombing, murdering, burning property, terrorizing everyone who refuses to join them. So maybe a few people do get kicked around by the Guard. Maybe they deserve it. Nobody beat you, did they?"

"No." She put her sandwich back on the plate, untouched. "Nobody beat me."

Yolanda bent to one knee by her chair and put her arms around her. "Mama, you're so tired. It's been an awful day. Would you like Maria to run you a bath?"

"Yes." She stood up. A bath. A sleeping pill. With luck she would not dream. She thanked Milan again, hugged them all, last of all Jadine, Jadine who had said barely a word, but whose eyes were wise and empty. Beatriz held her face a moment between her palms.

"Leave this country, little cousin," she said. "Before it kills you."

No one spoke for several moments after she left. Leon got up and helped himself to a handful of sandwiches, began to speak, saw his father's face, and thought better of it. He sat down again, eating with studied concentration.

Milan, who had not sat down at all, moved quietly to Alvaro's chair. "We must talk," he said simply.

The older man looked up, shook the last of his drink and emptied it. He did not respond at once. He'd been drinking since the early evening but he was not so much drunk as shaken. Badly shaken. No matter how much he talked about politics over the years, no matter how seriously he took it, he had never really expected the revolution to touch him personally.

"Yes," he said. "Yes, of course." He rose with effort.

"You'd all best get some sleep," he added. "It's been one long fucking day."

He took the rum with him into the patio. They closed the heavy doors behind them—doors they closed only for epidemics or hurricanes. What Alvaro chose to tell his family afterward would be up to him, but they would speak first alone, as men.

Alvaro put his hand on the other's shoulder. "I want to thank you, Milan," he said. "I want truly to thank you."

"You already have."

"Nevertheless . . ." He sat down by the heavy oak coffee table and poured a drink.

"You spoke with Davila, then?" he asked finally.

"We spoke very frankly."

"And they are looking for my daughter? For Pilar? That part of it wasn't a mistake?"

"*Exacto*." Milan reached, plunked a fresh ice cube into his glass. Alvaro was weak, he reflected. Pushy, blustering men almost always were.

"How bad is it, Milan?" he asked. "What the hell has she done? She isn't working for the Sandinistas, is she? She wouldn't do that. She says a lot of crazy things but she wouldn't. . .?" His voice fell away. The look in his face was almost pleading.

"Alvaro." Milan sat on the edge of the chair beside him. "It's not for a son to be giving his father advice, but I'm going to give you some now. Stop being innocent. Stop imagining that there's a fence around your world that will keep the shit out. There isn't."

His voice took on a soft, carefully measured edge: "Your daughter Pilar is a sworn member of the FSLN. She's in a cell led by a man known as Valerian, who broke with the hard-line Marxist faction from the mountains because they weren't blowing things up fast enough. She's got her little *rojinegra* bandanna and her machine gun and her book of Che just like the rest of them. And she's got a shantytown street rat's bastard in her belly, just to prove how dedicated she is, to keep the terrorist line clean and healthy, you might say—"

"Stop it!" Alvaro said harshly. "Damn you, Milan! God damn Jesus Christ, damn them all!" His glass crashed across the stones and he dropped his head into his hands. He was not crying, but he was close to it. "Jesus," he said again, several times.

Milan lit a cigarette. "I'm sorry, Alvaro. I was hard. Sometimes one has to be." He fixed them each another drink—not very strong. Alvaro was maudlin enough already. "Here."

"*Gracias.*" Alvaro sipped once and reached for the bottle. "Christ, Milan, you drink holy water, not rum." He fattened his own very generously and held out the bottle. "Have some, for Christ's sake. Next year the Sandinistas will have it all."

"No," Milan said flatly. "They won't. There may be nothing left, but they won't have anything. That I can promise you."

"God willing, my friend. *Salud.*" Alvaro leaned back in his chair. "You know," he brooded, "those crazy people who spend their lives on the beaches, smoking marijuana —maybe they're not so crazy. We work and work and work, and for what?"

Milan did not reply. It was two hours, maybe less, until dawn; the night was languid and still. Deceptively still. The city did not sleep. It huddled.

"I took the kids out of the fucking Catholic school so they wouldn't grow up to be nuns, can you believe that?"

"Yes," Milan said. He believed it; it was not relevant.

"I don't understand it, Milan," Alvaro went on. "I just don't understand it. She had everything. We gave her everything..." He looked around him as though searching, searching for holes in his house, for some unnoticed fault that had let the rain in. "She liked books; she had all the books she wanted. Even Marxist books. I let her buy what she pleased. She liked music. I got the piano. She never learned to play it. It was Yolanda who learned to play it...I had a quarter of a million cordobas in a trust fund to send her to graduate school in the United States, and she never even finished her degree.

"Do you understand it, Milan? Any of it? How it happened? We gave her everything and she spit on us and went to live with pigs. Gave herself to pigs. How do those things happen? How are they possible?"

"They happen," Milan said. "That is all, they happen. You put six perfect oranges in a basket and one of them rots."

Alvaro shook his head. "It's what they learn," he said. "That fucking university is full of communists. Pilar didn't get into all this shit by herself. I know she didn't."

"Yolanda went to the same university, *suegro mio*. And so did I." He leaned forward intently. "My father was in the National Guard for more than seven years, Alvaro. I know as well as any man in this country what kind of influence subversion can have. In the schools. In the churches. In the factories. It's all over; I know that. And I know it sucks in every ignorant, desperate son of a bitch around; it channels their hatred, and fills them with illusions of power, and allows them to believe that they are heroic and persecuted rather than weak and stupid. But the people who carry out the subversion are not stupid; maybe they themselves were once seduced, but I can assure you that it was willingly. They choose. The Sandinistas—the militants, not the would-be-revolutionary riffraff that hangs on their tails—they know exactly what they're doing." He smiled, faintly and bitterly. "Your daughter is sleeping with the man who blew up my factory."

"Oh, Christ. . . !" Alvaro threw his head back, gestured with his arm, vaguely, as though he meant to do something but could not determine what. "Davila told you that?" He spoke like a man with a claw in his throat.

"Yes."

"Do you know anything about him? Do you know his name?"

"Daniel Chillan."

Alvaro made another irritated gesture. The name meant nothing to him. "What the fuck is he?"

"What are any of them?" Milan replied. He recalled his talk with Davila, recalled the thin file in the colonel's hand. The record on Daniel Chillan went back eight years but until this week there had been very little in it. He remembered Davila's description: totally unprincipled, totally dedicated. An animal.

"He's a professional terrorist," Milan said. "He grew up on Marxism instead of milk. His father was a founding member of the Socialist Party and spent his whole life trying to radicalize it into armed revolt. The kid never bothered with the party; the guerrillas were more to his liking."

Alvaro shifted in his chair, muttered something under his breath. Anger was slowly, finally, edging the shock out of his eyes.

Milan went on: "Colonel Davila described Daniel Chillan as a pure revolutionary animal. Myself, I would be less exotic. I would simply call him a dirty little half-breed fanatic."

Alvaro looked at him, his face twisting. "And Pilar chose him—is that what you're saying? He's filth, and she knows it, and she chose him."

"Him," Milan said. "And what he is. And what he does." He paused, and added very softly. "And how it ends. That too is chosen, Alvaro. That, too."

After a long silence Alvaro shoved himself to his feet, put his glass down hard and unsteadily.

"She's not your daughter, Milan."

"No. Neither is she yours. Not any more."

"No. She's theirs, isn't she?" He laughed harshly. "You're hard, do you know that, Milan? You are the hardest God damn son of a bitch in Managua."

"Probably," Milan said, untroubled.

"But you are also right." He began to move toward the house, one arm thrown around Milan's shoulders. "Why should we take all the shit, you tell me that? We have to be hard. We're the only people who can save what's left. And there's only a handful of us, Milan. Only a fucking handful. We have to be hard."

Armando Davila was not a handsome man; nonetheless, he radiated a confidence, a worldliness, that almost made him seem so. He was heavy-featured and a little overweight, but his eyes were shrewd and his wit sharp. Like his friend Ennio Valdez he was a professional soldier, political only to the degree that was necessary for survival. Unlike him he remained—or believed himself to remain—personally removed from the more unpleasant aspects of his job. His children were in school in Costa Rica and it was widely rumoured in the Guardia that he would follow them if the revolution really heated up.

He smiled as Milan came in, rose to shake his hand, to ask about his father and offer a cigarette.

"So," he said, shaking out his match, "you still want to see Chillan?"

"Yes."

Davila shrugged. He had arranged it as he promised, but he saw no purpose in it. "There isn't much left to look at," he said.

"What have you gotten out of him?"

"Nothing. If he talks at all it's to tell us what mother-fucking pigs he thinks we are. Mostly he just takes it. They train their people well, Milan; you have to give them credit for that. They train them well. I don't think many of my own men would show that kind of discipline."

"Discipline, Colonel?" Milan asked. "Or merely fanaticism?"

"That depends entirely which side you're on."

Milan laughed. "You're becoming a philosopher, Colonel."

"No. Merely a realist. Shall we go?"

They moved into the corridor. "Tell me," Davila said as they began to walk, "did you see any demonstrations on the way down here?"

"No. Should I have?"

Davila laughed without warmth. "God knows, Milan. They're out every day, one God damn barrio after another. We had a near riot yesterday in Open Tres. All women, would you believe it? The fat cows can't even read but they think every prisoner in the country is one of their children."

He paused to exchange salutes with two white-uniformed members of the president's personal guard who were rushing past in almost unseemly haste.

"His Excellency must have run out of oysters," Davila observed dryly.

Milan did not smile, and the colonel went on as though he'd never been interrupted: "This morning I drove by one of the schools where the kids are on strike—twelve and thirteen-year-olds carrying placards bigger than they are. Over in Los Santos there are six of them sitting in the bell tower of a church saying they won't come down until we account for Danny Chillan and everybody else who's gone missing since Jacob's brothers dumped him down a well.

"What's a man supposed to think of his country, my friend, when even the women and children are out of control?"

"What are you doing about it?" Milan asked.

"We're doing what we can. It's not easy to deal with, you know. Not in Managua. There's too damn many people watching."

Milan cursed softly. Between Chamorro and the foreign press and the diplomatic corps and the Church and every other meddling band of bastards who stuck their interminable noses into things they did not understand, the government and the National Guard had little room to move. If they could just once act freely. . . just once. Three months would be all that it would take.

They turned, went down a flight of stairs into another long hallway. Milan had never been inside the bunker before, but he did not have to ask what part of it they had entered. The sounds were unmistakeable. Davila raised his voice a little, as though they were passing through an office full of clattering typewriters. At a door no different from the others except for a number—019—he paused. "Here we are. You're expected." Milan hesitated, and he made a gesture with his arm. "*Pase*."

"You're not coming in?"

"What for? I've seen it all before."

The room was small, heavy with old, overheated air and unshaded light. Inside the closely fitting mask, sweat ran quietly down Milan's face. He hated ugliness, and everything around him was ugly—the stained walls and the dirty table with its simple crude machine: a few clamps, a few wires, a generator that could shoot enough electricity into a human body to stop a heart or melt down a brain—unspeakably ugly, all of it, and most of all the prisoner strapped to that bare metal frame that looked like a discarded bed spring. His face, unhooded for Milan's curiosity, was unrecognizable, a pulp of cut and battered flesh, swollen and discoloured, human only by inference. His eyes were muddy with pain and fever; he looked at Milan with hatred but without much interest.

The man in charge of the interrogation was a sergeant, a big, beefy man who seemed to vaguely resent Milan's intrusion. "You want to ask him something?" he said. "Or can we get on with it?"

Milan stood back and waved them to go ahead.

He'd observed interrogations before, many times, and had taken part in a few. But he didn't have the patience. He couldn't do what the man beside him was doing: couldn't pace and shout and cajole and threaten, couldn't hammer out the same questions over and over and over again, until his voice itself became a weapon:

"The guns, Chillan? Where did you get the guns? Where did they land? The name of the village, damn you, do you hear me, I'll burn your motherfucking balls right off—where did they land? Who helped you? Names, damn you, tell me the names!"

The questions were laced with torture in no particular pattern—blows, shafts of electricity that flung the prisoner's body against its restraints like an animal against a tether. Quite suddenly the sergeant would pause, wipe his face, speak calmly:

"Listen, you damn little fool, don't you know we can keep this up for fifteen years? Haven't you had enough? Don't you want to go to the clinic? We'll send you to the clinic right now if you show some sense." His hand closed on Chillan's ankle. "This wound's gone all bad, don't you know that? It's a hell of a mess. It'll kill you. Just tell us where Valerian is, and you can go to the clinic. Or tell us who keeps one of the safehouses...just some little thing, all right, Chillan? That's fair enough, isn't it?...Isn't it...No? By Christ, then we'll take you apart, you scabby little son of a communist whore! Turn the power up, Alfredo, the fucking bastard's not awake yet!"

He began again, the questions always different, always the same: Where did you get it? Where did you hide it?

Where did you take it? Who helped you? Names, damn you, tell me their names...!

"He's useless." The guard threw up his hands, turning to Milan. "He's a fucking shithead. All he does is yell. If I didn't need his tongue I'd tear it out and make him eat it. Christ, what a shithead!"

Milan dug out his cigarettes and offered each guard one. What he was watching was obscene, but it was also quite extraordinary. It recalled to his mind a day of his adolescence when he'd been out riding and had found vultures tearing up a corpse: some animal, he was not sure what kind; it was bloated and foul, but dissolving, ceasing to exist before his eyes. He had watched, appalled and fascinated, marvelling how afterward it was as though the horrid creature had never been. The bones were scattered and meaningless, and the wind that passed over them was clean.

Chillan's body was shaking where it hung; blood trickled from his wrists, from a cut re-opened on his face, from the wound in his ankle that was burning and growing calmly dark with poison.

An animal, Milan thought. Dangerous once, perhaps, but not an enemy, not as men ranked enemies. An animal run to ground by history, whose bones the wind would soon pick clean...He felt unspeakably disgusted, but he also felt somehow strengthened, made whole. There was a kind of purity in such absolute violence, in such absolute reaffirmation of what was, and what was not, real.

He drew a last time on his cigarette, and then pressed the burning tip into the prisoner's genitals, turning it slowly until it went out.

"In Chinandega," he said, "we had a lieutenant who used to drip a little bit of kerosene on them, and set it afire, and then a little bit more...They talked."

In fact, some of them hadn't; some of them never would. But that wasn't the most important thing. The most important thing was how they disintegrated, how utterly they ceased to exist.

He walked through the long corridors and back into the brilliant Managua sun. He felt tired and soiled, but it did not matter. Tomorrow at first light he would take Yolanda and her mother back with him to Carazo. The American woman, too, if she wanted to come. They all needed to breathe again, to be away from the violence, to laugh, to ride until the sun fell into the sea, over lands that were clean and entirely their own.

20

There were children crying in the clinic, that long line of children that never went away but simply took on different faces until it seemed to Jadine a bizarre and cruel game, an unending treadmill of children. There were grown people, too, of course; and adolescents with strange wounds for which they gave even stranger explanations. But it was the children Jadine remembered; the children that she would write about, hunched over Pepe's wooden table in the back room with the smell of disinfectants heavy in the air. She looked at what she had written:

"Pablito is nine years old. Although he is suffering from advanced tuberculosis, he is responsible for earning a share of the family income, which he does by selling papers. He and the other five members of his family live in a shack made of boards, cardboard, and bits of tin. Because he is sick his family have given him their only bed: a mat made of rags which in the rainy season lies on a dirt floor in two inches of water. His mother lives by scavenging offal from the slaughterhouse sewers..."

She read it again, and tore it up. You couldn't say it quite like that. Not that harshly. People wanted to feel good when they read their missionary newsletters.

She wrote again:

"Pablo's mother is living with her third husband. One abandoned her before her first child was born; the second beat her and she left him. Pablito loves his new father and says that he is good to them, but that he may have to leave, too, if there is no work..."

God, she thought, that would really do it. She imagined the reaction to such a letter read from the pulpit in Kerry Heights—even if it went on to explain:

"The cost of abject poverty is not merely hunger and disease, brutal as these things are. There is also an appalling cost in broken families, prostitution, alcoholism, and despair..."

No. You wrote those things in sociology books, for the benefit of people who already knew it. You couldn't tell the Christians of North America that half of Nicaragua lived in sin. It would simply confirm what they already suspected about Latin decadence.

She scrunched the paper into little balls and threw it away. It wasn't going to be easy, writing these letters. She wondered how Pepe did it, and decided that probably he didn't have nearly as much trouble as she was having. Pepe was not cynical; he believed in people, in their immense capacity for good.

And also their capacity for evil.

That too. And that had surprised her. Father Pepe talked about evil as though it really existed; as though it were not just a theological abstraction but something you could point out on the street.

There had been a body in the clinic when she arrived this morning, the body of a young girl from Acahualinca, who had died there during the night; her family had not dared to bring her to Pepe until after dark. Two days before, they said, the National Guard had raided the barrio and taken her away.

Jadine made herself look at the corpse. Just once. Very

carefully, but just once. For weeks afterward she would not be able to dress herself or bathe or do anything which made her confront her own unclothed body without remembering, without contemplating again and again the fragility of human flesh, the strange sweetness of it, the absolute, incomprehensible brutality with which it could be violated and destroyed.

She asked Pepe—not because she expected him to have an answer but because she needed to say it—asked him: What kind of men did things like this? What kind of mind even *thought of* driving nails into the pelvis of a fourteen-year-old girl?

"Very ordinary men, Jadine," he said simply. "Very ordinary."

She started to protest but he went on:

"Oh, there's a few psychopaths out there; of course there is. The kind of power that the military has attracts them. But there are over seven thousand men in the National Guard, you know. Probably a thousand of them routinely use torture. Another two or three thousand use it sometimes. They're not crazy, most of them. They are ordinary human beings who've made choices."

It was very late. A weak bulb hung over the table where Pepe was eating a bowl of cold soup. His face was lined with exhaustion; he ate without interest, simply because it was necessary.

"We're terrible cowards when it comes to admitting to evil," he said. "We used to blame it on the devil and now we blame it on the id. But people choose, you know, Jadine. They choose clumsily, with insufficient knowledge, with fear, with all kinds of things which make the choices less than perfectly free. And yet they do choose. And some of them choose evil.

"It's not a Satanic thing. Milton was all wrong. It's small and shabby. It's taking away other people's food and labour and hope, eroding their minds, destroying their identities—using them, just using them—and saying: I owe nothing. I have no responsibility. I spit on you. I'm stronger than you and I spit on you...never acknowledging that everything that made my strength—my body itself, and everything I eat and wear and learn and enjoy exists because of other people—was made by somebody, cared for by somebody, planted by somebody, chopped down by somebody, put together in a house or a factory or a concert hall by somebody, its refuse carried away by somebody. . . It's saying that I share no common humanity with people whose work and attention and accumulated knowledge I live on; that some of them—maybe nearly all of them—simply exist for my use. Abuse is just a variation.

"Evil isn't at all complicated. It is nothing more than grinding people up for your own power or profit or self-gratification. It doesn't matter how—whether it's crazy-making or war-making or slave labour or prostitution or torture. We suck out their blood and their bones and then we throw them away. Nothing very Miltonic about it. No grand demonic defiance—merely a slow accumulation of selfishness and smallness and cruelty until we can let half the children born in our country simply die of starvation and disease; until we can pay someone who picks our cotton or sews our jeans less than we spend each month to feed our Siamese cat; until we can build brothels and porn factories and make sure there are people who will have to work in them; until we can order the use of pesticides that kill *campesinos* because we owe it to our shareholders to keep the costs down and we owe it to our wives to get promoted. And yes, until we *can* torture someone. Or pay the man who does. Or invite him to dinner. Or elect him or advance him or just pretend he doesn't exist. I suspect that by then it's quite easy. There's a logic to things, you know. We build ourselves block by block."

She did not answer. She thought about the girl whose body they had carried away this morning and buried in a hemp bag. No money for a coffin, or even a dress. Not even that little bit of dignity; of justice one did not even speak.

Block by block, she thought. Block by block . . .

"You're very tired," Pepe said. "You should go home."

She looked up sharply. "Me tired? What about you?"

"I enlisted," he said. "You didn't."

"Well, I did, sort of. Are you going home?"

He shook his head. He had a little house not far away, not exactly a shanty but not much more than one. He went there less and less. The last she had heard three stray youths were sleeping there.

"I stay here most nights now," he said. "Just in case, you know."

Just in case some more people came by darkness with their dying children. He was no doctor but he was a priest; he could at least give the sacraments. At least that.

"You're an amazing man," she said.

"Only from the outside," he said. "It's all a question of perception."

She took a taxi home, as she always did if it was dark. Twice her cab had been stopped by the Guardia, but her U.S. passport was like an amulet. So far. She was never particularly frightened, and she did not know if that were arrogance or genuine suicidal indifference.

The Zelaya family no longer knew quite what to make of her. Her decision to continue at the clinic—especially now, after Pilar had been identified as a Sandinista and everyone else in the family was trying to disassociate themselves from anything and everything that Pilar had ever done—her decision seemed to them desperately unwise and almost ungrateful. It did no good whatever to protest that what she was doing had nothing to do with politics.

No one except Leon would talk at all about the fact that Pilar had gone over to the guerrillas, and he would do so only when they were alone. He did not understand it, and he was of little help to Jadine, who did not understand it either.

"Maybe she just fell in love with the guy," he said once.

Jadine looked at him blankly.

"The guy she's running with. The guy who got her pregnant."

"Oh." Running with. As though they were coyotes or something. God, I hate male pretensions; I hate them so bad I can taste it!

"Pilar's got a mind of her own, Leon," she said.

He shrugged. "I know. Or at least I used to think so.

But, Jesus, Jadine—*terrorists*? It's one thing to condemn Somoza, to try and get a decent government into this country—even some kind of socialist government, if that's what you think you want. It's a whole other thing to go around blowing things up. To go shooting soldiers from ambush. Every time the Sandinistas kill a few Guardia, the Guardia goes out and kills a hundred innocent people. The Sandinistas aren't doing *anybody* any good. They're just . . . Jesus, I don't know what they are."

"I had a professor once who said that revolutionaries were eaters of chaos."

"That's good," Leon said. "I like that."

"Only somehow I can't see Pilar as an eater of chaos. I just can't. Can you?"

He sighed. "No. But then I can't see her as a Sandinista either. Papa says the authorities have absolute proof, but sometimes I wonder. I mean, to think that she's actually living like that? Sleeping in ditches and making bombs and screaming *Patria libre!* at some dumb bastard before she shoots him—really, Jadine, do you believe it?"

Believe it? Yes, remembering the banked fire in those eyes, remembering that mind whose unflinching honesty was almost cruel. Yes, I believe it. But I do not understand it.

Neither did anyone else. All the years they had lived with Pilar and been aware of her radicalism, they had somehow inured themselves to its dangerous implications. As of course they had to.

It was an impossible situation. You couldn't know, not really. And you couldn't quite not know. Your daughter had Marx and Lenin and Che Guevara stacked up in her bedroom shelves . . . but so did half the students in Latin America. She went out a lot, went to a lot of meetings, came home late and sometimes didn't come home at all; and common sense made you wonder about it, but common sense also reminded you that your neighbours' sons and daughters were doing the same things; some of them were a little radical but they weren't all Sandinistas, let's not be ridiculous about this. You weren't going to be melodramatic; you weren't going to say: Good God, they blew up a bridge last night and my daughter wasn't home; she must have done it. You weren't going to start thinking like that.

On the other hand, to really say that it wasn't possible, you had to say the revolution wasn't real; you had to convince yourself that the marches and the terror and the bullet-riddled cars and the bodies in the craters weren't there, that they were in some other country or maybe in a movie. And you couldn't quite do that, either.

So you just didn't deal with it, and one day the Guardia came to your door looking for your daughter and told you that yes, she was one of them, she was a terrorist, and you went into shock but you still didn't deal with it. Jadine was never aware of anyone having said, or commanded: We will not talk about Pilar. There was no ritual of banning, no pictures turned to the wall. There was simply silence. That which is not spoken of does not exist.

21

The hours turned slowly into days—how many Daniel did not know, but they came and they passed. His jailers gave him food sometimes, mostly gruel, which he gulped down greedily without noticing or caring what it was. If there was bread with it, or solid food, he could eat it only by tearing it up with his fingers and swallowing it whole.

It was no longer comprehensible to him that he had allowed himself to be captured alive. He'd had a weapon in his hand. He'd needed only to turn on them, only to get to his knees and turn on them, and they would have killed him. They would have eagerly, extravagantly killed him. But he had not done so. It was never a conscious choice. There had been a moment—an unimaginably brief moment—of being torn between the instinct to fight and the instinct to live, and the instinct to live had won. That was all. It had won. Pure, blind, animal response. Not cowardice, no; he was not about to accuse himself of that.

Just...not knowing, not imagining, not ever imagining that there was a limit to hope. Just wanting too much to live and believing, in the face of everything, that it would still, somehow, be possible. Even yet.

The cell was a hole in the earth with a rough stone floor. He was not tall, but he could not lie full length in it. There were no rats—an oversight, surely; or perhaps the stench had killed them, the stench of uncounted weeks and months and lives of excrement.

Sometimes, when he was not unconscious or too crazed with pain to think of anything at all, sometimes he thought about his life, gathered up fragments of it, like a child searching for treasures in a room full of broken glass. It was difficult to keep the pieces together; they kept shifting and changing and getting lost, and the guards never left him alone. He could hear the fat sergeant's voice pounding at him even in the darkness; once the man came and sat in the corner of his cell, just sat there, a great hulk in the closed space, quiet for once, just listening, listening for whatever Daniel might say in his delirium or his sleep. The presence was unbearable, and painful as it was to move he struck out finally, recklessly, and smashed his hand against the wall.

So, he thought. That too.

His mind and the will that sustained it were his only defenses, and all there was to nourish them—all there ever had been—was the reality of the world. He clung to the pieces of that reality as to the flotsam of a shipwreck.

Someone—not Paco, someone else—had told him once: In prison, you must erase all that you ever knew of beauty, or tenderness, or joy. Forget your lover, your children, your friends; forget the sun. Torture can be endured only if you do not remember that there ever was anything else.

But it was not true. Perhaps for some; people coped however they could. For himself, in a place like this, continuity was all there was. He could face his torturers not in spite of what existed outside of these walls, but because of it: Martin carving his dumb wooden animals which he claimed were cats or geese or horses but which always looked like tamales with legs. Amparo who would trade a month's supply of cigarettes for an old tattered poster of Fidel. Ana's tin stove in the Mercado Oriental, where no matter how broke or weary or frightened he was he could get a plate of black beans and a tortilla and his hair brushed out of his eyes.

Clariz.

Clariz beside him in so many stuffy meeting rooms and dark streets and *campesino* trucks. Clariz in the earthquake ruin where he had first made love to her—in broad daylight, in a blinding rainstorm; they had done it standing because there was nowhere to lie down without drowning; even in the rain her hair and her breasts smelled of jasmine. She was not a virgin, and that neither surprised him much nor wounded him much. It was enough to have her, to feast on her kisses and her beauty; he would not let go of her, could not, until suddenly the sun was crashing into the ruins around them and they fled. Both of them spent the night in sleepless terror, wondering if the other had made it home before the curfew.

Clariz...always Clariz; he shut the other name out of his mind, never think it, never speak it; Clariz who touched him as though the gods of the volcano had given her a book with his name on it and she had memorized every word. Clariz who with unmeasured generosity had given him food and books and weapons and cigarettes and pleasure, Clariz who would give him a child, and whom he had never given anything except his passion, his experience, and an expropriated bottle of French cologne.

Clariz beside him, running, black night, black painted walls, *Death to Somoza!* running, wind in her hair, brush in her hand, Christ, Manolito, I can't run anymore, I'm choking; running, falling, falling twenty feet away, twisting and falling, bullets striking like a thousand hailstones on a flower...*Clariz...!*

He awoke screaming, a single helpless scream that stumbled into sobs as he began to understand that it had been a dream, only a terrible dream; that Clariz was still alive, still free. For a few moments he was aware only of that knowledge, and of his limp, shattering gratitude for that knowledge. Then he noticed that he was in a bed, in a room with light and other people, that he was in excruciating pain. He raised himself a little to change position, and almost lost consciousness from the shaft of fire that went through his wounded ankle. It had not hurt much at all, the last while; he wondered why it did so terribly now. He sat up weakly, with great effort, and drew aside the cover.

He had, half consciously, feared what he saw, but the fear had not prepared him for it at all. His right foot was gone, severed well above the ankle; in its place was a blunt, bandaged stub, a grotesque white stick, wasted and awful, part of him now forever, irrevocable. Daniel Chillan, cripple.

Tomorrow, and the day after, he would think about what it meant to his whole future, if he had one; think about all the things he could never do. But now he thought only that he could no longer go to the mountains, or anywhere else; that he was finished as a Sandinista fighter. He began to cry.

"Eh, *compa*." The man in the bed beside him was half sympathetic, half cynical. "Don't take it so hard. At least you was under when they took it off." He waved a bandaged hand, of which only half was there. "I wasn't."

Daniel sank back in his bed, drenched with sweat and loss and desperate weakness. He had no idea what had happened; his last waking memory was of being in the interrogation room, too drunk with fever to be particularly aware of what was happening; observing from a great distance that he was going to die; feeling sorry, feeling grateful, feeling nothing at all.

He framed the question slowly; it was hard to speak. "How long have I been here?"

"A day. Two days. I'm not sure. What's the difference?"

No difference, he thought. No difference at all.

He was in the prison hospital for five more days. He had a bed, and a sheet over his body, and food; no pain-killers, nothing like the luxury of a bath; merely the extraordinary luxury of not being beaten or kicked or savaged with electric shocks. He used what small strength he had to do what he could to increase his chance of survival. He told his name to everyone he saw; he wrote it on the bottom of his plate and on scraps of garbage and around the toilet bowl. It was not necessarily going to be of any help to him; everyone here was either paid Somoza staff or prisoners as vulnerable as himself. He knew they might still kill him, and when two guards came to take him from the hospital all the fear came back, all the blind fear of having no defenses, of simply being dragged away and thrown out of a helicopter or shot like an animal. He told himself that they would not have gone to the trouble to cut his foot off if they meant to kill him, but he knew that wasn't necessarily true. Anything was possible; decisions changed from hour to hour, from officer to officer, from mood to mood. The guards were laughing, contemptuous; he grew so sure that they were going to kill him that he was half way down the prison corridor before he realized that they were taking him back to the interrogation area. To be tortured. Again.

He went crazy then. For a few minutes, until he exhausted himself completely, it took both of them to hold him, to get the hood back on him, to drag him into the room.

"Well now."

He recognized everything about the man beside him: the energy, the way of moving, the voice—above all, the voice, the voice that had ground away his being, the voice that he hated as he hated nothing else that lived.

"You're back again, are you? A little less of you this time, I see. You young fools have to learn everything the hard way."

The shackles closed over his wrists, his ankle; without hesitation or mercy, over the stump.

"No." He said it only once, aloud. In his mind he said it endlessly. No. No. No. It was not possible. He could not go through all of that again. He could not.

"By Christ, did you hear that?" the sergeant said. "The little bastard's got his voice back. We may get somewhere this time."

They began again. As though none of it had ever been. As though the days and nights of blinding pain had been merely a figment of his imagination. As though his refusal to speak had been an error in calculation, and if they ran over the figures one more time they would get the answer right.

The trail here was scarcely more than a footpath, and they were moving fast. Pilar minded her feet and kept her eyes on the shadow of the *companero* ahead of her. Sometimes a valley would open through the hills and for a few moments, until they passed it, she could see moonlight shimmer on the lake, see the small fading lights of a freighter bound for the San Juan.

She was wet to the bone with winter rain, and hungry. Her boots were soaked and they slurped with every step, as though they enjoyed it. It had been this way for a week, since they left the training camp in Carazo, but down there somewhere, only hours away if all had gone well, was Camilo Ortega and a hundred-odd of the best fighters the Terceristas had. And down there, curled against the lake, was Granada, the sleepy old city where nothing ever happened. The October offensive was six weeks old and still building; recruits were coming in almost as fast as the Frente could train them. They had fifty camps now like the one in Carazo, where Pilar had taught *campesino* kids how to read maps and they taught her how to read the mountains; where some learned the way to hold a gun and others learned the ways to capture a town and where everyone learned to share and to go hungry.

The very hardness of the life contained its own kind of mercy. You had little time to grieve for the living or the dead; very little time to take the images that were shut away in the nightmare corners of your mind, and look at them for what they were.

But since Carazo there were days of nothing but walking, and camps where they did not speak except when they had to, in whispers. The thoughts came remorseless then, sometimes, thoughts of Daniel—of others, too, but mostly of Daniel, of what hell he might have gone through, of whether he was somehow still alive. Of whether she would ever know.

The road dipped into a sheltered hillside overlooking a great expanse of lake. Valerian ordered a five minute rest. It was not much but she sat with her arms wrapped around her knees to shut out the wind, and felt the peace of the lake reach up to her like a benediction.

The Lake of Nicaragua was old, old and vast as an ocean. It had been an ocean once, long ago, before the land had risen up and closed it round, prisoning it forever with its great sharks and tiny islands. She could not see the islands from here, but she could remember them well. They spilled out from the old colonial city of Granada, green jewels tossed by a once unimaginably generous God, hundreds of them, wild with ibises and flowers, trailing their bounty into the sea like a mermaid's hair.

Her family had a cottage there, and as a child she had thought the islands a perfect haven for guerrillas. It seemed that one could hide anything in their jungle growth, escape any pursuit in the maze of channels that twisted among them. But it was not so. The *isletas* of Granada belonged to the rich; their pleasure houses clung to the rocky beaches, their boats idled like lilies on the water, at night sometimes the music and the laughter of their parties came muted and eerie through the darkness. Granada was the city of the Spaniards, the *conquistadores*, the old landed aristocracy that looked down their noses at entrepreneurial upstarts like Alvaro Zelaya. In Granada, all her life, she had listened to the endless variations of the palace quarrel: her father and his Somoza Liberals defending the democracy of the freebooter, the Granada Conservatives defending the oligarchy of the correctly born. In Granada she had overheard a jewelled dowager whisper to a friend behind her fan that *Somocismo* was corrupting the country: witness a man like Milan Valdez lowering himself to marrying a shopkeeper's daughter for her looks.

But the beauty of the lake, like its immense and ancient memories, was real. The beauty and the peace of its magical islands, of the cone of Ometepec and the distant ruined monastery of Solentiname, where they had dared to speak of Christ as though he still lived and cared about the world. It was a peace that touched her now in spite of anything.

It's not a personal fight, Valerian had said to her, back in Carazo. It's all of a piece and everything matters.

There was no longer any question that Daniel was in the

hands of the National Guard. Stories filtered quietly out of Montenegro, never quite exact, but yes, they thought one of the guerrillas had gotten out of the house; and yes, there had been shooting a couple of blocks away; yes, they had seen the Guard take prisoners, several prisoners; no, they could not identify anyone—how could you identify a beaten and bleeding captive through a milling bunch of men, peering through a crack in your wall, with the sun already going down? Ana Chillan went relentlessly from *cuartel* to *cuartel*, from office to office, from line-up to line-up, from blank contemptuous face to blank contemptuous face: I told you yesterday. We don't know where your son is. We have no record of him. Next!

But the pressure of resistance just kept growing. In Managua their friends had carried the coffins of Marta and Eduardo through the streets with Sandinista flags draped over them and the police had let them be. Other demonstrations they broke up with clubs and tear gas, and the following day there would be a demonstration twice as big. Somoza's power swung like a pendulum from repression to uncertainty to worse repression to greater uncertainty; brutal, detailed accounts of his killings were being read even into the records of the United States Congress, and maybe that didn't mean as much as it should have but it meant something. By these things the strength of a revolutionary movement was measured, and it was the strength of the revolutionary movement, in the end, that kept its people alive. Not all of its people, no. And not necessarily any particular person: state terror was too arbitrary for that; it had to be arbitrary to work. You held it back where you could, that was all.

Once, in the camp in Carazo, she had gone out alone into the trees and cried like a child, and Valerian had sat with her and talked to her for most of an hour, talked about small things in a voice edged with weariness. She reminded herself of how much he, personally, must have lost over the years. How many comrades. How many young kids won over and taught a few skills and buried before the year was out, a burden of guilt you carried because you led them; it didn't matter how right you were or how necessary was the struggle: you still carried it because you led them. . . How many young kids and how many old friends. . . he and Marta went back eleven years.

"You mustn't give up, Clariz," he said. "You mustn't."

"I haven't given up. I know he's alive." I feel his life like I feel the child inside of me. . . only I don't know any more if it's his life I feel, or just the child's. . . "I only wish . . . I only wish there was something I could *do*."

"You're doing your work," he said. "And that is helping Manolito as much as anything else you could be doing. You know that, *compita*. This is not a personal fight."

It was all of a piece, he told her. All of it mattered. "The revolution is for everyone. If it weren't, if it were only for our friends, what good would it be? Even Las Colinas looks after its own."

She got to her feet with the others, readied to move on, pausing once for a final look at the lake melting into the night sky and floating the moon like a flower.

Tomorrow Granada, she thought. And after that somewhere else, and again somewhere else, until it was done. All of it mattered. All of it would come together in time.

The day after they took Daniel from the hospital he admitted to having blown up the Valdez plant in Santa Rosa; to that first, then to other things. He no longer cared that it was shameful, only that perhaps the pain would stop, even for a little while, even for a moment. There was water in his lungs and he could no longer sit up without help. He could hardly talk but he could say yes, if that was what it took to end it: yes, he had made the bombs and planted them; yes, he had robbed the Altamira bank; yes, he had bought the guns, yes, but he could not remember where; yes, certainly, many of them, all of them perhaps—how many were enough? Yes, he would sign a confession. But he would read it before he did so.

They ignored that at first, and then they laughed: by Christ, they had one who could read. But in the end they took the hood off and put him in a chair and shoved the paper into his hands.

He read the document with difficulty. The words would not lie still on the paper and the light blinded him. He was not sure and did not care what it admitted to, only that no one was named in it except himself. Satisfied of that, he put his name to it: Daniel Chillan Santa Cruz. He held it a moment, stared at the clumsy, graceless words he had written, like the scrawl of an old man or a barely literate child, with a hand that once could have forged any signature he saw. He let the paper fall.

"Now let me be," he begged. "In God's name let me be."

But they did not, and he understood then that he had not spared himself, that he had only made it worse. He had let them know that his strength was utterly gone, and they closed like wolves. They beat him, though there was no part of his body left that was not blackened and raw with beatings. They dragged him across the floor by the stump of his severed leg. They threatened to blind him, to cut off his hands, to castrate him. They made endless, brutal mockery of his body, his race, his cause, his leaders. Sandino was a bandit and a murderer, they said, a petty thief with delusions of grandeur. Fonseca was a bastard, a faggot, a plaything of the Cubans. And Borge was crawling around on his hands and his knees in an unlighted cell in the bowels of Tipitapa, and there he would stay for the next hundred and twenty-nine years. *Sandinismo* was a joke, and here he was, the last dumb *hijo de puta* in the country who hadn't figured out that it was a joke.

He had nothing to hope for now but death, to hope that it might be soon, before he came apart completely, and left the pieces of his soul sticking to their fingers like shreds of rain-soaked paper. Mercy came only with darkness, and darkness came more and more easily. Sometimes he passed out so quickly that they did not even bother to send him back to his cell, merely threw him into a corner and brought in someone else. Or just left him; they had other interrogation rooms, other more interesting captives. He would awake to the sound of screaming or to the sound of laughter; once to the sound of a door banging, a strong, unfamiliar voice:

"All right, get out of here. Both of you, get the hell out!"

Someone untied the hood, lifted it almost gently from his head. It was a man in a colonel's uniform, heavy but attractive. Daniel's brain was too muddy to recognize him from the pictures he had looked at, the names of the Guardia officers he had learned. Once it would have seemed very important to know. Now he did not care.

The colonel freed Daniel's hands and gave him a soiled cotton blanket, which he drew over himself not out of modesty or the need for warmth, but simply for the illusion of protection that it gave him.

"I hate this barbarism," the colonel said. "I really do."

He offered a cigarette. Daniel shook his head slightly; he didn't want one, didn't want anything except to be left alone.

"I'll tell you something," the man went on. "I think your ideas are shit but I respect courage. I have always respected it." He paused, drew a chair close and placed one foot on it and leaned his arm on the chair's wooden back.

"I don't want to kill you, Chillan."

Then don't, Daniel thought wearily. That's simple enough, isn't it? Just don't.

The colonel continued quietly: "You don't believe me, do you? I can understand that. You've been through a lot. But the fact is, we aren't murderers. We're soldiers, that's all. Just like you."

It was hard to keep looking at him, looking into the light. Daniel closed his eyes.

"I have a son about your age," the colonel said. "In university. In Costa Rica."

The smoke from his cigarette drifted dreamily past Daniel's face and for the briefest moment it filled him with memories of his life, memories of freedom. The voice went on, soft and persuasive, and Daniel gradually understood that what was being spoken of was a debt, that he had somehow incurred a debt, that he owed something to this man who was speaking to him so patiently. What that debt was he could not possibly imagine, but he was very confused and very tired. The colonel had to shake him twice to keep him awake.

"I want to help you," he said. "You're a very gutsy kid. But you have to help me. I have to account to other people, too. Just a couple of names, Daniel. We both know it doesn't matter. Everybody that we didn't get in the first twenty-four hours has gone underground. But then it looks better, you see. I can say: yes, I did get some information. And I can say that's it; it's over. You go to trial. You get five years, maybe; you get out and you start taking potshots at me again..."

He laughed softly. "Crazy, isn't it? This life we both live?

"You've done your duty, Chillan, and so have I. I want you out of here. I'll settle for the smallest excuse to get you out of here. Because if I give you back to the other two, they'll kill you. The sons of bitches like it; I never could understand that. They enjoy it."

He finished his cigarette, dropped the butt and ground it under his boot.

"Just two names, Daniel. And then it's all over."

Daniel looked away. He had no strength left even to listen. It was all so meaningless.

"They'll kill you," the colonel said. "They want to. They talk about it."

Probably they did, Daniel thought. And probably they would. One of them. Both of them. All of them. He would die under torture or in the back of a truck, and his body would disappear into the lake or a crater or a lime pit with a hundred others.

And that was all.

Better people had died at their hands—younger, more beautiful, more innocent, more experienced, more gifted, more loved. They killed children and teachers and young girls with their eyes full of dreams and old men and cripples and guerrillas and it was all the same. They killed his father, and Oscar Medina, and Marta. They killed Fonseca; they cut off his head in the woods of Zinica and carried it back to Somoza in a sack, but his blood ran in the same rivers as that of the peasant women of Cua. Nobody could separate the blood any more; there was too much of it. It laced the landscape in a tapestry of loss and defiance, in patterns that had not been seen for three hundred years. That tapestry was all there was. It was the past and the future and it was Nicaragua and all that was left to him was not to damage it.

Los hijos de Sandino ni se venden ni se rinden... jamas!

Never.

"Let me help you, Daniel. Just two names."

"*Jamas.*"

It was slurred and the colonel didn't quite catch it. He bent forward, quickly, eagerly. "What did you say?"

"*Jamas.*"

The man was looking at him in blank incomprehension; he could speak very well but he could not hear at all; he had grown deaf from the sound of his own voice.

Daniel said it again. "*Jamas.*" And again, and again. How amazing that the man could not understand.

"Damn you!" the colonel said softly, bitterly. "Damn you to hell anyway!" He turned on his heel and walked out; the door all but shattered on its hinges behind him.

In the next room the two guards enjoyed a smoke and sat on the desk, talking about sailing. They stood up sharply as Davila came in.

He looked at them with barely veiled contempt. He was sick of them. He was sick of everything.

"He's a fucking basket case," the colonel said. "Get him out of here."

The door was almost closed when he added: "Take him back to his cell."

The sergeant was surprised, but he merely shrugged and continued on his way.

Fuck them all, Davila thought. Everyone was screaming at him, demanding the impossible. Get the Sandinistas, keep order in the streets, keep the lid on, but whatever you do, don't put this government into an impossible position; whatever you do, keep it out of the papers; but above all, whatever you do, get the fucking Sandinistas!

Well, he had gotten some of them. Let some other damn son of a bitch figure out what to do with them.

22

It was dark, and the house that was always full of light and Leon's interminable music was absolutely still. Jadine went numb with fear even before she reached it, and walked through the rooms like a thief, too terrified to call out. When she found Beatriz in the patio, sitting quietly, she was too limp with relief to remember for several minutes that Beatriz never sat outside at night.

"Where is everyone?" Jadine asked.

"At the concert."

Oh, yes, of course. Jorge Ibanez. The Spanish matinee idol with the melt-in-your-mouth voice and the come-to-my-bedroom eyes. One night only at the Ruben Dario Theatre—not a big stop on his tour but he loved Nicaragua's beaches and he always enjoyed the best of them as a personal guest of the president. His concerts were a national institution; everyone in the Zelaya house had bought tickets weeks ago.

"Didn't you want to go?" Jadine asked.

"No."

Jadine sat down. She was glad that someone was at home.

"Are you hungry?" Beatriz asked. "Maria isn't here; I gave her my ticket. But she left you a salad and some cold chicken from supper."

"Maybe later, thanks."

They sat quietly, Jadine content to relax, to drink in the stars and the silence. Since she started going to the clinic every day she had become increasingly aware of the elegance of this house; of how cool and peaceful its rooms were, how lavish. Of how safe it was. She felt both guilty and relieved, coming back here every night to a good meal and a warm bath and a bed with sheets. To space and to silence. Down in the shantytowns, the roosters challenged each other all night long. For two years, Pepe told her, he never knew more than perhaps an hour of unbroken sleep, until he finally got used to it. She wondered what it took to get used to the shantytowns; wondered if she ever would. Wondered if she really wanted to. She thought sometimes about going home—thought about it simply because the possibility was there, like the possibility of suicide—quite a lot like it, actually. Pepe would never forgive her for either.

"Jadine," Beatriz began softly, "are you happy doing what you're doing? At the clinic? Do you want to stay there?"

"Yes. For a while at least."

"Alvaro has an opening for you. In the head office, here in Managua. He asked me to. . . ask you about it."

"Oh." She was silent for a long while.

"He said he can wait for a couple of weeks if you need . . . if you've made. . . some sort of commitment. . . ?"

Some sort of commitment? Yes, probably one could call it that. Some sort of something or other, some sort of life, some sort of reason for being.

"I'm sorry, Beatriz. I can't. I simply can't. I appreciate the offer more than I can say. I truly do. But I. . ." She couldn't go on. She couldn't say: I've done it all before. I've been there. I've been there and I couldn't stand it, and

I don't know where the hell I'm going now but it's not to anywhere I've been before. Not ever. Not ever again.

After another silence she offered tentatively: "Perhaps I should...just...find a place of my own...? I mean, I have to anyway, sooner or later..."

Beatriz paled. Even in the patio light Jadine could see it. "But why, Jadine, why? Why would you want to leave us?"

She faltered. "But...but won't Alvaro be angry if he offers me work and I refuse?"

"Oh, perhaps he'll be angry. For a day or two. But if you leave...Oh, Jadine, don't even think of it! The city is so unsafe! What do you suppose the Guardia will think of you—a woman, a foreigner, who has a respectable family here but lives on her own and works in the barrios?"

Jadine had never considered that.

"You mustn't leave, Jadine. You mustn't. Alvaro would never forgive you. He might not even permit you to come to see us. And people would not understand. I know it's common in your country but here it would be seen as something very bad. They would think you are immoral. Or an agent for the Sandinistas. Or both."

Good God, Jadine thought. All that for not wanting to live off a cousin who disapproves of nearly everything I do?

Beatriz reached over the oak table and mixed them each a drink.

"Please, Jadine. Every night I think about my daughter. I wonder where she is. I wonder if I will see her again..." She paused, and went on: "Stay with Father Pepe. He needs you; my husband doesn't. There are plenty of *nicas* who know some English and who can spell well enough and who need work. And I'll tell Alvaro that. I will support you. But please, please, don't leave this house."

"All right," Jadine whispered, and added softly: "Thank you."

She watched Beatriz a moment. It had occurred to her before that her cousin was lonely, but that loneliness now seemed bottomless.

"Beatriz, why didn't you go to the concert? You always liked Jorge Ibanez."

Beatriz made a small, shrugging gesture. "I just didn't want to." She was silent a moment, brooding. "I used to ask Pilar the same question. So many times. And she would say: I just don't want to. Now I understand...

"I saw something unbelievable today, Jadine. Something I never imagined could happen. I had to go to the National Guard headquarters to renew some of Alvaro's import permits—we'd forgotten all about them. There was a demonstration. They were women—somebody told me they were from all over the country. They were asking for justice for political prisoners, asking about their children who had disappeared. They marched right on the National Guard headquarters. The guards were all over the place—they had machine guns, clubs, I don't know what else. And the women just kept coming.

"The traffic was at a standstill for blocks; there was nowhere to go. I sat in the car watching them and thinking: they have to stop. They have to. But they didn't. They just kept on.

"Alberto was scared out of his wits, telling me to lie down in the back of the car in case there was shooting. But I couldn't. All I could do was ask myself if I would have that kind of courage. If my daughter was in prison, could I carry her picture on a placard into the faces of men with machine guns...? I don't know, Jadine. Do you think I could?"

"Yes."

"And chain myself to the barracks fence? That too?"

"*What?*" Jadine whispered.

"Six of them," Beatriz said. "They broke through the guards—I guess that was what they'd planned all along, to get to the gates or the fence. They had chains and padlocks and they chained themselves in a row along the *cuartel* and then just stood and chanted: *Donde estan? Donde estan?* Where are they?

"They were poor women, mostly. The one who led them wore old running shoes and a cotton dress and carried a picture that someone had drawn by hand, with crayons... maybe of her son; I don't know..."

The silence fell like cold rain.

"Somehow," Beatriz said finally, darkly, "somehow I

just couldn't stomach the thought of listening to Jorge Ibanez dying for love."

The concert ran late, and afterward there was an official reception at the villa of Somoza's mistress; those who did not make the guest list held gala parties of their own. Shortly before midnight Alvaro phoned to say that he and the others would be home very late.

"I could eat that chicken now, I think," Jadine said. They went to the kitchen and made coffee. A scrunched end of *La Prensa* protruded from the garbage can, undoubtedly the object of Alvaro's wrath. She could guess why. She had seen it on the street, waved at her by clamourous paper boys: *GN Patrol Ambushed at Esteli*. The Sandinistas were striking all over the country, sometimes twice in the same day. They were capturing Guard posts now; a week ago they had taken the city of Granada—taken it and held it for half a day. They ran up their red and black flag and made reckless speeches about freedom in the dust of the old colonial square; they gave flamboyant interviews to the international press, and posed for news photos with scarved faces and captured M-16s, and vanished like foxes when the Guard stormed in with tanks and helicopters. Somoza made a great boast of how easily he had gotten the city back, but what people talked about was the fact that he had lost it at all. It was the first city to fall, they said; it would not be the last.

Beatriz noticed her glance, and said wryly: "Did you see the front page of *Novedades* today?"

"No."

"Jorge Ibanez. Why Latin American women are the most desirable in the world."

"I'm crushed," Jadine said.

They laughed. Beatriz dug the paper out of the garbage can, brushed the coffee grounds off it. Leon would have to learn to stop leaving it lying around, she said. She folded it very neatly, like a napkin. Without looking up she said:

"They're going to win, you know."

Jadine stared at her, the coffee cup halfway to her mouth.

"Nothing's going to stop them."

"Beatriz, you aren't. . .?"

"I'm not anything. I'm telling you what I see. They're going to do it."

She looked up; their eyes met, just for a moment; then Beatriz looked away, as though shaken by her own words. She went and put the paper in Leon's room. When she came back, they spoke for a while of other things, and said good night.

But Jadine thought about what she had said for a long time before she slept. It did not seem possible. She remembered the Panamanian on the plane: a few hundred guerrillas, he had said. And a great deal of subversion. She hadn't known what he meant by subversion. She still didn't, but she had the feeling it had a lot to do with women chaining themselves to command post fences. With Father Pepe talking about evil. Maybe even with herself. Maybe to live here at all was to be subversive.

She sighed, and curled on her side to sleep. None of it made any sense; none of it. But the Panamanian had definitely been right about one thing: It was not over.

Epilog
December, 1977

The jail at Tipitapa was called the *Carcel Modelo*, the model prison; Ana wondered if the irony was apparent only to the prisoners and those who came to see them. A female guard searched her rudely; another—a man—methodically went through the little bags of food she had brought, almost with distaste. He unwrapped everything, broke everything into pieces as though he expected to find bombs inside. The *nacatamales* and tortillas he gave back to her, mangled; the candy bar and the half-dozen cigarettes he put into his pocket without a trace of shame.

She took the soiled paper bag in silence, burying her anger, burying everything except the need to see Daniel. She knew that it would do no good to beg or make demands, to remind this man that it was Christmas, or that people had gone without food to buy these few small things for her son. She simply followed him, avoiding his eyes because it was better that he did not see the hatred in hers.

He led her through a heavy door into a large, barred room. People were already there, mostly women sitting with husbands or sons. She waited, aching. It had taken weeks to get permission to see Daniel. The authorities never gave a reason for their refusals. They did not have to, and she did not have to guess. They just wanted the more obvious signs of torture to be gone.

The lawyer—he was a good lawyer, hired by the Frente—had been appalled at Daniel's condition, appalled at the mockery of a trial, appalled at everything.

"They had accusations they'd tortured out of other people, and a confession they'd tortured out of him. There was nothing I could do. It was over in five minutes."

Five minutes. One-third of a minute for each year of prison they had sentenced him to serve. Enough, no doubt, for a barrio street rat.

She stood up as the door opened, moved toward it, all but running as she caught the first glimpse of him. She wasn't going to cry; she was determined that she wasn't going to cry, and perhaps she wouldn't have, except that he did. He hobbled into her arms and buried his face against her and sobbed like a child. It seemed a child's body that she held, so gaunt she wondered how he lived, so raw with hurts that she could not embrace him as she longed to do, with all her strength and all her pity; she could only hold him as though he were made of broken glass, steady him, and stroke his hair, and cry.

"Danito...Danito, my poor child, oh my poor little one, *mi pobrecito*..."

Her baby, the last of her babies that lived, the one that God knew why was the strongest, the most sure, the one she'd always worried about least...

He struggled to calm himself, took her face between his palms. Standing straight, they were the same height; he was not a child; he had turned twenty-three in this nightmare place.

"Mama...are you all right? Is everyone all right?"

"I'm well. I'm always well." She found the strength to laugh a little, foolishly. She kissed him, brushed shags of hair from his face, wanting to weep again for what she saw there. His face had always been thin, too sharply chiselled to be beautiful, but the lines of it had been clean and straight. They weren't any more.

"And you, Danito? How is it with you? *Que tal?*"

"I'm alive," he said.

For a moment she could not speak, could not do anything. She wanted to scream. She wanted to smash everything in reach—every wall and window and iron gate, every guard who tended them, and more than that every linen-suited smiling son of a bitch who paid the guards and trained them and armed them and turned them loose on people without land or power or any defenses except what they could fashion for themselves; turned them loose and said: Do what you like. You will not have to answer for it. No laws, not even the laws of warfare, apply to them. Do what you like.

He shifted his weight, his fingers gripping her shoulder so hard that it hurt. He could not stand very long on one foot. She helped him to a chair; the small effort seemed to exhaust him. Or the pain. When it eased a little he started asking questions, begging for news: of his brothers, of the Frente, of everyone they knew.

"Naldo and Martin are well. They're both in hiding. They're safe. Give me your hand, Danito."

He did so, unthinking, and tensed like a cat when she pressed the small wad of paper into his palm. His eyes sought hers, eyes dark with exhaustion and suffering and yet so alive, so hungry for the letter that she felt a sudden unexpected flash of jealousy, of loss. It passed. He was grown; he had a right to his own life.

"Valerian told me," she whispered. "Not her name, but he told me there will be a child. I don't know where she is, but he said to tell you she is well.

"He also sent a message of his own. He said to say that we are with you; that we will always be with you. That we do not forget."

"Thank you." He bent as though to ease a cramp in his injured leg, and slipped the paper inside the ragged bandage that still wrapped it. "Thank you," he said again, and put his head in his hands, shaking softly like a small, beaten animal.

She talked to him, made him eat, told him all the news

she had that was good. She told him about Granada; told him the story that was going around the Frente, how Valerian had smuggled thirty rifles into Granada in a hearse, himself driving it, solemn as a priest would you believe, not a speck of dust on his fancy black hat, with mourners yet, and flowers, and a stolen coffin packed with guns. Right under the Guardia's nose, right up to their gates. They never suspected a thing until the mourners started shooting and a farm truck armoured with paving stones and sand bags rolled out of a side-street to pick them up. It was beautifully done, she said. And after they'd taken the *cuartel* a few Granada youngsters ran into the plaza and painted Somoza's name on the sides of the bullet-riddled hearse, and laid the fancy wreaths all around it, and tied a tattered red and black scarf to the radio antenna. The dictatorship, they said, was dead.

It was sheer defiance, of course it was, and some of the foreign journalists shook their heads over it, but it said everything about the people's outrage, their readiness, their faith in the Sandinistas.

"All over the country it's the same," Ana said. "The Guardia thought the raid in Montenegro would break the whole offensive. It didn't even stop us in Managua."

"Things are going well, then," he said. It was partly a statement, partly a question.

"Yes," she said. "Thing are going very well."

"*Pues...*" He smiled, just a little. "That's what matters."

There were a few scraps of broken *nacatamal* left; he ate them right from his palm. She urged him to take another, but he shook his head. He would keep the rest. Likely as not, she thought, he meant to share them out among his comrades; there were five other political prisoners in his cell.

She had so many things to tell him, but already it was time to go. He took her hands, thanked her for all that she'd done. He'd be all right, he said. He'd be all right.

"Daniel..."

The guard was standing over her like judgment.

"I'll come again as soon as they let me." She wrapped him in her arms, and it took all her will power to let him go. He wasn't all right. He needed medical care and he needed decent food and he needed someone to talk to when the nightmares wouldn't stop; he had a long way to come back from, such a long way; and all she could do was lie on her bed every night thanking a God she only half believed in that they hadn't killed him.

She cried all the way back to Managua, but nobody noticed. On the bus from Tipitapa, many people cried.

It was agony to wait, but Daniel did not take the letter out until he was sure that it was safe, that there were no guards about who might see him. The note was very brief. It had to be, to be small enough to hide in cigarettes and pocket flaps and the toes of shoes. He read it once quickly, then again very slowly, savouring every word.

"Manolito: I miss you. When I heard that you were alive I couldn't sleep for joy; now I cry because you're hurt and in prison. Don't lose hope. We're getting stronger every day; there is a fire in this country now that nothing will put out. I'm well. It's hard living in the mountains but I've grown used to it. If you were here I'd be very happy. I think of you all the time. Clariz."

He folded the note and hid it away again. He would destroy it, he had to, but not yet. Not quite yet.

He laid his head back, remembering her beauty, remembering her moody eyes and her touch that melted down all his bones. The memories drowned him in loss. He would be old, maybe, when he saw her again. If he ever did. Old and crippled and what could he say to her then? They had promised to trade stories. Every time they met, they said, they would tell each other where they had been and what they had done. What could he say? Territory held: one wooden bunk. Enemies captured: two thousand cockroaches and a rat...

But the struggle went on; it went well. *We are getting stronger every day*...And she was free. She was still out there, not too terribly far away, still fighting, still Pilar, Sandinista, woman of rain and *rojinegro*, woman of flesh and firedreams and morning. She was still free and the revolution had not been stopped, it would never be stopped, they were going to win, they had to.

The cell was hot and crowded, foul with time and unwashed bodies, almost dark now. The other prisoners talked quietly, or sat alone with their own thoughts, their own wounds. Carefully he took out the bag of *nacatamales* that he had tucked behind his bunk. He had food to share, news to give them, everything Ana had told him, detail by detail, small fragments of courage against the hunger and the filth and the pocked stone walls. It had to be, somehow, still possible to live.

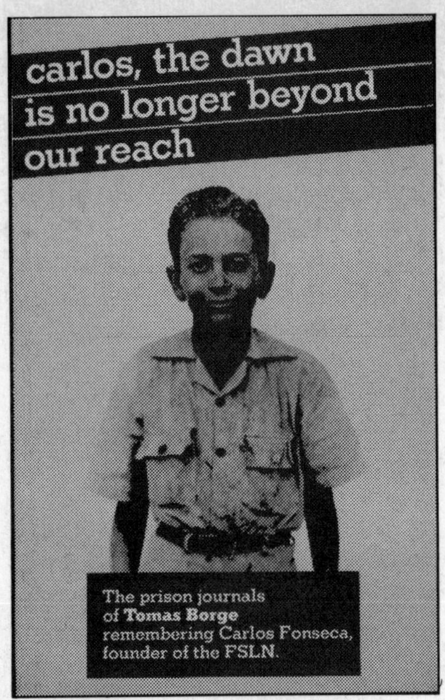

CARLOS, THE DAWN IS NO LONGER BEYOND OUR REACH

by Tomas Borge

Translated by Margaret Randall

Carlos Fonseca was a founding member of the FSLN and a hero of the Sandinista movement. Tomas Borge was a close friend of Fonseca and wrote this lyrical remembrance of his *companero* upon hearing word, while in jail, of Fonseca's death.

Borge intersperses recollections of Fonseca with accounts of events in recent Nicaraguan history, events that influenced Fonseca or, as was increasingly the case, events that Fonseca himself influenced.

Tomas Borge is the last surviving founding member of the FSLN and is currently a member of the nine-member directorate that governs Nicaragua.

Fall 1984, 96 pp., illustrated, CIP
$ 5.95 paper ISBN 0-919573-25-8
$11.95 cloth ISBN 0-919573-24-X

SANDINO'S DAUGHTERS
Testimonies of Nicaraguan
Women in Struggle
by Margaret Randall

In July 1979, when the FSLN led the revolutionary armies to victory in Nicaragua, women made up 30 percent of those armies. Now in its fifth printing, *Sandino's Daughters* is the remarkable story of the women who fought in and won the Nicaraguan revolution.

After the war, Margaret Randall interviewed scores of these women: field commanders, rank-and-file guerrillas, messengers, intelligence agents, keepers of safe-houses, and many others. Randall captures the personal and the ordinary, along with the revolutionary.

1981, 240 pp., illustrated, CIP
$ 7.95 paper ISBN 0-919888-33-X
$14.95 cloth ISBN 0-919888-34-8

Printed in Canada